Under Siege

Also by C.K. Crigger

Painter's Bay Series

Buried Bones

The Woman Who Series

The Woman Who Built a Bridge

The Woman Who Killed Marvin Hammel

The Woman Who Wore a Badge

The Woman Who Beat the Odds

The Woman Who Inherited Trouble

The Woman Who Went for Broke

Novels

Ault's Heir

Black Crossing

Hereafter

Letter Of The Law

Liar's Trial

Lost Girl Lake

Madame's Daughter

The Yeggman's Apprentice

Yester's Ride

And many more...

Under Siege

PAINTER'S BAY
BOOK TWO

C.K. CRIGGER

WOLFPACK
PUBLISHING
— EST 2012 —

Paperback ISBN 979-8-89567-113-9
Ebook ISBN 979-8-89567-112-2
LCCN 2025932993

Under Siege

One

If there was anything Rio Salo disliked, opening the front door of the Painter's Bay Hotel to a stranger in the dark of night headed up the list.

Although, she couldn't help thinking as she eyed the man standing on the porch with a nice leather valise in his hand, the danger in that must be over. If only someone could convince her heart since it was galloping like a runaway horse. Lord knows there'd been enough to fear in the last month or so to last a lifetime. Maybe two lifetimes. Besides, the two men who had wanted to kill her were dead. And she, though wounded, was very much alive.

"Hello. I'm Quinn Callahan," the man said. "I have a reservation."

He stood at a respectful distance, which she found reassuring.

Rio hoped he didn't hear the breath that gusted out of her. A relieved breath. "Indeed you do. Come in, Mr. Callahan." She introduced herself and, spinning the contraption she was still using to help her walk—deep

1

furrows from being shot in both legs having made the thing a necessity—she led the way to the registration desk in the small lobby.

Boo, her little curly-haired dog—white, which had led to his ghostly name—cavorted around the stranger like a small mop and she heard him chuckle.

"I hope you'll excuse this late arrival," Mr. Callahan said to her. "The train was delayed, and I walked here from the depot." His attractive chuckle came again. "You've got a fine little welcomer here, Miss Salo. Is he always so friendly?"

She reached the desk, the contraption thumping with every stride, and pushed the register toward him. "Not always. But he's certainly not aggressive unless provoked." Like when someone tried to attack her, not that she figured to tell Mr. Callahan this particular story.

"I'd best not provoke him then." He took the pen she handed him and signed the book, even though a quick glance indicated it might take a magician to decipher the signature. He smiled at her when she thanked him.

"I don't suppose the kitchen is still open." He looked around the darkened lobby, toward the hall leading past the equally dark dining room, then to the stairway leading to the second floor. A single lamp shed only enough light to prevent anyone from falling.

Rio sighed. She was tired to the bone and wanted her bed. Pressing on, she did her best to keep her innkeeper face pleasant. "I'm afraid not if you're looking for a hot meal. If a sandwich will do, I can provide that." Even though the thought of holding a knife seemed almost more than she had strength for.

"I would very much appreciate a sandwich. Whatever you've got will be fine."

She reached for a room key to hand off to him, figuring any one would do. The rooms on the second floor were basically alike, except for the room that had belonged to her father, her own wee cubbyhole, and the one at the end of the hall. That one was larger, looked out over the lake instead of the road, and had more impressive furniture. She planned to charge a little more for it. So far, since her father had died and she'd reopened the hotel, no one had taken the room.

To her surprise, he stopped her. "Do you have a ground-floor room? I'd rather not be upstairs."

She'd been thinking to move her own things into the one downstairs room, but had put it off until her legs healed. There was no hurry, she supposed, judging it best to accommodate a guest. Switching to the key to room four, and no, she didn't know why it was called four since it was the only guest room on this floor, she handed the key to him. "Just down the hall. There's a bathroom across from it, so you should find it convenient." Taking a lamp from under the counter, she struck a match and lit the wick before passing it to him.

"I'll drop off my valise," he said. "Then, if you'll just put a sandwich on a plate, I'll pick it up at the kitchen and take it to my room. It's late, and there's no need for you to stay up and fuss. If you'll excuse me for saying so, Miss Salo, you look tired."

Tired? She figured she looked positively haggard if anyone cared to be so blunt and she'd just as soon Mr. Callahan hadn't mentioned it.

"That's very thoughtful of you," she said stiffly. "Give me a few minutes." A wave of her hand indicated the contraption. "I don't move very fast using this thing."

As he could see for himself and although his expression showed he'd like to ask the particulars, he refrained.

Thankfully, he nodded and strode off down the hall in the direction she pointed while she turned into the roomy kitchen, going to the big ice box and taking out the things she'd need. The bread was today's bake. She sliced off two pieces, buttered both, and piled on stacks of thinly sliced roast beef, cheese, chopped lettuce, onions, and horseradish mayonnaise thinned into her own special sauce. On the plate, she added two dill pickles and a few radishes. And then, because he'd been thoughtful about not having to light the dining room, she put a piece of her spiced apple cake with caramel sauce on another plate and put everything on a tray.

When she turned around, he was leaning against the doorjamb watching her. Straightening, he entered and took the tray. "Looks good. Thank you," he said. "And good night."

Boo followed him out. As she put things back in the icebox, Rio heard him say, "Not this time, little fella," and his door click shut. Boo came pattering back to her, hurrying to see if she'd saved a bite of beef for him.

She had. "I think you made a friend," she said to him. "But we'll check in the morning. Let's go to bed, shall we?"

First she had to finish locking up, front and back. In back, when she stepped out on the enclosed porch, the night was quiet except for the nightly chorus of crickets, frogs, and the splash of waves hitting the lakeshore.

Stars were out, and though mid-June, the night was cool.

A shiver wracked her. Tomorrow would finish the transfer of property, meaning the hotel and the land it stood on, from her murdered mother's name to hers. Free and clear, thanks to her father paying the taxes on it all these years.

A wry smile creaked across her face. He hadn't paid those taxes on her behalf. Not by a long shot. He'd intended for the hotel to belong to him. Rio's death had been in the plans, but the cancer got to Elias first. And no matter what, whether her half brother Eino ever turned up or not, there had been nothing he could have done about it.

But the shiver came again, little bumps breaking out on her arms like a warning premonition that all might not be as well as it seemed. What did Anna Golz always say? Something about not counting your chickens before they hatch?

Leaving the contraption at the bottom of the stairs, Rio, laboriously pulling herself via the banister, arrived on the second floor and walked quietly down the hall to her room. Dr. Clement had told her to go ahead and practice walking on her own, and she was doing much better. As long as she could take her time and build up weakened muscles, he promised that by the end of July she'd be moving like she'd never been shot.

She'd make that sooner if she could. It was a vow she made to herself.

At check-in, she'd placed the two traveling salesmen who'd signed in for the night on the other side of the landing, preferring some separation between them and her own room. Even so, she could hear the whiskey salesman snoring like the weekly lumber train's locomotive pulling the grade up from the bay. Too much sampling of his own wares, she figured. But with her door closed, the noise shut off.

It took only minutes to rinse her face at the washstand and don a nightgown. Boo leapt onto the bed with her, a stretch for a little dog like him, and settled against her back. She pinched her lamp's wick to kill the light then lay staring at the moon through her window, tired beyond speaking but sure she'd never sleep until the hearing was over.

The next thing she knew, before she could even make plans on what she should wear to court the next day, it was morning and time to get up.

Dressing in a light muslin skirt and blouse with one of her enveloping chef's aprons wrapped around her slender body, by the time she had pancakes, sausage, and eggs sizzling on the stove, two early fishermen, and the two salesmen were ready to eat and be on their separate ways. She served the meals in the dining room, and while thankful for the business, was grateful there weren't more customers as she'd worked without the contraption's aid. She'd already cleared the tables and tidied the kitchen when she remembered her new guest.

"Boo?"

The dog rose from his pad and looked at her.

"Have you seen Mr. Callahan this morning?"

Boo waggled his floppy ears, which Rio took to mean no. Her fine dark brows—a stark contrast to her pale flaxen hair, drew together.

"I wonder if I should see if he'll be wanting breakfast. Wash will be here soon, and I need do something with my hair and change clothes before we catch the morning train. I can't appear in a courtroom looking like a ragamuffin." She shook her head. "But I don't want to awaken our guest if he's sleeping in. That would be rude."

Boo's sudden gallop to the doorway gave a moment of warning. When she turned, the *he* in question was leaning against the doorjamb. Had he heard her discussion with the dog? If he had, he probably thought her ready for the looney bin.

"Good morning, Mr. Callahan," she said, aware of heat rising in her cheeks. "Are you ready to order breakfast? There's a menu on the small table as you enter the dining room. Choose any table you like. I'll be there in a minute to take your order." She was proud of how collected she sounded considering he'd taken her by surprise.

"Do you know how to make a western omelet?" In the light of day, she saw that his eyes were gray, but not colorless gray. More like the hue of the storm clouds that came out of the north. And he watched her intently, waiting for her answer.

"Certainly," she said. "Would you prefer pancakes with that? Or toast? And may I suggest hash browns or a fruit compote?" Rio was a bit offended. Did he think her ignorant of basic fare?

"Yes," he said.

She blinked. "Yes?"

"Yes to the hash browns and fruit, with toast. And plenty of black coffee, please."

"Very good, sir." She turned to the stove, thinking he'd go on to the dining room, but he didn't. He remained standing at the doorway. After a moment, she said, "Will there be anything else?"

He shook his head, but then cocked a brow. "Are you alone here? Don't you have help?"

For some reason the question raised her hackles and made her uneasy. "I do have help. Of course, I do. I'm only alone until my employees arrive."

Maybe he sensed something in her sharp reply because he said, mild as milk, "I'm glad to hear it. I didn't want to be the cause of you having to use that helper thing I see parked in the corner."

Rio glanced at it. "The contraption."

"It has a name?" He smiled a little and pushed off to make for the dining room.

As he did, his jacket swung open. Not far, but enough she spotted the small revolver in a closely fitted holster tucked under his left arm. From the outside, it wasn't visible at all, a testament to his well-tailored jacket.

But this wasn't the old days, like before the turn of the century when most of the men around Painter's Bay, the loggers, cattlemen, railroad workers, and a few independent miners—everyone but the Chinese, really —went armed. Nowadays, only a few carried a gun everywhere they went. Why did Mr. Quinn Callahan? And now she thought about it, where did he come from? He had some kind of accent she didn't recognize. And what was he doing here? Why had he chosen to visit the Painter's Bay Hotel?

Boo, she was startled to see, was following the man down the hall to the dining room. She heard Callahan say something, whereupon Boo gave that funny little "ruff" that he seemed to think was an answer. The man laughed.

Maybe, she decided, she didn't have to worry about the looney bin after all. It appeared he talked to dogs too.

Still, she'd have to fetch Boo. He wasn't allowed in the dining room. There were customers who were apt to complain and actually, she didn't approve. But first, she took a few deep breaths, hoping to settle her ruffled feathers. After a minute, she poured coffee from the pot into a carafe and put it on a tray along with a cup and saucer. No cream or sugar. He'd said black, she remembered. Moving carefully because of her legs, she carried the tray into the dining room.

Mr. Callahan had chosen the table closest to the kitchen. To save her a few steps? How very considerate of him. As for Boo, his ratty old ball was rolling across the empty room with him chasing hard behind it. As Rio watched, the dog caught the ball and ran back to drop it at Callahan's feet.

The man didn't seem to be put-off by the slobbers on the ball, for he picked it up and rolled it again.

Rio thumped the tray onto the table. Fortunately, she'd had the forethought to supply a napkin. She handed it to him. "He's not supposed to be in here," she said.

He wiped a splash of coffee from his sleeve before looking up at her. "I won't tell anybody if you won't."

She carried on silently from there, but she called Boo out when she'd served Mr. Callahan his breakfast. After that, she left him to his own devices, catching sight of him only once when she went to the herb patch for some thyme. He was down at the corral where she kept the hotel rental horses patting the friendly pinto on the neck.

Eliza, the youngest of Anna Golz's daughters who'd joined what Rio liked to call 'the team,' had arrived in time to pour Mr. Callahan more coffee and tend to any customer needs until her sister Blanche arrived. Blanche would start prepping for the evening meal for which as of last night they had twelve reservations, plus any diners who might drop-in. Blanche would also be in charge for the day and cooking on her own for the first time, while Rio attended the court dictated probate hearing on her inheritance. Rio couldn't help worrying about Blanche's new responsibilities, though they didn't seem to faze the other girl. Not too much, anyway. Blanche had already shown herself plenty capable of taking care of business. Right from her first night on the job, in fact, the night Rio got shot in plain sight of a roomful of people.

Rio shuddered as upstairs in her pokey little room she washed and changed into the best clothes she owned, a fitted dark-red skirt and short jacket over a white tucked shirtwaist. She brushed, rolled, and pinned her pale hair into something resembling a pompadour hairstyle, and dabbed rice powder over the red slash that remained where Sheriff Thor Donaldson had slugged her, breaking the skin. Embarrassing, she thought, for a judge to see someone—especially a sheriff even if he was crooked as a dog's hind leg and a proven murderer—had taken his fist to her. Last, she pinned a straw hat with a frothy swirl of tulle and a couple fanciful feathers on top of her hair.

When she'd made her torturous way down the stairs again, she found Washington Ames, timber boss

—all around boss really—for the Salo logging crew, waiting for her. He was wearing his good suit, the one he'd worn to her father's funeral last month. Out of his ordinary logger duds of caulked boots, worn britches with the bottoms cut off, and a red plaid shirt, he looked good. Very good. Not that he didn't always look good to her, with his dark hair and deep blue eyes.

And, according to the expression on Wash's face, Rio thought maybe she looked all right to him too.

"Ready to go?" he asked.

"Almost." She felt uneasy about leaving Blanche in charge for the day, but she had no choice. The probate hearing demanded her presence. Poking her head into the kitchen where Blanche was already at work, she said, "Are you all set?"

The other woman nodded at her. "Sure. You go ahead. I know what to do. And don't worry about Boo. Tommy already took your dog home with him. They will have fun together."

Rio sighed her relief. "Well, we're off then."

"Good luck," Blanche said.

"Thank you." Would she need luck, Rio wondered? Mr. Brackman, her attorney, assured her everything was in order. But all of her experiences lately warned against taking too much for granted.

She and Wash went down the swept path to the lakeshore where the hotel boats were tied up. Wash helped her into one of them, just like she hadn't spent hours getting in and out of boats by herself all of her life. But not with wounded legs. Today was different. She hadn't been in a boat since the shooting. Whereas normally she rowed customers back and forth to town, today Wash untied the lines and took the oars as a matter of course. Rio felt positively pampered.

Arriving in town, they caught the train bare minutes before it left the station. Rio settled onto the seat, her excitement starting to rise. The train whistle blew and the wheels began their slow clacking as they started off.

Neither of them looked back. Maybe they should have been paying more attention because as it happened, Rio caught the merest glance at a man who swung aboard the train as it left the station. What she didn't see when they reached Spokane, was when he jumped to the ground a half-minute before the train came to a full stop and he slipped around the corner out of sight.

Two

"Where do we go from here?" Wash asked. Instead of allowing the conductor to lend a hand, he simply plucked her from the train step and lifted her to the ground. "The courthouse?"

Rio felt a little unsettled as her feet touched the passenger loading—or in this case—unloading zone, and forced her sore legs to move her quickly out of the way of other people waiting to disembark. "Mr. Brackman asked that we meet in his office first thing so we can go over how the hearing is supposed to work. Best if there are no surprises, he said. We should have time. But I've never been to his office." She retrieved a letter from her pocketbook and, unfolding it, held it up for Wash to see. "Do you know where this is?"

The letterhead on the stationery gave an address.

Wash shook his head. "Nope, but that doesn't matter. We'll hire a hack and have him take us there. The drivers always know right where everything is."

What a relief to have Wash accompany her and

take charge. Especially when he whistled an eardrum piercing shriek that Rio believed made her eyeballs shimmy. A cab clustered together with a half dozen others lined up along the road pulled his horse over and stopped beside them.

He spat out a stream of nasty looking tobacco juice and said, "Where to?"

Rio read off the letterhead address and with a delay barely long enough for them to seat themselves in the vehicle, they started off. It didn't take long. Just over the bridge that crossed from the depot on Havermale Island to the downtown where tall buildings crowded side-to-side. People rushed in and out of the buildings, crossing streets in a way that made Rio wonder why they all didn't get run over and trampled underfoot.

Once into the city core, Rio gawked, impressed and a little frightened by the height of the high structures, the crowds, the streets filled with horses, wagons, and even a few—a very few—horseless carriages, their motors sputtering and making clanking noises. They emitted a powerful stench that made her nose sting.

It had been a while since Rio had been to Spokane. No, she thought, thinking back, more than a while. More than two years. It had been when Eino was preparing for his jaunt back east to visit relatives. He, with Elias agreeing, had declared his clothing too shabby to present the appearance he wanted the world to see. But, being the kind of men they were, the tailor in Painter's Bay didn't have the expertise they insisted on. Nothing would do but that he visit Spokane's finest. However, afraid Eino might be cheated, Elias insisted Rio accompany the party, seemingly on the supposition that as a nineteen-year-old female she should be able to judge the quality of the tailor's product. Funny, really, considering her father's general opinion of her. Why she should have any expertise in the first place was a mystery. The only clothes she got she made for herself.

Mr. Brackman had his law office on the second floor of an imposing clinker brick building on Fourth Avenue. The building had electric lights, she was delighted to see, and as she and Wash slowly, due to her legs, mounted the stairs to the office, she heard a telephone ring behind one of the doors. Sometimes, she believed, sighing heavily, it would be worthwhile to live in a city, simply for the availability of electric lights and telephones. It would be years before they got to Painter's Bay, if ever.

They found Mr. Brackman's office easily enough. His name, emblazoned in gold leaf on a frosted glass window set in the door, promised exclusive service. Wash knocked. A female voice called, "Come in." Once inside, they found a secretary sitting at a desk in a small reception area. She looked up as they entered.

Rio couldn't help noticing her eyes went straight to Wash. Well, he was looking particularly handsome today. Who could blame her? Then the woman's gaze shifted to Rio.

"Good morning, Miss Salo," she said. "Mr. Brackman has been expecting you. If you'll wait here, I'll let him know you've arrived. He's anxious to speak with you."

The heels of her stylish shoes clacking on the polished wood floor, she hurried off before Rio could say a word.

"Anxious? What do you suppose has made him

anxious? And how did she know who I am?" she whispered to Wash.

Though he appeared a little uncomfortable and out of place in this building with art on the oak-paneled walls and the sumptuous Persian rug centered on the floor, Wash seemed to be doing his best to look at ease.

He eyed a seascape painting and said, "Brackman probably described you. I'd bet he doesn't have many pretty brown-eyed blonde ladies asking for him. And she probably knew you have an appointment and a court date today."

Pretty? Wash said I'm pretty? Rio's heart went hippety hop, though she said, "Oh. But I'm the anxious one."

He grinned. "I don't blame you."

Rio gripped his arm and leaned close. "Wash, I'm scared. I don't think..." She paused and started over. "I do think something is going to go wrong today."

He smiled and shook his head. "Nothing will go wrong. Why would it? He's got all the right paperwork, we found your mother's bones, there's nobody got a reason to contest the will. Everything will be fine, Rio. You'll be fine."

A retort was rising to her lips. Something along the lines of saying it would be the first time in her life things went right. She didn't have time to deliver it, though, as Mr. Brackman stepped into the room just then and beckoned them into his office.

The attorney shook their hands before eyeing the pair of them with approval. "Mr. Ames, I'm sure you'll make a good impression on the judge. Rio, my dear girl, you most definitely will." His expression changed. "There is one thing—"

Here it comes, Rio thought. She'd known there'd be something.

"A friend of Mrs. Bliss, my secretary, is a clerk in the records department at the courthouse. He let Mrs. Bliss know that yesterday someone was poking into the files regarding deeds to the hotel property. Of course, Mrs. Bliss then reported to me." He held up a hand as if to keep her from interrupting, although Rio had no such intention. "No one seems to know who this person is. At first, my guess was that it's someone connected with the late Mr. Thor Donaldson as he'd seemed bound he was going to be taking over the property when your father passed on. Then I learned the person is a woman."

Rio cringed at the mention of the late sheriff's name, and she didn't miss the way Wash's eyes narrowed. "A woman?"

"Yes. A dark-haired woman with sharp features wearing a green suit." The attorney pretended not to notice their reactions and went on. "I wish I felt safe to consider this as someone's simple curiosity, considering the matter was reported in the *Chronicle*, both just after the shooting, and again when the sheriff died."

This time Wash winced noticeably. He'd been the one to fire on the sheriff, wounding him, but not quite in time to prevent the sheriff from shooting Rio first. Donaldson developed sepsis a few days later and died. Nobody Rio knew had been heartbroken at his demise, she least of all. Which raised the question of what sort of woman would be associated with Thor Donaldson.

Something about the way the attorney spoke worried her. "I take it there's more to the story."

Mr. Brackman breathed deeply, folded his fingers

17

into a tent shape and shook his head. "There is. I'm not quite sure what it means, however. But this morning when I entered my office, a couple things just seemed off."

"Off?" Wash said.

"Yes." Brackman pivoted his chair and pointed at the twin oak four-drawer filing cabinets behind his desk. "For instance, one of these cabinets was unlocked, with the drawer gaping open. Just a tiny bit. Maybe a quarter of an inch or so. But that isn't the only thing."

Rio looked at Wash. He raised a brow.

"Do I understand you routinely keep the cabinet locked?" she asked. It stood to reason those files were private.

"Indeed I do. More than that, all the paperwork recording old contracts, wills, judgments, action taken, is routinely stored away from the office in a vault at one of the banks. Only active work is kept in this cabinet, which is locked after every opening. The office is locked as well except when I'm in it, and the building is secured at night. Plus, the building tenants as a whole chip in to pay a night watchman."

"I guess the second thing has to do with security?" Wash asked softly.

The attorney sighed. "Good guess, Mr. Ames. You probably didn't notice, but the door to this office has been pried open, bypassing the lock. And when I looked through the open drawer, the divider holding information concerning clients whose name starts with an S had been rifled. Both the old Serrano and the Salo files were stored there until the probate process is settled. Both files were empty, except for a document stating the date and time of today's hearing."

Rio's eyes opened wide. "I was the target? They got everything?"

"No, no," Brackman hastened to say. "I imagine someone is very disappointed. You see, they got nothing. The files were already empty."

"Empty?" Rio repeated.

"What would've they taken?" Wash demanded. "And what would they do with the papers if they'd gotten them?"

Brackman's chair creaked as he tilted it back. Oddly enough, it struck Rio that he seemed rather complacent.

"Previously," he said, "all the original paperwork setting forth the deal between Mr. Serrano and Elias Salo putting the hotel in Serrano's hands were taken from the archives and put in the file. Then there was Serrano's will passing the property to his daughter, Juanita Serrano Salo. And a couple months later, her will, with all the legally necessary permissions, passing the hotel to you, Miss Salo. All of those items were there. Fortunately, I took the relevant papers home with me last night to study before the hearing today. Had they gotten hold of the information, they might have slowed the proceedings, made complaints, taken the information and delayed matters until it could be rescheduled. Or, more likely, simply destroyed them. In which case, we would've had a difficult time passing through probate. As it happens, whoever attempted to get at them got nothing."

"But who would do such a thing?" Rio blinked and added, "And why, now that my father is dead. We all know he intended to take the hotel from me." She was aware of Wash moving restlessly, as if he'd like to jump up and take some kind of action.

Brackman frowned. "That's the question, isn't it? Offhand," he said, "I've got to wonder if your half brother is as dead as he's purported to be. Because if he is, we've got another case of a missing body making it difficult to declare death and right of survivorship for the rest of the property." Standing up, he fetched a leather briefcase from a desk drawer and tucked it under his arm. "But that's for later. One thing at a time. We should get to the courthouse and prepare. Mr. Ames—" He gave Wash a meaningful look. "I know you're a good friend to Miss Salo. There is always a bailiff on hand to keep order, but I hope you'll keep a watchful eye on proceedings, as well. This break-in has me worried."

Wash nodded. "I will." He smiled, a mere lift of his lips, at Rio.

The whole notion of being the object of an unknown someone's attention set Rio's insides to quivering again, just when she'd thought she'd gotten past that particular reaction.

What's more, her left leg ached fiercely from the walking, especially dealing with the stairs, and, she suspected, from the knowledge there might be somebody beyond the late Sheriff Donaldson who wanted to shoot her. Well, besides Eino, she supposed.

Mr. Brackman hustled them out of his office, but instead of going out the same way they'd come in, he led them through an almost invisible door at the end of the hall and down a narrow set of stairs to where they exited the building via a back door. To Rio's surprise, a closed hack awaited them.

While Wash kept a watch, the attorney helped Rio into the vehicle and climbed in beside her. Wash, seeing the way was clear, followed. They set off at a brisk pace.

"I arranged this when I discovered there'd been a break-in this morning," Mr. Brackman said. "I've worked with this particular driver before. He knows just what to do."

Apparently, that included turning into a narrow alley that led them two blocks south, then onto Fifth Street, and then north toward the courthouse. Even so, they were a little early when the hack stopped and the driver let them out.

Stepping down, Rio's eyes widened at her first glimpse of the preposterous courthouse. "It's a castle."

Brackman laughed. "It is. Come inside."

The grounds surrounding the courthouse held a good many folks wandering around wearing serious expressions. Rio assumed she wasn't the only one alarmed by whatever proceedings were going to happen to them next. Right now she felt as if her stomach was tied in knots, especially when the elevator she entered almost swooped her feet out from under her as it started moving, then again as it stopped. The attendant opened the door, which was when she discovered she was hanging on to Wash.

He grinned down at her. "That was fun."

Not so sure, Rio shook her head.

The attorney walked briskly to a courtroom door which he opened just far enough for all of them to pass inside. They made their way to the front where a small table had only enough room for his briefcase and papers and accommodated two chairs for them to sit. Wash was delegated to a bench just behind them.

They'd no more than settled when the door opened

again and a few people filed into the room. Rio had never seen any of them before, but Brackman nodded to several. There were no women. Rio began to feel like a llama in a chicken coop.

Proceedings began at last, and her palms started sweating. She turned to look at Wash, just in time to see the entry door swing closed. She glimpsed a man mostly turned away from her. Had there been something familiar about him? She thought maybe so, but the judge entered the courtroom just then and she had to stand and face front so lost sight of him.

The bailiff made his pronouncements and they all sat. At this, the proceedings began. Rio's moment of curiosity faded as if it had never been.

Rio tried to listen and make sense of everything the judge and Mr. Brackman said. *This injunction, that deposition.* She didn't understand half of it. Every once in a while the judge would ask a question, and her attorney would answer. After a little time, they got down to business. These were the parts she actually knew something about. Her nervousness eased—until she had to rise, make some sort of oath, and allow the bailiff to hand her into a chair set on a slightly raised dais.

The judge leaned toward her. "Don't worry," he whispered. "You're all right." His lips barely moved and his expression never changed. His next words were louder, loud enough people in the room could hear. "Tell me," he said, "whatever you might remember of the last time you saw your mother. I believe you were eight years old."

Rio took a deep breath, hoping her voice wouldn't shake. Sad hope. It did. "Yes. Eight. I'd finished washing dishes after the dinner service and the hotel dining room had emptied. My father was standing at the bar with a whiskey glass in his hand. I remember being awfully tired and was on my way to bed but he was staring at me in a funny sort of way and I thought maybe it would please him if I told him good night."

She stopped, not really wanting to continue.

"Did it please him?" Judge Thornton asked.

After a moment, she said, "Not particularly. Nothing I did ever pleased him."

The judge frowned. "What happened?"

"He said something. I don't remember what. Something not nice." Not true. She remembered very well, but nobody else needed to hear this part. "My mother happened to walk past and overheard." Her lips trembled. "They quarreled, yelling at each other. After a little bit, Mama told me to go on to bed. I remember crying and saying I didn't want to leave her, but she gave me a little push and told me to go. So I did. That's all."

Judge Thornton looked out over the silent people in the courtroom. "Do you remember the color of your mother's dress?"

"Oh, yes." Rio didn't hesitate when it came to this. "Her dress was new, for one thing, and she looked very pretty in it. The background was cream-colored printed with small bunches of multicolored flowers. She was wearing earrings, small ones with pearls and sapphires, and a plain gold band wedding ring. I know it had a date engraved on the back. The date my father and mother were married."

"And did you ever see your mother again?"

"Not alive."

"But later?"

"Yes. Five weeks ago when I happened upon a cave on Salo property. It is on a hillside opened up by a landslide. I found her bones."

"And did anyone else witness this?"

The audience seemed to hold their collective breath.

"Yes. A Federal Customs Agent, Mr. Beckett Ferris, who was tracking opium smugglers crossing Salo land, and the Salo Timber Products logging boss, Mr. Washington Ames."

Wash, called forward, took her place in the witness chair and reported what they'd found in the cave. It had proved to be a grave holding her mother's bones.

"There was a bullet hole in her forehead," he said.

Mutters in the courtroom forced the judge to stare out at the observers, his visage stern, until they quieted.

The judge had the bailiff read Beckett's deposition next. Then, with Rio back on the stand, demanded she explain why and when the three of them were in a position to make this discovery. Consequently, she had to touch more closely on the opium smuggling ring Beckett had broken up. They went on to the murder of one of the Salo logging crew first, then to the Chinese cook, and finally the attempts on Rio herself.

Rio didn't like where the next hour of testimony led. The part where the judge asked her about when her father was dying and he admitted to killing Juanita Salo and that everything he'd ever told Rio about her was a lie. Dr. Clement's avowal of hearing Elias say these things, a deposition like Beckett's, was read. Then the part where Sheriff Donaldson shot her, in plain sight of a roomful of people was discussed.

After what took another two hours, time which seemed to Rio never-ending, the wills, the special dispensation of Elias Salo's control over his wife's property, and subsequently his daughter's estate, were examined. Only then did Judge Thornton say he was ready to make his declaration.

Rio drew in a deep breath.

"I believe all criteria have been met and satisfied. The estate of Juanita Serrano Salo passes to her daughter, Rio Salo, without encumbrance. The property known as the Painter's Bay Hotel belongs solely to her as does anything still undeclared of her mother's estate."

Rio stood, turned, and almost fell into Wash's arms.

Three

Rio's ordeal didn't end with the judge leaving the bench. Clamor arose in the courtroom. Unfettered clamor now the officials had gone. In a surge, a half dozen or so men gathered around her and the table where Mr. Brackman was assembling his documents into order.

Wash, steadying Rio on her feet, eased her behind him in an effort to stem the rush and protect her. For his trouble, he received an elbow in the ribs, a staggering shove from a much larger man, and a series of name-calling from the others.

They were trying to reach her, Rio realized. Eyes dilating, her heart fluttered. Why? Were they crazy? She grabbed Wash by the back of his jacket and held on.

Brackman finished stowing the papers and moved between the men and his bewildered clients. He had, she saw, a great sense of command as he announced, "Settle down, fellows. Give us some time and I'll answer your questions."

Eyes narrowed, Wash's expression set and he made his own announcement. "If any one of you gets too close to Miss Salo, you're going to learn it was a bad idea. Back off."

"Say, buster. Who'er you? Her bodyguard?" one demanded. This one wore a shabby suit, a curled mustache, and a strange-looking hat with pins and papers stuck in the hatband. At least he apparently took Wash's warning at value.

"Come closer and you'll find out," Wash said.

"Oh, yeah?" said another. "Why don't you get out of the way and let her talk? You too, Brackman."

"Hey, lady, the lawyer said you got shot in the leg. Can I see your wound?" This one, more impertinent than the others, got jostled aside.

The men started a new round of shouted questions and recriminations that Rio made no sense of whatsoever. She buried her face in Wash's back.

"What the hell? Do something, Brackman," Wash demanded. "Who are these jackanapes, anyhow?"

Brackman let out an audible sigh. "Newspapermen." He turned to Rio. "I'm sorry about this. I expected a reporter or two, but I didn't realize there'd be mayhem. Not all of these are local."

"You could've given us some warning," Wash said, his face set.

Rio agreed. A few feet away, she saw someone pointing a large, unwieldy camera at her. She ducked away.

"Yes," Brackman said. "I see that." He held up a hand. "All right, men, this is how we're going to act. Each of you will have a chance to ask one question. I will answer it. At the end, if there's anything else I think you need to know, I'll tell you." His stern gaze landed on one of the men. "You. What's your question?"

"What made old man Salo give up his rights to his wife's estate?"

"Weren't you listening to the testimony? The original deal was made between his wife's father and him. He sold the run-down hotel to Benedict Serrano for money to buy a large parcel of timberland. The deal came with the understanding Mrs. Salo had the right to dispose of it when and if it became hers. Salo signed off from claiming any husbandly rights. He also claimed his wife had run away, which only a few weeks ago was proven a lie. She was murdered and he murdered her. Since Miss Salo was a child at the time, his child, he avoided any question of inheritance although even then it should have come directly to her."

There was a great deal he left unsaid about the deal, for which Rio was grateful.

The questioner scribbled on his pad, the pencil moving at a great rate of speed.

Rio, standing slightly behind Wash, noticed how tense he was.

"Why do any of you care?" Rio's question burst from her. "Frankly, you all seem a gathering of ghouls."

"Why do we care?" A man's eyebrows rose practically into his hairline. "Because of the newspaper reports on your attempted murder at the hotel, of course. Right in plain sight of everyone, which seems pretty much unhinged. That was big news, especially when it came to light the sheriff of the county was a criminal and head of opium smuggling ring. He attacked a defenseless girl."

Another man agreed. "Big news! Didn't you know

that? Didn't anybody tell you?" Then he glanced around. "That wasn't my question. Not my real question."

Brackman ignored him.

Rio hadn't known her ordeal had been big news, having been laid up during the early furor. And afterward, even when she reappeared in the hotel, folks mostly had avoided talking about the shooting.

"That doctor,"—the next man in line spoke up—"he said he heard your father say he should've killed you when he killed his wife. Your mother. Did Salo really say that? Did you hear him?"

Feeling as though she'd been turned to ice, at her attorney's nod, Rio said, "Yes." Stark. Enough. Though most of the newspapermen abided by Brackman's specifications, more questions came, some aimed at her. And some at Wash, especially when they found out he was the one who wounded the sheriff.

"You killed him," the next man said. "It just took him a while to die. How do you feel about that?"

Brackman said, low, for Wash's ears alone. "Careful how you answer."

Shrugging, Wash said, "I'm glad he's dead. I'm sorry I had to be the one who did it."

More questions peppered the conference. Some were couched in language that would've made Rio's ears burn if she'd led a more sheltered life.

Finally, seeing Rio was flagging and that Wash grew more impatient with every utterance out of the reporters' mouths, George Brackman had had enough. He didn't want anything to go wrong here.

"Here's my final word on events." He waved his arms over his head to make sure he had everyone's attention. "You may have noticed this whole hearing has smacked more of a trial for a dead man—Sheriff Thor Donaldson—than a simple probate hearing to prove a husband gave up any rights to his dead wife's property. Moot after all this time, a process fourteen years in the making. But neither Judge Thorpe nor I wanted any question raised as to the rightness of the decision. It's settled. We all hope Miss Salo will go on running the Painter's Bay Hotel for many years while serving up her superlative dining experience. You should make the trip to Painter's Bay and try it. That's all."

With that, he pushed ahead through the men with enough confidence they parted way for the three of them.

Outside the fancy castle-like courthouse, to Rio's surprise they found the same hack they'd arrived in waiting for them. She collapsed inside, sinking onto the seat. Finally, she summoned up a smile for the attorney. "Remind me not to read any newspapers for the next week or so."

Brackman chuckled. "I may need the same reminder. But their interest in you will pass. It won't take long before there's some new event to draw their attention and they'll go to yammering after someone else."

"God willing," Wash muttered under his breath. And louder, "I'll be glad to get back to Painter's Bay. Got a batch of logs coming down the flume tomorrow to dump in the bay, and I need to be there to see the sticking points are greased. Don't want anybody getting killed."

Greasing the flume was an extremely dangerous

job. Rio shuddered at the necessity. "I hope you're not planning to do it yourself," she said.

He shook his head. "Zhiyu volunteered when I said I'd pay whoever did it an extra two dollars a day."

Rio hoped the young Chinese man knew what he was in for.

Back at the attorney's office, Rio had papers to sign and her attorney's bill to pay. Seeing the total, panic turned her mouth dry as she wondered how long the $2626.00 she'd found in the secret compartment of her father's armoire would last. The hotel had better pick up business fast at this rate. And she still had questions she hoped Mr. Brackman had answers to.

The woman who'd greeted them in the morning filled the ink pen Mr. Brackman supplied and laid the papers out on the desk. "You should read them," she whispered. The attorney and Wash stood in the doorway discussing something just then, so it was just the girls.

Rio's chocolate brown eyes opened wide. Mr. Brackman wouldn't try to bamboozle her, would he?

Mrs. Bliss must have guessed her apprehension from the expression on her face. "Oh, Mr. Brackman would never do anything against your interests, Miss Salo. He always tells me to remind the clients to read before they sign." She smiled.

Rio did have one more question, though it didn't stem from the straightforward paperwork. She signed the last paper and looked up at the attorney as he claimed his swivel chair.

His eyebrows raised. "Something you want to ask?"

"Yes. Why did my father want the hotel so badly he killed my mother? Do you know? And why, after so many years, did he want to kill me? Was it because of Eino when my mother omitted him from her will?"

Brackman only shrugged. "I'm sorry. I can't tell you. Anything is possible, I suppose. I take it maternal love was not involved between Eino and your mother."

A short laugh burst from Rio before she could stop herself. "Maternal love? No. Definitely not. I remember Mother having to protect me from him. My father never tried to stop him from hurting me. It did not endear him to her." She went silent for a moment. "After she was gone, I fought back."

Two pairs of eyes stared at her. Brackman's a little shocked, Wash's questioning. "How did you manage that?" he asked.

Color rose in her face. "One day I put a few chopped rhubarb leaves dressed in a spicy vinaigrette on his sandwich after he'd tried to break my arm. Oh, not enough to do permanent harm. Just enough to make him sick and teach him a lesson."

"Did it work?" Brackman asked.

Rio nodded. "It did. I told Eino what I'd done and said I'd do it every time he hurt me. Since I did all of our cooking by that time—and Eino liked to eat—he got sneakier, but less physical after that."

The men laughed to think of a little girl threatening her teenage brother and winning the battle, but she didn't laugh with them. To her, it had been a matter of survival and staying whole.

Wash, taking pity on Rio's hard-used legs, soon got her outside to the street, where he whistled for a hack to take them to the station to catch the train. They didn't speak of the hearing, with each caught up in their own thoughts. Not until they were about to reach the depot at Painter's Bay.

Rio yawned, holding her hand over her mouth in an attempt to hide it. Wash grinned down at her. "Tired? It's been a rough day, hasn't it?"

She nodded. "I keep hoping everything will straighten out in this county now. I hope the next man elected sheriff will be both honest and fair. I hope the hotel and restaurant will thrive." She thought a moment. "And that my legs get well fast and I can start sleeping through the night."

Wash's grin flashed, but only briefly. "Your legs will be fine. Doc Clement says so, and he ought to know. And if the last couple weeks are anything to go by, I'm pretty sure you needn't worry about the restaurant." His mouth twisted. "I've got to admit I've got my doubts about a new sheriff."

"Has anyone applied?"

"Not that I've heard. Somebody said the country commissioners even sent out notices back east asking for applications."

Rio blinked at this news. "Really!"

"Really." He fell silent as the train slowed. The engineer blew the whistle, loud over the squealing of wheels as brakes were applied. Then he said, "I know one man who'd stand a good chance if he'd apply."

"You do?"

He nodded. "Trouble is, I don't know if he'd want to take on the job."

"Who is it?" Did he mean himself? He'd be an excellent sheriff, but she'd hate to have him in harm's way. "Who?" she repeated.

The train lurched to a stop, casting her forward out

of her seat. Deftly, Wash caught her and sat her back upright. "Beckett Ferris," he said, his eyes watching her face.

"Oh." She didn't know what else to say. What did he want her to say? Wash had acted strangely in the days after she was shot. Stiff with her. Stiff with Beckett. Even a little stiff with Win, Beckett's young brother, who'd himself still been recovering from being shot. The Ferris brothers had moved on a couple weeks ago, and only in the past two or three days had Wash showed signs of returning to the steady, reliable man she knew so well.

Thought she did, anyway.

She shuddered. She was glad Thor Donaldson was dead. Glad! He'd not only killed two men that she knew of but had tried to kill both Win and herself. Wash had said he regretted being the one whose bullet ended up killing Donaldson, but she was grateful he hadn't hesitated.

Still, she wondered. Did he hold her to blame for having taken a man's life?

"What do you think?" he asked, his gaze holding her as he waited for an answer.

"About Beckett for sheriff?" She wanted to be sure. And to have a moment to think.

His expression suggested impatience.

She wouldn't lie but took a moment to get her legs under her in preparation of standing. "I think he'd make a fine sheriff." She ticked off attributes. "He's got experience, considering his time as a customs agent. He's got grit. He doesn't back down from characters like Thor Donaldson. And he takes care of his brother." She stood. "Against him is the fact not many people know him. He wasn't here long enough. Not that that should be a consideration if the commissioners are sending word all over the country."

They eased out into the aisle between seats and slowly made their way to the exit.

"Hell," Wash muttered from behind her. She didn't know why.

Getting from the depot to the town pier as it jutted into the bay took what remaining energy Rio had. At least the Painter's Bay boat, painted a distinctive green with red trim, remained right where Wash had tied it this morning. The lone fisherman standing on the dock as evening shadows drew in around them saluted Wash and nodded to Rio. Before he could speak, his fishing rod bent as the hook caught, and he lost interest in talking as he reeled the fish in.

Rio was relieved. Wash helped her into the boat and took to the oars. He made short work of crossing to the hotel. The last of the light had faded by then. Lights shone in the windows. A laugh carried across the water. Frogs croaked. A fish jumped only inches from the boat, water splashing as it went back under. A breeze had cleared any smoke released from the sawmill's burner and the air smelled of verdant greenery and, even at a distance, freshly cut logs.

Rio sighed, glad to be home. For the first time since morning, she thought of Blanche and wondered if, untried though she was, the girl had been able to keep up with the flow. Rio was confident. The young woman learned fast and didn't fluster.

"You'll eat in the dining room tonight?" she said to Wash as he docked, jumped out and tied the boat.

His mood seemed to have eased. She decided the

effort of rowing the boat had helped. "Is that an invitation? I don't know. What's on the menu?"

She laughed. "Yes, it's an invitation. If Blanche followed the plan, there's a choice between brown sugar glazed pork chops and spicy braised chicken breast with honey/ginger charred carrots and rice. The only problem with the chicken is convincing Blanche not to cook the juice out of it."

Rio was happy to let the subject of Beckett Ferris drop.

IN THE TWO days he'd spent at the Painter's Bay Hotel, Quinn Callahan had oriented himself to the area, spending hours in daylight the first day, and later in the dark, examining the trails and paths around the hotel. Mostly in the dark, come to think of it, given he'd taken the train into Spokane for most of one of those days. He didn't mind admitting the result of this excursion had been a surprise.

This was pretty country, different from the flatlands where he came from. Where what they thought were mountains back home were no more than hills here. This morning early, he'd hired one of the hotel's four horses to take him around. At the stable, a small boy had managed to saddle the horse and bring it out to him.

Evidently, they grew stout kids around here. He'd passed the boy a nickel tip, and you'd have thought it the most delightful experience the kid had ever had.

Tonight Quinn had other plans, some taking him in a different direction. So far, he'd stayed away from the logging company's headquarters located at the edge of

Painter's Bay, believing it had nothing to do with his business. But nothing else had developed either, and he was already tired of this infernal waiting. He was ready for action. Ready to complete the job. Meanwhile, the more he could learn about the people, the better and faster his work would be done.

For instance, as far as he could tell, Washington Ames, whom'd he'd gotten a few locals to talk about, was as honest, hardworking, and as likable a man as you'd hope to meet. Not a man to be associated with the villain on his list.

And the woman at the hotel? Folks hereabouts were all too eager to talk about her. About how right in front of a roomful of people, the sheriff shot and almost killed her. And about how Ames's defense of young Miss Salo had ended up with the sheriff dying. And now, just as he'd arrived, he'd learned she owned the hotel.

She did. Not the brother. Which might make his job more difficult.

Quinn had slipped away from the hotel just when most of the first seating of restaurant diners had finished and were leaving. If anyone spotted him, they'd think he was one of them. Someone simply cutting through the woods while taking a shortcut back to town. Not that he expected anyone here to know him or his purpose anyway.

Still, as he walked through the woods, a sensation of being watched raised the short hairs on the back of his neck. No stranger to the feeling—he knew it came with his line of work—Quinn kept a sharp lookout. He wasn't the only one likely to be here with the same purpose in mind. Others had a stake in this as well.

A burst of light blasted across his eyes, taking away

his night vision. He flung up a hand to shield his eyes, and didn't see the knife coming at him until too late. There was a stabbing pain, a quick sensation of weakness. He struck out, landed a blow, but his arm was already going numb by then. The blow glanced off bone. So did the next and the one after that. Each got weaker. The attacker was fast. The knife flashed. First into his side, going for a kidney. Next, into his chest, but the knife had struck his gun in the shoulder holster and missed the heart or lungs.

He knew that much, but it didn't help him now.

Quinn stepped back only to find his legs had gone to jelly. He went down in a heap.

"Here," a voice called out. "Enough. You got him."

The attack stopped as quickly as it had begun.

Just as quickly, the light faded. Not only the bright light, but all the light.

Four

B y nine o'clock, the hotel was quiet. The last of the restaurant customers, a single man who paid his bill with nickels, finally departed. With the kitchen properly cleaned, the weary Golz ladies left soon after. Out in the lobby, where the bar held sway in a nook, Rio could hear men still talking. The bartender and one other—yet another salesman staying for two nights, she thought.

Relieved beyond measure, Rio sank down at the desk in her office. Or what she called an office. It was a small storage room off the kitchen where she had arranged a desk, a chair, and an old locking cabinet for her paperwork. At the very back of the room, essentially hidden by the desk and chair, she'd squeezed in a cot for times when her legs just wouldn't support her any longer. She'd already had to use it more than she'd liked.

After two weeks, the routine still felt odd following so many months off as she waited for her father to die. He'd demanded her full attention and hadn't cared about the hotel.

Boo, who'd stuck with her like a burr since her return from the city, lay at her feet, nose resting on his paws while keeping a close eye on her. His fluffy tail wagged fiercely as she reached down to pat him. Soon her attention returned to adding up the restaurant order slips for the second time. Finding the sum totaled exactly the same as before, she gave a crow of satisfaction.

A fuss at the door alerted her. She looked up as Mr. Turner, the bartender, stuck his head into the room. "Thought that feller wasn't ever going to bed," he grumbled. "But I'm leaving now."

"Thank you for your work tonight, Mr. Turner. I appreciate your handling of the bar and keeping the guest...um...entertained." The barkeep, as she well knew, told some highly diverting stories to amuse people. Especially drinking people.

The man flushed. "What's good for you is good for me," he said. "Good night."

He had a hand on the doorknob when she followed him into the hall. "Mr. Turner?"

"Yeah?" He stopped.

"Have you seen one of our guests, a Mr. Callahan, this evening? Eliza Golz said she didn't remember seeing him in the restaurant for the dinner service."

Turner shrugged. "Don't know him," he said. "Don't guess I've seen him."

"Oh, all right. Well, good night, Mr. Turner. Take care on your way home."

He touched two fingers to his forehead in a sort of salute and left. She guessed he didn't need her advice. He'd been walking around on his own for forty years before she was born.

He told the same story as she'd gotten from the rest of the employees. The situation struck her as odd. Eliza, the only one who'd had a good look at Mr. Callahan from when she served breakfast this morning, had made a point of mentioning his absence to her, which had roused Rio's curiosity.

"He's a fine-looking man," the girl had said, blushing so violently Rio had thought her hair, which already had a touch of ginger, might catch on fire. "And so polite. He talked to me real nice. Wasn't fresh at all this morning when he asked me where the best hiking trails might be."

"Hiking trails?"

Lips pursed, Eliza nodded, which led Rio to believe she might have been a little disappointed about that.

Rio put the night's receipts in the safe bolted to the floor behind the desk and file cabinet. A storage bin for potatoes used to occupy the space, their scent still strong. Her nose wrinkled.

"Did you ever notice spuds have a kind of musty smell?" she asked Boo, slamming the safe door shut and twisting the dial. "There. Done. Come on. Let's lock up." She wondered some if Callahan planned on showing up in the middle of the night and ringing the bell for attention. She'd have to rise and unlock the door then. The thought irritated her. Traipsing up and down those stairs—especially with her legs still not right—taxed her energy. It had been one of the reasons she'd planned to take the ground-floor room.

Finished at the front, with Boo following her through the lobby, past the dining room and then the kitchen to the back while checking that lamps were out and the kitchen fire properly banked, she moved on to

41

the porch. They stepped outside, Rio taking a deep breath of the night air. Scented with pine, cottonwood trees, and lake water, it helped ease the cares of the day. And finally allowed her mind to drift back to everything that had happened. Meaning her appearance before the judge and the clamor of the newspapermen. And last, best of all, culminating with the worry about claiming the hotel erased.

Startling her, Boo shot off the porch without making use of the steps, barking and dashing toward the path leading to the loggers barracks and cook shack.

Rio knew Mr. Turner would've gone that way only moments ago. Had her warning been needed after all? Had he had an accident? Fallen? A worse thought struck. Been attacked?

Or, more likely, had her dog sensed an animal and gone to run it off.

"Boo," she called softly. "Get back here."

But he didn't. Even when his barking stopped.

Her eyes adjusted to the dark as she stood at the top of the steps. Another minute passed. Slowly, she reached behind her for the shotgun propped behind a horizontally halved wooden barrel where she planted some of the herbs she used for cooking. She pulled the gun toward her, the scent of rosemary rising as its butt brushed against the herb.

Kept loaded, the gun was meant to discourage varmints.

But she knew it also worked to protect against villains or thieves.

Treading softly, she went down the steps and followed the path Boo had taken. Maybe fifty yards into the woods, she heard something and stopped.

Panting? *Yes.*

Footsteps? *Yes.* She thought so. Not Boo's, though. Certainly this was something, or someone, heavier. Fear, a familiar companion these days, touched her. Then a flash of white raced toward her. Rio almost fainted with relief.

"Boo, where have you been? What's going on?" *Relief?* Yet she whispered.

The dog looked back from whence he'd come, and her gaze followed his. Movement. More panting. Then two men emerged on the path. One supported the other.

Even in the dark, she recognized both and went to meet them.

"What's happened? Mr. Turner? Mr. Callahan?"

"Could use some help," Turner said. "Found this feller in the woods. This the one you was asking about?"

"I'm afraid so. What happened to him?"

"Dunno for sure. He says..."

Callahan, swaying despite Turner's supporting arm, managed an answer for himself. "Knifed."

"Knifed?" Rio's voice rose. "You've been stabbed?"

"Stabbed and sliced," Turner answered for him. "He's dripping blood like a slaughtered steer."

"Dear God." Rio thought a moment. "My legs. I can't really help." She barely kept herself upright, let alone bearing other weight. "Maybe I can rouse the salesman."

"No." Callahan could barely speak, but speak he did.

"He's right," Turner said. "Ask me, that feller was talking too much, too fast, like maybe he was keeping me out of the way. He coulda done it. I don't trust him."

43

Rio didn't trust Mr. Callahan either. "Who did this to you, Mr. Callahan?" she asked.

But he didn't answer.

She sighed. "It's not far to the hotel. Keep going. I'll run ahead and prepare your room and fetch my aid kit." Although from his weakness, she figured it would take more than her scant knowledge and paltry supplies. At least she'd renewed the items since they'd been used when Win Ferris was shot and his brother refused the doctor.

Callahan, she thought, would welcome Dr. Clement. Or if he wouldn't, she'd still insist.

Stripping the blanket from the bed and putting a worn but clean quilt down over the sheets, she set out the kit and poked up the kitchen fire for hot water. The boiler in the basement had gone out hours ago. Going around the room lighting lamps, she was as ready for the patient as she could be. The rigamarole reminded her all too vividly of events from a month ago with Win.

Hearing Turner grunting with effort, she awaited them as they tried the steps onto the porch. Callahan hadn't made a sound until then. Now he did. A soft curse. Boo rushed in ahead of them, his tail, which normally curled over his back, drooping around his heels.

Rio made sure to lock the back door once they were inside and brought the shotgun in with her.

Callahan fainted the moment he lay down.

"Hellfire." Turner said, his alarm showing off his vocabulary. "He gonna die on us?"

"Not if I can help it," Rio said grimly. "Mr. Turner, I hate to ask this of you, but do you think you could row over to town and fetch Dr. Clement? Look at his skin. I'm afraid Mr. Callahan has gone into shock."

Looking down at the wounded man, Turner nodded. "Don't want to, but I reckon I'd better."

Rio bit her lip. "Do you want a lantern?"

"No. But you might keep a watch for me, comin' and goin'. And don't let that there scattergun outta your sight."

Rio had another of those trills of fear run down her spine. "I will. I won't," she promised, answering both his demands.

And she did, until she couldn't spot Turner and the boat on the lake anymore. Then she turned back to Quinn Callahan.

It was easy to see where the knife had done its damage. One wound was a slice down his arm, as if he'd thrown it up to block a thrust toward his chest. The second showed a stab, an indication the knife-wielder had tried a horizontal jab between the ribs. It appeared to Rio that since there was no bloody foam issuing from either his lung or his mouth, the blade had glanced off a rib and slid around his rib cage until the shoulder rig holding his small pistol stopped it.

Why hadn't he taken out the pistol and shot the man with the knife?

She removed the gun and laid it aside. Deeming the shirt—a fine thing made of softest cotton—far beyond repair, she wrestled him out of what remained of it and used the rags to make pads to sop blood. While propping him up to remove the shirt, she found a jagged cut in his belt. Evidently, the attacker had tried first for a kidney, but the belt Callahan wore had deflected the blow. Deflected, but not a total miss. If all had gone as the attacker had planned, he'd be dead.

And he might yet be.

When the water warmed, she washed away the blood that had dripped from his arm onto his hands, where she discovered broken and bruised knuckles. He must have gone down fighting, a point in his favor.

There wasn't anything else she could do for him. Except keep him warm. She remembered how young Win Ferris had complained of the cold, so she tossed one of the blankets loosely over him. He moaned once but didn't open his eyes.

Then she went outside to keep watch for Mr. Turner and the doctor, taking the shotgun with her. Boo followed, cuddling on her lap when she seated herself on the bench. They were quiet. Nothing happened to disturb the woods around the hotel.

It seemed like forever before she heard the quiet splash of oars and a boat with two men in it came into sight. They alighted and hurried up the path, Dr. Clement taking long strides and surging ahead.

"Let's get to work," he said.

RIO WENT to sleep in a chair with her head resting on the mattress where Quinn Callahan lay. Sometime in the night, she'd leaned over—or fallen over—in the most uncomfortable position possible. She hadn't meant to fall asleep at all. She'd intended to keep watch to make sure the patient's bleeding didn't start again. However, the day, which had begun very early in the morning, had taken all the sap out of her.

Fingers tangling in her hair awakened her. Sort of. Her first thought was to wonder where in the world she was since all she could see seemed to be flesh. *Male flesh.*

She shot upright. The fingers in her hair went up too, only to slowly drop and pull pale strands down around her face. Like a witch, she supposed, looking into Callahan's wondering gray eyes. Daylight had just begun to brighten the room.

"Mr. Callahan, you're alive," she said and felt her face get hot. What a stupid thing to say.

"I am." He seemed to think about it. "Though somebody tried for a different result." He moved a little, grunting with the pain.

She shoved her chair back, out of his line of sight. "Who did this to you?"

"Who?"

"Yes. The who that tried to carve you like a turkey—and nearly succeeded." She was deliberately harsh. "Who was it?"

"I don't know. It was dark under the trees." He shook his head, wincing with the movement. "Seems like the first thing I remember is a blinding light. So bright I didn't see him until it was too late to dodge."

Possibly true, but when his assailant tried to shove the knife between his ribs, they had to have been face to face. Remembering Callahan's hands, he'd even had time to land a blow. Something didn't quite add up.

"Was it a stranger? Why would a stranger try to kill you?"

He hesitated. "I don't know."

He was lying. Oh, maybe not about a stranger, but about why somebody would try to kill him.

Rio didn't like the idea. Not one bit. She most certainly didn't want a guest in her hotel who was mixed up with people who wanted to murder him. A murder right here on her doorstep? No, indeed. People were bound to think it too dangerous to stop in at the Painter's Bay Hotel, especially after what had happened to her just a few weeks ago. She'd be out of business before she got properly started.

So she went right ahead and said what she was thinking. "You're lying. You may not know who, but I figure you do know why. You should tell me. We need to put a stop to this."

He closed his eyes. "What you need to do, Miss Salo, is look the other way and keep quiet. I'm fore-warned now. I'll take care of—" He stopped. "Where's my gun?"

She gestured toward the bedside table. "Here."

"Be a sweetheart and stick it under the pillow, please. I like to keep it handy."

Sweetheart? Her mouth tightened. *Handy?*

And the nerve of him, telling her to look the other way and keep quiet about what happened to him. But who could she even tell?

A sort of despair shook her as a new thought struck. "So you think he's going to come right into the hotel and finish the job?"

"Don't know. Try maybe, if he finds out he failed the first time and I'm still alive."

He had a point. Angry, she got the pocket pistol from the table drawer and stuffed it under the pillow, ignoring the way he grimaced as she jostled his shoulder. "Don't you go waving this thing around or firing it off for the fun of it. I'll have you know I've had about all I can stand of guns and killings around here."

"So I've heard." He sounded dreamy now. Whatever Doc had knocked him out with was still holding sway. "I'll make you a promise. I won't shoot anybody unless I absolutely have to."

"How kind of you." Sarcasm oozed from her voice, but with that, Rio had to be satisfied. What could she do, after all? Certainly not throw him out of the hotel. Not in the shape he was in and there was nowhere else in Painter's Bay he could go. Besides, he'd already paid for a week's stay.

She'd already flounced out of the room before what he'd said registered.

So he'd heard?

Just who had been telling him about the shooting in her hotel only a few weeks ago? How much did he know?

Five

Usually, Rio would've bewailed the lack of overnight hotel guests over the next couple nights. Until she discovered having Blanche Golz and her two younger sisters on the premises made Quinn Callahan's bare presence a difficult secret to keep, let alone his state of health. The credit—or blame —was due to Boo frequently standing outside the door to room four as if thinking someone should let him in to comfort the patient. More than once she had to shoo him away. And with a small dog's stubborn persistence, it was hard to change his mind.

In a matter of hours, everything changed and she found herself wishing just the opposite. One after another, every room filled. The restaurant kept both Marie and Eliza hopping to keep up while in the kitchen, both Rio and Blanche had the challenge of preparing epicurean—or so she liked to think them— meals. And charging plenty for them too.

But it did mean no one had time to pay attention to Boo's curious behavior.

During the afternoon of the third day since Calla-han's wounding, she stood at the hotel lobby desk taking the rental fee on the last of her boats from a hard-faced man who didn't strike her as someone intending to spend a few peaceful hours fishing.

What is he up to? she asked herself. *He and the other new guests?*

Oh, she had an idea all right. A guess. And it wasn't reassuring.

Though the summer always brought new people to the lake seeking respite from city heat, that was more likely to happen on weekends and include families. These were not that kind of guests. Besides, summer didn't truly begin until July.

So many fishermen, none of whom she'd ever seen before, put the hotel finances in the black almost imme-diately. But as actual fishermen, their activities struck her as almost funny. While seeming to troll the lake, they never caught a single fish. Their rented tackle came back dry. Rio would've had to be as dense as a rock not to notice.

The thought lodged in her mind that she had more to worry about than making a profit.

What were they all after? Or who?

On the fourth day, when told the last small room had gone for double the usual price, a man asked to examine the most expensive one before he committed. Rio didn't miss the way the way his eyes lit up when he entered her father's old room and spotted the armoire. He surged forward as if he couldn't wait to fling open its double doors and explore inside. On the spot, he handed over the price of one night's stay, though not without complaining at the cost and attempting to bargain down the price.

Rio refused.

His actions were suspicious enough to make her wonder if he knew about the secret compartment fitted into the cabinet. The compartment no one was supposed to know about. Except, with Elias dead, Rio herself and, most probably, Eino, if by chance nobody had killed him. In fact, she'd only learned of it by spying on her father before he died. And she'd been told Eino was dead. Of course, she'd also been told he was alive. She had no idea which was true. Both assertions had come from the old sheriff. The one who tried to make her dead too.

Rio could've told the fellow the compartment, while it *had* contained a stash, money and some extremely private papers, contained nothing but some lint. But she didn't bother. Just to see what happened, she decided to let him waste his time looking. He left the next day early, even before the Golz girls arrived and without his breakfast. He didn't appear happy. She had the feeling he might be reporting to someone else and that someone wouldn't like the results of his investment.

Early on the fifth day of Quinn Callahan's seclusion, Rio knocked on his door. At his, "Enter," she went in, Boo crowding in front of her. She found Callahan not only out of bed, but washed and fully dressed with the small pistol in the holster already settled under his left arm.

"You're up." A stupid thing to say. Rio figured now he'd think her an idiot—if he didn't already.

"I am." He smiled at her. "I had a good nurse."

"Oh—" she started, but he interrupted.

"I mean Boo." He grinned. A very pleasant grin.

"Of course," she said, and couldn't help smiling back. "I knew that."

Boo had kept him company for several hours a day, the dog's absence from the premises enough to cause some of her regular dinner patrons to ask his whereabouts.

Her smile faded. "I'm glad to see you on your feet. Are you sure you're well enough? Dr. Clement said—"

He cut her off. "I'm good. I heal fast."

When she'd looked at his wounds yesterday, per the doctor's requirements, they had looked better, but not so well he should be putting a strain on the stitches. Especially considering how weak he'd been when Mr. Turner had helped him to the hotel. Mr. Callahan had lost a lot of blood in a very short time. His recovery struck Rio as miraculous.

"I hope you really are fine. And that you do heal fast." She heard a sharpness in her words and was a little shocked at how cold she sounded. But then her dark eyes narrowed before continuing the thought.

His left eyebrow cocked as if asking a question.

She answered clearly. "Because I have acquired a strange array of people showing up at the hotel over the last few days."

His eyebrow climbed higher, asking another question without actually speaking. If she continued, would it disappear off his forehead?

Quinn Callahan sat on the edge of the bed. He wasn't smiling now. "You want to explain why I should care?"

"Oh, I think you know why, sir. You see, every

single room in this hotel is taken." Maybe that didn't quite speak to his question though. "Which, before you ask, is extremely unusual, particularly in mid-week at this time of the year. You know, before the heat strikes. More unusual still, at least two of these men—they're all men, you see—have accents just like yours."

Rather odd, some sort of lilt. She'd never heard the like.

"I don't have an accent," he said.

Ignoring this nonsensical comment, she watched his right hand move up and touch the butt of the small pistol.

"The oddest thing is that while some of these men take hikes, they don't even change into boots. They wear their clumsy city brogues and heavy woolen suits into the woods and come out looking as if they'd been attacked by wolves." She snorted. "Others rent my boats and 'go fishing,' or so they say. But they forget to bait their hooks or even bother to cast their line into the water. I've told them they should go out into the deeper part of the lake to dangle their hooks, but they don't. These so-called fishermen bypass the most likely fishing spots and row for the areas where boats can make a shore landing. As for the hikers, if there's an inch of land around the hotel they haven't examined, I'd be surprised."

He blinked.

"Does that make sense to you?" Pausing again, she waited for him to say something.

He didn't. At first.

Quinn pondered a bit, then said, "Have you drawn any conclusions about this so-called odd behavior?"

Her lips tightened. "Yes. I have."

"What sort of conclusions?" Though still speaking softly, his voice had lost all the lightness present earlier. His face had gone a couple shades paler, but those gray eyes had turned darker. And narrower. Definitely narrower as he sought her reaction.

Rio sighed. "Mr. Callahan, no matter what you may think, I'm not an utter fool. You've been looking for something, and so are they." She paused before adding, "Or someone. I know it. You know it. Right now, they're looking for you. Or your body. Only instead of just one man with a knife, there are a half dozen."

He swallowed. "Have any of them said anything to you?" Wisely, he gave up on denying her claim.

"Not yet. But I've seen them looking at me, me and the people working for me. I expect this is the last day they'll wait. They've been searching the woods but by tonight they'll know the only place you can possibly be, if you're here at all, is in the hotel. Right under their noses. And then they'll be poking those noses into every nook and cranny. With knives most likely accompanying those guns everyone..." She eyed his shoulder holster with its small but lethal gun. "Including you, have been trying to hide."

Her voice, she discovered, had gotten louder. She said, lower now, "These guests don't seem to realize seeing men with guns is not unexpected around here. I'm afraid we are not so 'civilized' as city dwellers. We recognize danger when we see it."

And I hope I see it in time to dodge this time, she added, but only to herself.

He went quiet. His hand went to the gun again. Finally, he said, "And I guess you see danger now. Sorry. If I'd—"

"If you'd what?"

But this time he shifted whatever he'd meant to say to out-and-out disrespect. "You'd best mind your own business, Miss Salo. Tend to your cooking and ignore whatever you fancy is going on."

Tend to her cooking? He spoke to her as if she were a...a...well, she didn't know what.

His stern advice made little coils of fear tie knots in her stomach. And anger, too. Just what had he started to say?

But it turned out he was done talking. No wiser than she'd been before, she left in a huff, calling Boo out of the room with her.

Rio's retreat came just in time as Blanche and Eliza appeared, striding up the narrow lane that led to their family's farm. In unison, they mounted the porch. Blanche clutched a flat basket of eggs; Eliza lugged a tall, round basket overflowing with leafy greens. The tops of a handful of scallions waggled over the top.

The porch screen door slammed as they entered and walked past her into the kitchen.

Blanche's sweet, but plain face, Rio saw at a glance, glowed red with wrath, with Eliza's not much better. Both women set their burdens onto the work table with a decided clunk.

Alarm made Rio's dark eyes widen. "Oh, no! What happened?"

"Men," Blanche said, a word of loathing.

"Men? Did someone accost you?"

"These out-of-towners." The loathing was still there. "Why, the Chinese workers around here are a much better class of men."

Rio didn't have to work to catch on. "Do you mean the men staying in the hotel?"

"Yes," Eliza said. The word hissed.

"Which of these despicable men did it?"

Eliza's voice shook. "That greasy looking fellow. I don't know his name. I don't want to."

"Are you hurt? Do I need to..." Rio couldn't even finish.

"Need to what? Throw him out?" Blanche scowled at her, Eliza's expression following suit. "Excuse me, Rio, but I don't think there's anything you can do. I doubt you're up to giving any of those men the boot if they don't want to go. Most particularly since you're still fragile yourself."

"I've got a gun. I know how to use it."

"And I'm getting one for myself," Blanche said. "Just don't forget they all have guns too. So maybe a good, stout whip would be a better choice."

Eliza turned to her sister. "May I borrow it from you if you're not with me?"

"Yes. No. Get your own." Blanche stared down on her smaller sister. "You're apt to need it. Tell Marie too."

Rio wasn't sure how much good a whip would do. Blanche, though a stalwart woman, would have to be prepared to wield it fast and hard.

Even with her father's old .44-caliber Smith & Wesson pistol, Rio didn't feel entirely safe. Besides, it was heavy and she couldn't carry it around with her all the time. She might better get one of those little derringers. Maybe one of those would suit. Then she remembered the .32 pocket pistol Wash had taken from the Chinese fellow and given to her. Better on all counts.

She blinked and came back to what Blanche was saying as the woman began extracting eggs stained with the yolk of a broken one. "It was that runty little twerp with the smallpox scars who is in the room with the greasy guy at the end of the hall. I hope you're barring your door at night, Rio. I wouldn't put anything past either of them."

Eliza had the wits to actually explain. "We weren't expecting anybody to be on our path so early. Anyway, Scar startled us both when he stepped out from behind a tree right in front of us. Blanche nearly walked right over the top of him. She's taller than he is."

Blanche nodded. "Right away, before I could even back away, he'd yanked the egg basket out of my hands and started pawing through it. Broke two of them, the jackass. I yelled at him and he just sneered. His greasy partner grabbed Eliza's basket of greens." She huffed, short and hard. "Pulled his hand out quick with a worm attached."

Eliza proved able to laugh at him now. "He acted like it was a rat or something. Blanche said to him, 'What are you looking for?' and he said, 'Just checking.' I said, 'Checking for what?' but Blanche told him to scat and he did." Hauling greens out into a metal basin to be washed, she laughed again. I had a hunch she'd laughed then, too. "He walked off still shaking his hand like he'd picked up a turd."

A smile finally quirked as Blanche shook her head. "What could they possibly have been looking for in our baskets? Checking for what? And why?"

Rio compressed her lips, deepening the dimple in

her left cheek. "Pure intimidation, I should think. I don't know what else it could be. Or why they wanted to intimidate at all." She busied herself with the fire in the huge cookstove banked from the night before.

"What were they doing out there so early, anyway? I thought those men slept late." Blanche, calmer now, wrapped an apron around her plain dress and went to work washing the greens while Eliza wiped the eggs clean.

"I don't know," Rio said, but that wasn't true. She did know. Looking for Quinn Callahan or some sign of him, that's what. Most probably all these hotel guests were. The why of it remained a puzzle. And he refused to explain.

And why anybody would paw through the two young women's parcels of food stores while looking for a man was a complete mystery.

———

WHEN TAKING a room in the Painter's Bay Hotel, the terms of service were clearly printed at the sign-in desk. Breakfast, being served only until eight a.m., was complimentary to a room's occupants. Rio didn't do a noon meal and concentrated on the evening meal. She charged for dinner, welcoming anyone, meaning anyone hungry as long as they paid their sixty-five cents, for a meal served *table d'hote*. The term meant, as she'd had to inform more than one ignorant of the French, a set menu. No *á la carte* meals. In-room hotel guests paid a dime less. On Friday and Saturday nights, reservations were preferred. Not everybody, she'd discovered, at times to her dismay, adhered to this request.

But this schedule did allow for not only herself, but the Golz women to have some daylight hours for themselves. As long as she and Blanche got the dinner prepped in time, that is.

By noon on this fifth day, the hotel had gone eerily silent. As she sat on a stool behind the high lobby desk, Rio heard waves lapping at the shore through the open double doors facing the lake. Gulls squawked as they winged overhead. A boat, maybe not as securely tied as it should be, knocked rhythmically against a dock piling.

Having totaled a column of figures, wincing just a bit at the cost of hired labor—the Golz family taking more of the profits than herself this past week—she set her pencil down and closed her eyes. Not only did her head ache, but so did the newly healed wound in her left leg. While the constant pain had ebbed and she walked almost as well as ever, she had a way to go before she was back to normal. Such a relief, she was thinking, not to need the contraption. Maybe tomorrow she'd have time to return the silly thing to Dr. Clement. It would be nice to see Molly, his wife, as well.

This peace didn't last long. A voice, loud and boisterous, broke the silence. Her eyes flew open.

"Who's in charge here?" A man walked through the outer door toward her, already demanding attention. "I'll want a room. Your best room. Chop, chop."

Like a tinny echo, "Chop chop," sounded from behind him. It came from an invisible source.

Best she could, Rio blinked away the ache. Or denied it, anyway.

She sat up straighter on her high stool. "I'm in charge. What can I do for you?"

"Can't you hear? I said I need a room. Your best room." He paused to look around, his heavily mustachioed lip lifting in what looked like total disdain for her poor little Painter's Bay Hotel. "Make that two rooms. My friend here will need one of his own."

His invisible friend?

Well, while this was no Palace Hotel, she admitted, like the one destroyed in San Francisco last year in a horrible earthquake and fire, it was hers and she didn't like the way he regarded it.

She eyed him, catching brief sight of a smaller man —a much smaller man she'd only heard as an echo— almost hidden by the loud-mouthed one even though he was thin as a fence post.

"I have only one room available. I'm afraid you and your friend will have to share. Or one of you will need to look for other accommodations." It pleased her to say that, as she'd taken instant umbrage at his loud voice.

He scowled, heavy dark eyebrows drooping over sagging eyelids. "I didn't see no other hotels when we went through town."

Rio forced a smile. "No. I'm afraid this is the only one, although," she added thoughtfully, "I heard Mr. Newsome from over in The Falls is laying the foundation for a new one there. It'll be finished by fall. For the hunters, you know. Quite rough and ready."

He gagged on his own ire. "Yeah? Well, you'll just have to kick someone out. Get at it, girly."

"Or," she added as if she hadn't heard this last part, "you can buy tents and gear from the hardware store in Painter's Bay proper and camp in the woods. Be sure to ask permission first. It's up to you."

She looked back down at her paperwork, which is

when she caught a glimpse of the little man, who'd stayed all this time behind the big guy, slipping away toward the stairs. Meanwhile, the big man continued yelling at her. A ploy she recognized right off, meant to hide a clandestine peek, if not plunder, of the rooms upstairs. Did they actually even want a room? A single room, let alone two?

Boo, who'd been sleeping on a rug tucked under the tall lobby desk, woke up and began barking. He chased after the little man, getting underfoot and showing his teeth.

"You on the stairs. Return to the desk immediately." Rio's stern call rang out, loud and clear.

The little man stopped and looked back at his companion. The thin guy shook his head.

Except for Boo, silence fell. Rio met the thin man's eyes. A level gaze, or so she hoped, even though her insides shook like custard pudding. What neither of these men knew was that with the lobby desk hiding her hands, her right fist already gripped Elias's old .44, which lay on the shelf just beneath the desktop. She had complete confidence only a second would be needed to lift the gun and discourage any threat against her.

Maybe he guessed she wasn't as defenseless as she first appeared as he forced something that served as a smile onto his face, accompanying it with a choked laugh that turned into a loud bout of coughing.

"Now, now," he said. "No need to get all wrothy. If you ain't got two rooms, then I'll take the one you do have. Even slip you an extra buck for it. Suit you?"

She kept her hold on the gun. Her eyes narrowed

and she assumed as menacing of an expression as she could manage. "Why?"

"Why what?"

"You're not the first stranger in town to take a room lately. There's a batch of strange men congregating here in my hotel," she said. "What are you all looking for?"

He chuffed. "How should I know why anybody else is here?" He looked around. "This hotel ain't exactly a summer resort, you know."

As a matter of fact, that's *exactly* what the Painter's Bay Hotel was. One that did most of their business between July and October.

Rio shook her head. "Then why are you here? I ask again. What are you all looking for?" There was no patience left in her. Time he either spoke up, paid up, or got out. And she knew which she'd prefer.

The thin man hemmed and hawed for a full half-minute.

Oddly, before he started speaking, Rio noticed the little man had resumed his position hiding behind his partner. She still hadn't gotten a real good look at him, but Boo, bless his valiant heart, kept a steady eye on him.

"Not what," the thin man said at last. "Who."

"Who?" *Oh, no*, Rio thought. She could guess what came next.

Turns out, she wasn't wrong.

"There's this fellow." The thin man leaned forward to rest his elbows on the desk. Behind him, the little man copied the move, only he had nothing to rest his elbows on. It didn't seem to matter. A most peculiar thing.

"Um-huh?" she murmured. "Does this fellow have a name?"

He frowned. "Welp, I don't know what name he might be using, but he ain't hard to describe."

Rio, her impatience growing since she had things to do besides sit here and yap, made a hurry-up motion.

He didn't like it, her showing the initiative. His voice boomed out again. "His name, it's Callahan. At least that's the name he uses most often. He works for whoever pays him the most. Word is he's in these parts on some kind of hush-hush business that you don't need to stick your nose into."

She schooled her features to reflect bare interest in the subject, thankful for once that she'd learned this tactic to protect herself from her father's cruelty. His and her half brother Eino's.

"Is that right?" she said.

He glared at her. A muscle worked in his jaw, moving jowls that sagged as if he'd lost weight recently. "It is. He's a good-lookin' fellow. At least most of the ladies seem to think so."

Behind him, the little man nodded.

"Dark hair, funny color of eyes. Dresses like a gent."

Rio shrugged. Funny colored eyes? No, she hadn't seen a man with funny colored eyes. "I haven't seen anyone like that."

And whether she had or whether she hadn't, she had no responsibility to tell him.

"You sure?" He eyed her. Maybe sensing something in her too careless dismissal. "Chances are he's been hurt. Maybe even hurt bad."

And just how would he know that?

"I repeat. I haven't seen anyone like that. And I'm

sure I would have, whether a summer visitor or a local. Now, if you'll excuse me, I've got work to do. Either take the room or not. It's up to you."

Though she turned away, he stopped her when he hauled a five-dollar bill out of his pocket and proffered it. "I'll take the room, two nights for the pair of us. But there's something else."

Reluctantly, she took the money. What else could she do? It was more than she charged.

"I'm thinking maybe you've heard about a dead man being found in the woods," he said.

"A dead man?" She gaped at him. "Not lately. Not in my woods. Nor any dead men found in any of the woods nearby," she replied tartly, turning the register toward him. The page with Quinn Callahan's name on it had been torn out and destroyed days ago, when she'd realized these men were looking for him. "If there had been, I'm quite certain the news would've gotten about." Just to show he didn't scare her, she eyed him closely. "Though why you'd be asking me, I don't know."

But she did.

Six

The next morning, as soon as the breakfasts were served, eaten, and cleaned up after, Rio donned a clean blouse, wheeled the contraption down to the dock, and wrangled it into a rowboat. By the time she got it stowed she had sweat forming under her corset. The day was already turning hot. Looking out over the bay, which thankfully bore no sign of chop on this windless morning, she had doubts about her strength. A month ago she'd whizzed back and forth across the bay to town several times in a day without thinking twice. Now she wondered if just rowing over would bring on exhaustion.

"Boo," she said, sharp-like, having decided she'd never know if she didn't make the effort, "we're going for a ride. Get in the boat." She'd chosen the lightest one belonging to the hotel and refused to rent it to anyone this morning.

The little dog stood to attention and cocked his head.

From his attitude, he apparently questioned her

now, she thought, a little disgusted. But she really did need to see and speak to Dr. Clement. and not on account of her own mostly healed wounds. "Get in," she repeated.

He did. She did too. Carefully. Then sat a moment and caught her breath before loosing the lines. Pacing herself, she began rowing.

After nearly a half hour, they approached the town dock. An empty slip beckoned her in, but even better, a man stood at the dock's edge watching her coast into where a cleat offered a place to tie the boat. Rio recognized Mr. Meadows, the undertaker, as he loomed out over the water with his arm upraised, his shadow making him appear twice as tall. Boo barked.

"Afternoon, Miss Salo," Meadows called out. "Throw me the line and I'll tie'er up for you."

He sounded friendly. A surprise, because she'd only really met him when her father died a while back and Mr. Meadows had taken care of his body. He'd been cool and professional then.

"Thank you, sir. I appreciate that." She tossed the line, gratified when the weak throw reached him. Luckily, he had long arms and caught the line before it dropped into the water.

"Seen you coming," he said, "and thought to ask if you're doing all right after, you know..." He seemed bashful about saying the words, as if they might be indelicate. "After your pa dying and you getting shot."

Taken by surprise, she told the truth. "I'm coming along, Mr. Meadows, thank you for asking. I'm not completely recovered, but almost. I made it here. Not sure I'll make it back." She smiled ruefully to show she wasn't serious, though she was. "Could you help me get this contraption out of the boat, please? I need to return it to Dr. Clement."

"Sure." It took no particular effort from him, with his long arms. And it gave him an excuse not to look at her when he said, "I got something else on my mind. Something that might concern you. Or maybe the woods around the hotel. Figured I ought to ask seeing as it came handy."

Since Rio didn't really know him, she couldn't tell if the lugubrious expression on his face was natural or something he put on, but she didn't like seeing it.

"Me?" she said. "Something that concerns me? What is it?"

Accepting his hand as he helped her from the boat —and happy to have the aid—she stepped up onto the dock. Boo jumped out to join her.

Meadows didn't look happy. "Something that's never happened before in all my years in the business of taking care of dead folks."

She had a premonition. "Have you been threatened?"

At this he looked startled. "Threatened? Why, I guess you might say so. What I've had is three different men, all strangers unknown to anybody in town, barge right on into my mortuary asking if I have the body of a youngish fellow, not a local boy, ready for burial."

"Do you?"

"No. And so I told 'em. But here's an even queerer thing. To a man, they insisted on looking through my mortuary."

"Did you tell them no?"

"I did. But like I say, they insisted. At gunpoint."

Rio stopped pushing the contraption and stared at him. "They did? At gunpoint?"

"They did."

To her surprise, he didn't appear as discombobulated as one might expect. He waved the idea away. "I soon put a stop to that."

He didn't say how.

"Thing is," he said instead, "I heard one tell this little feller with him that I was as dim and deliberately unhelpful as that woman at the hotel. Since you got the only hotel around, I figured they must be talking about you, so I thought I'd ask. Miss Salo, have you been having trouble with a bunch of fellers, strangers, dressed in city duds, that came in on the train a few days ago?"

Rio found it a relief to answer. "Yes. A plague of them, though so far no one has pulled a gun on me." Her mouth twisted. "But every room in the hotel is full and if I had more capacity, those rooms would be full too. I've had to turn some of my regulars away, poor fellows. An unusual situation to say the least. While some of the men are overly boisterous, Mr. Turner, who tends the bar in the evening, is mostly able to keep them in line. They haven't bothered the Golz ladies too badly. Those women are quite capable of handling most anyone that tries. That's not to say I'm comfortable around them."

Meadows nodded. "They asking nosy questions? Trying to pry into dark corners?"

"I couldn't have put it better myself."

"They have any luck?" he asked.

Rio shook her head. "Evidently not. I think if they

had, they would move on. But the odd thing is, they seem to be waiting."

"What for?"

"No idea. I wish I did. They act like they're looking someone who they expect to be here, or to soon show up. I don't who, or whether it's a friend or a foe. Or why. But I am afraid they're dangerous and becoming more so every day."

Afraid they were? She knew they were. Look at poor Quinn Callahan. Yet she figured he played a part in this and might be just as dangerous as the others.

"At least they haven't bothered any of my regular dinner customers yet, and I can only pray they don't." She sighed. "Our people won't put up with it if they try."

This seemed to please him. He smiled. "No. They won't." The smile faded. "This is another sign we got to find somebody willing to run for sheriff. Meanwhile, we need a town marshal. And we need him before these out-of-town riff raff decide to take over the place."

Someone motioned to the mortician from across the street just then, calling out that he was needed at the Blue Sky logging camp right away. Right away wasn't a real meaningful term, however, since the camp lay ten miles from town.

Meadows's mouth tightened as he waved acknowledgment. "That don't sound good. You take care, Miss Salo. Try not to let those fellows get you down. Best to do as they say if you can."

She nodded. "You too, Mr. Meadows. And thank you for the information."

He sped off toward the funeral home, no doubt to hitch his team. Rio continued on to the doctor's office, pushing the contraption down the street, to where Molly Clement stood in the doorway laughing at the sight of her.

Part of her mission got left undone. It turned out Dr. Clement, like Mr. Meadows, had been called to the Blue Sky logging camp as well. There'd been an incident.

THE RETURN TRIP across the bay was every bit as onerous as Rio had feared. In plain fact, though Boo bounced in and out of the boat as if urging her to move, after Rio pulled her craft in tight against the dock she had to sit a few minutes to summon the energy to get out. Her arms, she discovered, were like jelly, shaking and weak from the effort.

It wasn't until she heard yelling coming from the hotel that concern got her moving. She hurried.

Boo beat her into the building. He dashed on through the lobby and ran ahead toward the kitchen, little legs working like pistons.

Rio, on the other hand, stopped to listen. "What in the world?" Pausing at the lobby desk, she reached around and retrieved the .44 stowed at the back of the shelf. A woman's voice rose above the man's. Not Blanche. Not Eliza. Not even Marie. It was Anna. Calm and steady Anna, and she was yowling like a fishwife. Rio also recognized the man. The tall fellow who'd insisted on, and paid extra, for her best room.

She snapped the revolver's chamber open and checked the load before continuing to the kitchen, her footsteps drowned out by the loud voices.

The man's name as he'd written it, she remembered, was Howard Smith. His small lickspittle partner apparently didn't have a name since Mr. Smith hadn't signed for him. A quick scan, as she cautiously peeked around the corner, showed the little man sitting on the floor with a hand over his mouth trying to staunch the bleeding. He looked like Rio imagined a vampire from Mr. Bram Stoker's novel.

Eliza stood behind her mother. She looked scared—and mad. Even from the doorway, Rio could see bruises forming on one of her wrists and a scratch on her cheek.

But it was Anna who claimed Rio's immediate attention. The older woman had her arms pitched and ready to strike. She held a cast iron skillet with both hands on the handle, poised for a fast backhand should the need arise. It wouldn't, Rio concluded, be her first blow as the lickspittle, to his detriment, had already found out.

"You touch my daughter again and you'll see what a good German mother does to punish the man," Anna was saying. "This one," —she cocked a thumb at the little man, "—he lost a tooth. So far. That's nothing. He's lucky I didn't brain him."

"Maybe I'll just shoot you," Mr. Smith said and waggled a small pistol just to show he meant business. If he'd been a bear, Rio figured the remark would've come out as a growl.

Even Boo recognized the sound as such and did a little growling himself.

Anna noticed the dog then. She saw Rio, too, standing in the doorway with the revolver cocked and ready to fire. She shook her head, just the least little bit.

Rio had heard enough. "I suggest you do not fire

that pistol, Mr. Smith, because then I will be forced to shoot *you*. And after you, I'll shoot him." She indicated the pop-eyed little man. "Don't think for a moment I won't."

"The hell," he said.

She smiled, a mere twitch of the lips. "I've survived my father trying to kill me. I've survived the sheriff trying to kill me. And I survived my half brother's dirty tricks too. Buster, you're nothing but an ordinary, run-of-the-mill vermin I'd have no problem shooting. Oh, and since this gun I'm holding is a .44-caliber, you may be sure it would make a dreadful mess at this distance."

"I'll clean it up," Anna said. "Me and my daughter. Clean it so good nobody can ever tell what happened."

She meant every word. Anna never said anything she didn't mean.

And Smith believed it too. Slowly, he lowered his pistol and turned to glower at his bleeding companion. "Get up. You ain't hurt that bad."

The little man, speaking for the first time within Rio's hearing, tried to talk through a mouthful of blood. Garbled almost beyond understanding, she thought he said, "She knocked out my tooth."

A tooth did lay on the floor in front of him.

Smith saw it too. "Pick it up and stick the cursed thing back in. And get up. You look like a toad, sitting there."

He had, Rio decided, a better eye for description than she'd thought him capable of.

She didn't lower the revolver. "I shall expect the two of you to pack up and leave immediately. "

"My business ain't done..." Smith started, but Rio knew how to waggle a gun and make it look good just as well as he did. Maybe better. Her weapon was certainly more commanding.

"As far as I'm concerned, it's done. I'll give you five minutes."

"I only stayed a night. You owe me..."

"I don't owe you anything. You're lucky you and your friend aren't laid out in a corner of my woodshed waiting for the undertaker."

He decided not to argue, maybe because she spoke so quietly. He lent a hand to his partner and hefted the little man to his feet. "Go pack our duds," he said. The toad-like man nodded and took off at a shambling run. Smith backed away then, retreating to stand at the bottom of the stairs where he waited for his companion.

She waited with him, saying nothing, the revolver lowered, but ready for any untoward move he might make. Only a couple more than the five minutes she'd allotted passed before the little man came back down the stairs toting a single carpetbag.

Smith nodded. "Don't suppose we can use one of those boats to cross the bay."

"You suppose right. There's a trail around the end of the lake. The walk only takes about an hour."

The gun proved the incentive to get them going, Mr. Smith cursing first Rio, Anna and Eliza Golz, then the little man in a steady stream of invective so potent he sent himself into a long bout of coughing.

Eliza waited until the pair disappeared from sight before turning to Rio. The girl's expression was one of profuse admiration. "Mercy me, Miss Rio, you looked... you looked just like a steely-eyed spitfire out of a dime novel. Would you really have shot him?"

Rio took a breath. "Yes."

With a stern look, Anna hustled her daughter away.

Rio, feeling as if her legs would no longer support her, made it back to the kitchen where she sank down onto a chair. Boo jumped into her lap and cuddled against her. She pressed her forehead into his fur.

A minute later, hands clapped. Her head shot up and she spun around.

"A steely-eyed spitfire," Quinn Callahan said from where he leaned against the doorjamb. His gray eyes glinted.

"You were listening all this time?"

"Just since the scrunty little fellow screamed. I take it that's when the older lady clouted him with the frying pan."

"Ah." She hadn't even heard that part of the furor.

"Things got real dicey about then. The lady and the so-called Mr. Smith were both hot under the collar, while the young lady was hollering something about a whip. I'd just decided I might have to take a hand when you showed up like an avenging angel and saved me the trouble. Not that Smith thought that's what you were." His grin grew wider.

"No. I expect not." She glanced around. "I'm surprised no one else came to see what the racket was about. They're normally plenty nosy."

He sobered. "The hotel is empty at the moment. All the men are out making a final survey of the woods for their lost parcel."

Rio couldn't quite decide whether he meant himself or someone—or something—else.

Callahan moved to where he could see out the window. "And the outbuildings. They looked through them too. I heard the kid who takes care of your horses complaining to his mother when one of them left a gate open and he had to chase down the sorrel."

How had he heard that? She eyed him, her dark eyes serious. "Did anyone see you?"

Callahan shrugged, then winced as his stitches evidently pulled in protest. "I'm good at staying out of sight. Don't worry. I don't intend on bringing trouble down on the people working here."

Rio winced. "The Golz family is having a very bad day. I'm afraid they'll all quit. Not that I can blame them. They didn't expect this. But I can't run this place without them." Her measured speech, she noticed, had turned into a virtual wail.

What he said surprised her. "Don't worry. I think you'll find they're loyal to you."

Only later did she wonder if his good intentions not to bring trouble to the people working here included her.

So-called Mr. Smith, he'd said. Rio had an idea he knew more about the pair she'd evicted than he was letting on.

Seven

Washington Ames surprised Rio with an early morning visit the next day, something he'd omitted doing in the days since she was laid up and unable to walk. He'd taken overt charge of the Salo Timber Products logging crews, then and ever since. Clearly there'd been no need for him, with his experience, to take direction from her so their daily conferences had gone by the wayside. Those had only ever been an act set to reassure people and keep the business running during Elias's final days anyway. Now they didn't need to pretend, and as long as no one raised the question of who actually owned the business, they were going under the assumption Rio did. And she left it in Wash's charge.

When he knocked his special knock outside the porch door, it set Boo to bouncing with joy. He liked Wash.

So did Rio. She'd often thought—and maybe hoped —there was something between them. Now she wasn't

77

so sure. He'd kissed her a few times but the only thing she was sure of was that they were friends.

Smiling, she beckoned him into the kitchen. "Wash, it's good to see you. Seems like forever since the probate hearing. Is everything all right? I heard there was a logging accident at Blue Sky yesterday. A death. Not anyone we knew, I hope." One of their Chinese workers had gone to work for Blue Sky as it was closer to his home.

He grimaced. "A couple men were involved. White men. One dead, one hurt. The company isn't giving out any names yet. Not saying much about the circumstances either."

The Salo crew was Chinese. They didn't mix much with the white crews. Chang had been the lone exception.

She shook her head. "Bad news. Let's hope the hurt man recovers." She pointed to a chair. "Coffee? It's almost done."

At this he smiled. "You bet."

When they'd settled at the table, Wash chomping on a cinnamon roll Rio had just taken from the oven, a ritual resumed. Wash talked about the number of logs coming out of the hills. He talked about holding some back for later in the year. Or about maybe forming a braille to be floated out of the bay and downriver to the big sawmill that paid better than the smaller one in their own bay.

"You must do what seems best to you," she said. "I trust you. Everyone trusts you to do right by them."

"Well then, I won't. There's such a thing as loyalty. The men here need the jobs. Besides, I figure labor would almost cost more than we'd make. By the time expenses were paid, the extra profit wouldn't go far." He fed the last little tidbit of his roll to Boo, folded his hands and turned his gaze on her, his blue eyes serious. "There's something else."

She'd suspected there might be. Her breath caught. "What is it?"

"Are you doing all right, Rio? Is the hotel too much, too soon after...you know?" he asked.

She did know. An odd question, though, she thought. Oblique. "What makes you ask?"

"Word has been getting around about some unsavory characters jumping off the train and heading for the hotel like they knew right where it was. They causing you any trouble?"

She didn't say anything. Just looked at him.

"Folks are talking about seeing these same fellers combing the woods like they're following a treasure map," he said.

"A treasure map? That's interesting." Although she didn't believe a treasure map to be the item of interest.

His gaze sharpened. "Some of them have gone into The Dry Well Saloon, buying rounds of whiskey and talking to people. They don't seem to be worrying about money. Old Jimmy Baker got so drunk he passed out in the road. Worst part is, turns out the old coot didn't have anything they wanted to hear. Folks figure he might've been buffaloed out of pure spite. And I heard about a couple who forced their way into Meadow's mortuary and demanded a look at any bodies he might have on hand. Well, he's got a fresh one now, and it's got a bullet hole in it."

It took a moment for that to sink in. "A bullet hole?"

she echoed and sat up straighter. "Do you mean the fellow from Blue Sky was shot?"

"I do."

"I thought you said there was an accident. And there are two men. Is the other one shot? Do they know who did it? Do they know why?"

"I didn't say anything about an accident. You assumed. I said one of the loggers was killed. Both were shot. No. Nobody knows who did what or why they did it."

"Is anyone investigating?"

Wash shrugged. "Dunno. Not that I know of, but if we don't get someone appointed to keep law and order around here pretty soon this whole county will go to hell." He didn't mince words.

"Maybe you should take the job on," she said, but he chuckled and shook his head.

"I've got a job. I'm a logger, not a lawman. Anyway, eyes are looking toward your hotel when these things happen. Everybody knows the ones who invaded Meadows' mortuary are staying here in the hotel. So are the ones out prowling the woods and poking into folks' barns and sheds. They know the Blue Sky boys had a shouting match with a couple of the strangers."

"Are people blaming me?" If she sounded astonished, well, she was.

"Not yet, but don't be surprised if they start.

"You're behind the times and only partly right." She bit down on the words. "A couple of those men are not staying here anymore. I threw them out. I don't know about any of the others. I know they leave their rooms right after breakfast and don't come back until dinner-time. What they do between those hours is up to them. Sometimes they go out again at night."

Wash gawked at her like a kid at a rodeo. "You threw them out? Two men?"

It did Rio's heart good to see Wash's flabbergasted expression. "I did. They'd been harassing Marie Golz. Anna defended her daughter and there was a shouting match. After a round or two, it all became a bit violent. Anna used a cast iron skillet on one of them."

Wash was starting to smile. "She did, huh? Guess she wasn't messing around. How, Rio? How did you manage to throw them out?"

"They could see my gun, which was pointing at them at the time, was cocked and loaded and ready to blow them in half. All I had to do was squeeze the trigger."

His eyebrows went up. "They believed you?"

"Oh yes. They believed me." And after a few seconds, Rio could tell Wash believed her too.

He drew in a breath and leaned forward, taking one of her hands. "You've got to be careful, Rio. These men, we don't know who they are or why they're here. We don't know what they'll do. Most likely they've already killed one man and wounded another. And you say one of them took after the Golz girl. Think." He squeezed the hand, as if he didn't already have her attention. "You're here alone with them at night. It's hard telling what one, or all of them, if they're in cahoots, might take it in their heads to do."

As if Rio hadn't thought of that herself. As if she didn't keep her door locked, with a chair under the knob. No wonder Boo, always on alert, was in the room with her. Yes, and her dad's old .44 Smith & Wesson right there on her nightstand, ready to pick up and fire.

"I'm careful," she said. "But the sooner the commissioners can appoint a sheriff, the better I'll like it." Sometimes she scared herself, thinking about what could happen. But she refused to admit as much to Wash.

He surprised her again, more dramatically this time, when as he got up to leave then hesitated. He set his mouth and had one more thing to say. "What do you think about calling on Beckett Ferris to come back as acting sheriff? At least temporarily. He's got the right kind of experience. Might be possible he can take a leave from customs enforcement and take the job until we can have a county election."

She didn't know what to say. When Beckett had packed up Win, his young brother, and left to continue his customs agent job of corralling opium smugglers, things had been tense between him and Wash.

"I don't know as he'd want to come back here." Schooling herself to hide her feelings, Rio frowned. "I don't think he has any great fondness for the area. After all, it's where his little brother nearly got killed. And me. Win told me Beckett blamed himself, thinking he should've caught Sheriff Donaldson before things went so far."

"Fond of the area?" Wash smiled, a rueful kind of smile, and shook his head. "Maybe not, but he'd come if you asked him."

"Me?" She touched her chest with her thumb and shook her head. "Not my place to ask."

"You should. He'd come for you," he repeated. His

smile faded then and he turned and left, closing the screen door quietly behind him.

For moments, she stood and stared at Wash's departing back as he walked into the woods. What had he meant, saying that about Beckett? There were things she hadn't told him regarding Beckett and she felt guilty about that. Should she have? Plus there was what Wash said about the people now filling her hotel causing worry to the local folks. The visitors were argumentative when they'd had too much to drink, and they encouraged others to the same behavior. They all drank too much. Aaron Black, who owned the saloon in town may have liked the added income, but his regulars weren't appreciative. And Mr. Meadows had been browbeaten into letting them search his mortuary. Then there were the loggers from Blue Sky. Wash had said the local men had taken to carrying guns, something they hadn't done regularly for ten years or more.

She could only conclude her guests were a dangerous bunch and she couldn't wait to be rid of them. The sooner the better.

But while Wash had said nobody seemed to know who they were or what they were doing here, somebody must. But who? And why?

The one thing she did know she planned to keep to herself. She hadn't told Wash or anybody else about the man who'd made a hotel reservation, arrived late, and promptly almost got himself killed.

She hadn't told anybody about Quinn Callahan.

Eliza and Blanche were the only ones who'd seen him. And her bartender had probably saved his life. Neither had asked about him later, nor had she ever mentioned him. As far as they were concerned, he'd left almost as soon as he arrived, just as most of the overnighters did.

But Rio knew differently. He was waiting for something to happen and expected it soon.

So did the men looking for him.

What?

————

WASH JOGGED down the path between the hotel and his cabin without hearing of the flight of fledgling birds seeking to escape a hawk. He didn't even notice the rabbit that darted across the trail in front of him. He swore softly under his breath as he went, mind dwelling not only on what he'd said to Rio—and what he'd *not* said—but also on the previous evening.

As boss, he had his own quarters separate from the Chinese crew. He liked his privacy just fine as a general rule but last night had brought him an unwelcome visitor. One he'd hoped never to deal with again.

He should have told Rio. Guilt rode him hard, knowing there'd soon come a time when she'd find out anyway.

He should have told her what he'd learned about those men staying in the hotel. About the danger. As for the mention of Beckett Ferris, well, that had been an experiment. One he hadn't gotten a clear answer to.

It could wait, he decided. He'd be careful. They'd gone through some tough times together and he wouldn't deliberately hurt her for the world.

————

RIO PREPARED the hotel breakfast service, putting a second batch of rolls in to bake. She beat eggs to make omelets, then changed her mind at the last minute and decided to scramble the eggs, whipping them to a froth and adding just a bit of dry biscuit ingredients and some finely chopped green onions. Small dishes of early strawberries that the nearby Indian children picked and brought to her door in the evenings were portioned, bacon sliced, cooked, and kept warm to put on plates. She didn't think there was a point to the normal niceties she provided, seeing them largely wasted on her clientele. Besides, Wash's visit had put her behind and this was Blanche's day off.

Full of mother-issued orders on how to protect herself, Marie arrived to wait tables. "Eliza told me all about that awful little toad man," she said to Rio as she tied a crisp white apron over her dark dress. "And Father told me not to put up with any guff. He said I should tell him if anything strikes me wrong and he and my brothers will take care of it."

Rio caught her breath. "No. Not your father or brothers, Marie. Tell me. Those men are dangerous. I think they've already killed a man who crossed them."

Marie's big blue eyes widened and her already fair skin blanched. "Killed a man? Who?"

"I think so. I don't know his name, but I think they killed the man who worked for Blue Sky Logging. They're less likely to harm me than they are to hurt your father." Or so she hoped.

They watched a trio of men clump down the stairs, yawning and already bawling for their coffee.

Rio couldn't help smiling. "Did Eliza tell you how

your mother whacked the toad man a hefty blow with a frying pan and knocked out his tooth?"

"She did, when Mother wasn't listening. Told me you threatened to shoot them too." Marie giggled. "I wish I'd been here to see it."

Rio shook her head. "Hmm. See if you can still tell me that after breakfast is served."

Nine assorted men soon gathered in the dining room, slurping their coffee and eyeing Marie's lithe figure as she rushed around the room like a darting hummingbird. Rio chose to make an appearance then, walking to the center of the room where she rapped on a metal pan with a large spoon. The resulting racket quickly brought the men's attention to her. One of them whistled and more laughed as if he'd made a joke.

"I have an announcement." She waited until their noise died away. "Some of you are not included in this message. Most of you are. Pay attention."

"Speak up." A scar-faced man whom she vaguely remembered had signed his name as Marciano made a hurry-up motion.

Rio complied. "You may be aware I evicted Mr. Smith and his man yesterday after the little fellow assaulted one of my workers. You all should know this will not be tolerated. You will act with respect to the people here at all times. If you can't do that, I'll expect you to leave as soon as breakfast has been eaten. Understood?"

Someone at the farthest table guffawed. "You think you can boss us around? A little snip like you?"

She eyed him. "Have you spoken with Mr. Smith? Yes? Then you should know I can."

"I ain't Smith," he said as if it were a boast, and laughed again. "And he ain't either."

No surprise. She'd suspected as much. They all probably went under assumed names.

"Be aware. Next time I won't hold fire," she shot back. "You've all been warned. Comply, leave, or prepare to be shot. For your information, I use either a .44 Smith and Wesson revolver or a 12-gauge shotgun with double ought buck. Those are your choices."

Spinning, she headed back to the kitchen, hoping she wasn't limping too badly. Dead silence followed her out of the room.

She found Anna waiting for her in the kitchen. A smile wreathed the woman's face as she reached forward to embrace Rio. "Thank you."

But it still took several minutes for Rio to stop shaking.

Eight

Two of Rio's hotel guests, if guest was the proper word—she'd begun thinking of them more as a plague regardless of the money they brought in—stayed close to the building all day. Wherever or whenever she looked outside, she spotted at least one of them. Taking turns, the two men paced between the back porch and the horse barn at least a half dozen times before noon, then regularly after that.

One fellow took up residence on the broad front porch. He dragged a chair to the corner where he could sit and watch both the road and the beach and dock. Every so often, the other man would make a sashay around the building. He'd go upstairs, walk up and down the hall a couple times, then return downstairs to repeat the sequence. Once she saw him try the door to Quinn Callahan's room, only to find it locked. When he caught her looking, he snatched his hand from the knob, grinned at her, and left.

These new actions did plenty to arouse her suspicions. They certainly seemed to be expecting something new to happen.

Not a sound came from Quinn Callahan's room. Rio had begun to wonder if he was in there at all, although she hadn't seen him go out. Boo, however, didn't bother to go sit at his door, so she believed the room must be empty. Rio gave her dog a reward for the tip off, taking him outside to play fetch and once to let him wade in the lake. The man on the porch eyed them like a hawk watches its prey.

Why? The question gnawed at her. Their actions, while they'd been suspicious since their arrival, had been stepped up. Whoever they were looking for had them thwarted and they were in a hurry to change it to their liking. She suspected they weren't going to wait passively for much longer.

"C'mon, Boo. What say we amble on down to the boats?"

As a test, Rio and an eager Boo walked out on the dock where she pretended to peer into the distance. Shading her eyes with her hand, she waved at a non-existent somebody in the trees across the inlet.

The watcher jerked erect in his chair.

"Well, well. If that isn't proof of something, I don't know what is," she said to the dog. "Enough, Boo. Time for us to go in." Pacing slowly back to the hotel, she passed the man without looking at him and went directly to the kitchen to begin tenderizing some beef steak intended for the night's dinner service.

She wasn't so busy she missed seeing the porch sitter hurry down the beach and onto the dock the moment he felt she was safely out of sight. He rushed to the end of the dock, straining to catch sight of whoever she might've been signaling.

She grinned. "See, Boo? I told you. Something is going on. Look how we tricked him into giving himself away." As a reward, she tossed a meat scrap which he caught in midair.

Boo looked up at her and made a gruff little sound.

At five, Eliza and Marie arrived at the hotel to prepare the dining room for dinner service. Eliza carried a quirt, a sturdy thing with good whipping action. She slashed it about as the girls emerged from the path, making it obvious to any would-be pesterers that she wouldn't put up with their shenanigans. Marie wore a whistle on a leather thong around her neck, ready to blast the noise into the face of anyone who accosted her.

Rio greeted them thankfully. She'd been a little afraid they'd refuse to work after the morning's experience.

"Did you have any trouble getting here?" she asked.

Marie snorted. "Mother and her frying pan put a stop to that, I think, but she said I should have the whistle anyway. Just in case."

Rio had been afraid the frying pan incident might have roused Smith or the toad into sneaking back and escalating the hostilities.

"And Blanche agreed to me borrowing the whip," Eliza said. "She said I should aim for their face."

Rio still worried. "You'll be careful going home, won't you? I mean extra watchful. Ready to run."

"Father is coming to walk us home," Marie said, "and a couple of our brothers will come with him. Father doesn't want Tommy out by himself either."

"Good." Rio sighed her relief. "That's good." One worry eased, at least for tonight. But what about the next night? And the next, for however long they were here? One of the men, the scar-faced one in number three, always kept to the background and didn't say much within her hearing, but he still seemed to command the others' respect. Maybe she could ask him when he—they—planned to leave. They'd already been here several days, a visit that seemed without purpose.

Thus resolved, she went back to slicing onions thinly, cutting carrots into precise coins, and gathering herbs from her garden. She made a huge Waldorf Salad, hulling and chopping the walnuts, making the dressing, and putting celery upright in cold water to plump the ribs. She'd chop the apples last so they didn't turn brown. A chicken and rice soup was ready for a first course. Potatoes were peeled and placed in a large cauldron to cook. She'd made custard tarts with caramel sauce this morning. A simple meal. She had no guests except for these untrustworthy men, and no other dinner reservations. Not only did she not have the inclination, but didn't see a need to go all out.

By a quarter to six, most of the guests had gathered in front of the nook housing the bar. They kept Mr. Turner busy pouring the cheaper brand of whiskey and drawing beer from a tapped keg. Bottles of wine stood on a shelf behind him, but these men were not wine drinkers. They were talkative, though. If she stood in the kitchen doorway, she could hear the rise and fall of their voices.

Extra talkative on this night, she thought, although she wasn't able to make out a single sentence. Only a word or two at a time. *Tonight,* for one. *Orders,* for another. *The boss. Doesn't matter. He'll pay.*

Who will pay? What doesn't matter? Nothing she heard was reassuring. Later, she'd ask Mr. Turner if he had put those snatches of conversation together and knew what it all meant. But she'd wait until the men went to sit down to their dinner.

On the dot of six o'clock, Rio struck the metal bars of her chime apparatus with a wooden mallet. The mellow sound announced the start of dinner service. A few minutes later, the six guests that worried her seated themselves at various tables and the Golz girls toted in the soup. Happily, four single men and a party of seven had turned up without reservations so the girls—and Rio—were plenty busy. The courses followed, but it was during the main course Rio had a few moments to talk with Turner, who'd brought the used bar glasses into the kitchen to be washed.

She didn't have to ask. He volunteered.

"Something's up, young miss," he said, looking over his shoulder to make sure no one had crept up on them. "I listened to them fellers talking. A couple are stirring the rest up. Their talk sounded as if they got a plan in mind for tonight, and it ain't gonna be nice."

"A plan or a plot? What kind?" She plunged the dirty glasses into a tub of hot, soapy water and swished them around.

"Don't know. Maybe a plot. Something that don't bode well for someone. But, miss, there's a look in that gray-headed one's eyes. Shifty. He looks one way and then another like he's got something evil in mind." He hesitated, worry wrinkles showing on his face. "Miss, I think they might be intending on taking over the hotel."

"What?" It came out louder than Rio intended. Shock made her go rigid. Her hands, soapy water and all covered her mouth as if to muffle any sound. "They wouldn't dare!"

His narrow-eyed stare held that opinion in contempt. "Oh, I think they would. I doubt there's anything to stop them. Pretty certain you can't. Pretty certain you'd be better off not to try."

"Are you sure that's their plan?" Her voice trembled.

"Not sure, no. They was fairly close-mouthed through the first round of drinks tonight. The second and third rounds got their tongues to flapping louder, but still not so free as usual. From what I did hear, somebody sent the one they call Marciano a telegram today. No idea what it said, but it sure enough started some kind of stink."

Rio became aware of soap suds dripping down her chin and grabbed a towel. "Do you suppose it's because of what I did?"

Turner's face went blank. "What did you do, young miss?"

"I told them if worst came to worst, I would shoot them with my shotgun if they bothered any of the hotel workers."

A grin cracked his craggy face. "Did they believe you?"

"They better have," she said, grim as the reaper herself.

Eliza bustled into the kitchen, ready to begin serving the salad course, the last service before dessert and coffee. Her eyebrows lifted as she realized Rio and the bartender's conversation seemed serious. "Is anything wrong?" she asked.

Best not to tell her. Rio's split-second decision drew Turner's approving look.

"Nothing of note. The salads are ready and I'm just going to dish up the custard. It'll be ready as soon as you pick up the salad plates."

Eliza nodded and piled plates onto a large tray, just as Marie dumped a load of dirty dishes onto the counter and followed with a second tray. Six extra diners had come for dinner service after the others were served, but all the local people had gathered apart from the room guests. Their presence may have kept the others in check.

"They're awful quiet tonight, Rio," Marie said. "It's making me nervous. Kind of like before a thunderstorm."

"Is it? In that case, as soon as you finish serving the meal, I want you to go on home. Don't stay to clear up, or to wait for your father. Just leave everything. And be sure Tommy goes with you. I can easily handle anything else the guests need. There aren't that many of them."

After a brief argument, they agreed. Aware of the sharp glance Turner gave her, she was relieved when he didn't say anything. If he'd tried to talk her out of it, she might've given in and agreed with him. But no. This was all Rio could think to do to keep the Golz family safe.

As for Turner himself— "You too," she said. "In fact, go now."

"And leave you by yourself?" He sounded outraged. "I can't do that."

"Yes, you can. You must. I think I know what they're up to, and I won't be in any danger. It's best though, if no one else is here to protest. As long as no one loses their temper, all will be well. I'll be angry and inconvenienced, but that's all." She hoped she sounded convincing.

He shook his head.

Rio had a moment of panic, no matter what she told Mr. Turner. But she had to convince him he needed to leave and let things happen as they may. Because she had one thing she needed to do right away, while they were all still in the dining room.

She shivered. She had to warn Quinn Callahan and get him out of his room and away from the hotel. Plus erase any sign he'd ever been here.

The custards got dished up any old how and set where the girls could reach them. She spoke fast, hardly looking at the bartender. "Please," she said. "I don't want anyone hurt on my account. I know just what to do and where to go and if I need help, I'll run to the logger's camp and fetch Wash Ames and the Chinese men. Trust me. I won't let this get out of hand."

Turner was still shaking his head, then a light seemed to dawn. "Does this have anything to do with the feller who got stabbed last week?"

"I think it may. I think these men want to see if he's here in the hotel. Well," she said. "He isn't. He wasn't hurt quite as badly as we first thought and left two days later. If I open the place up and let them look, everything will be fine. I'm sure of it."

She hoped she was a good liar, although it didn't sound all that plausible to her. And maybe not to Mr. Turner, either, going by the way his brow crinkled.

"He left a couple days later?" he said.

Rio nodded. Vigorously. "Yes. I should have told you. He slunk off without so much as a fare-thee-well."

He stared at her moments longer. Moments that almost had her counting down the seconds, then he nodded. "All right. If you say so." He turned to go, then spun back and Rio barely got her face blanked of the fright growing stronger by the moment. "You're sure?"

Her smile felt like cracking ice. "I'm sure."

Within minutes, the girls rushed in, already removing their aprons and throwing them into a laundry basket. Eliza took up the whip and Marie slipped the chain with the whistle on over her head. They chattered and told her goodnight five times and then they fled into the evening where daylight lingered. Turner went with them to where the path broke, he going one way, the girls taking the path past the barn to pick up Tommy going the other.

Boo sat looking up at her.

"Just you and me," she whispered. "And your friend Mr. Callahan. If we can get him away in time."

A ping from the dining room summoned her to the desk where she collected money from the local diners, all ready to go at once. All had come by boat and soon were on their way across the bay to town.

That left her six hotel guests, and they were taking their time about finishing their meal. Marciano called for more coffee, so she went around the room filling cups. Someone, she observed right away, had closed the hotel door while she'd been to the kitchen. She acted as if she didn't notice and made her way back to the kitchen.

They'd start soon, she thought. Probably as soon as

they were sure no one else would show up for dinner. Hence, she thought, the discouragement of the closed front door to the hotel. She had to get Quinn Callahan out of here and put him somewhere they wouldn't find him. He couldn't hole up in his room much longer. But where should he go? Where should she go?

Rio had the key to his room. Taking a last look around to be sure no one was watching, she crept to the door and stuck the key in the lock, turned it fast and slipped inside the moment the door opened. He was there, lying on the bed propped against the pillows. An open book lay beside him. The small pistol he usually carried in the shoulder holster pointed at her. His face was set.

"Get up," she whispered, just as if she didn't see the gun. "Gather your things. You've got to get out of here. Quick. They're coming."

He didn't move nearly as fast as she'd prefer although at least the pistol's bore moved away from her midsection. One eyebrow went up. "They?"

"You know who. As soon as they can count on being undisturbed, they're going to search the hotel. And if they find you...well..." She left the rest unsaid.

Sitting up, Callahan shoved the pistol into the holster and strapped the apparatus into its usual position. He dropped his feet over the side of the bed. "What makes you think they—whoever they are—are looking for me?"

"Please." She eyed him scornfully, her dark eyes snapping. "I'm not stupid, Mr. Callahan. Nobody else has been cut to pieces and spent days hiding out in this hotel room."

"Hiding out?" He said it mildly although she could tell he was offended.

"What else would you call it?"

"Taking it easy and letting myself heal."

She made a sound somewhere between a snort and a cluck of her tongue. "Get up, you silly man. They're coming for you. You can't be here. Be quick."

At least he finally stood up. As soon as he was erect, she rushed forward and straightened the bed, long practice making her fast. Bed-making was, after all, a chore she'd done from the time she was five. His carpet bag was on the floor beside the washstand, half open. Fortunately, he appeared to be a tidy man. Or perhaps, it occurred to her, just a man always prepared to make a quick getaway.

Besides the book and a shirt in need of washing, he'd evidently kept everything in the bag except his shaving things. She scooped the mug, brush, soap, and razor into the bag, tossed the shirt and book in on top and looked around. Ammunition for the gun lay on the bedside table. She threw that in too, regardless of stains or smells. Every trace of him just needed gone.

He stared at her in wonder. "You mean it."

"Of course I mean it. Put your shoes on, for goodness' sake. We're going outside." Still carrying his carpetbag, she brushed past him and put her ear to the door before cautiously opening it.

"Clear." She was whispering again. "Go out onto the back porch. I'll be with you in a minute."

She was cursing herself. She had to get Boo and put him on a leash, something she should have done as a first step. Marciano, she remembered, didn't like her dog and she wasn't about to leave Boo to his mercy. She didn't think he had any.

"Go," she said, and he said, "Yes, ma'am."

He took the carpetbag from her and went.

Nine

❦

When Rio had been very young, there'd been plenty of times when she needed to escape Eino's persecution. When he played tiger and deliberately scratched the blood out of her, for instance. She still bore scars on her arms and one on her face. Or like the time he pounded her little finger with a hammer under the pretext of needing her to hold a nail. The digit healed crooked, as it remained to this day.

Pranks, Elias had called them, especially when someone—a guest at the hotel, perhaps, or even someone he was doing business with—caught sight of the boy in action. More than once strangers had stepped in to prevent more physical harm, but the minute they looked away, Eino'd be back at it.

At any rate, she'd found a hiding place. One close enough to the hotel that she could reach it in minutes. If, perchance, her half brother had landed a blow in her stomach, she usually had enough strength to reach safety.

And he had never discovered her hideaway which, she remembered, had aggravated him something awful. No one knew.

The memory of those times came to her as, carrying Boo in her arms, she fled. Loud voices were coming from the dining room. The men were on the move.

Frantic, she spotted Callahan standing in the shadows. He had the carpetbag in one hand. In the other, he had her 12-gauge. Evidently, he'd heard the men gearing up for a hunt.

She went past him without stopping. "C'mon," she said. "Hurry."

Following the same path the Golz girls had taken only minutes ago, she went fast, dodging into the shadows where possible. Boo struggled in her arms, but she held on. "Hush," she murmured into the dog's fur. She found herself wishing he had black fur instead of white as he gleamed in the darkness like new-fallen snow.

Mr. Callahan grunted once as if he were in pain as a pine cone rolled under his foot and he lurched to the side, but Rio didn't stop and neither did he. She did look back and could tell he was struggling to keep up.

"Not much farther," she whispered, not sure if he heard her.

They reached the barn. Rio ducked off the beaten path, going around a tall, noisome manure pile just before they reached the corner. There she stopped for a second and looked back.

Nobody in sight.

Quickly, she swerved around the side of the barn and kept on, moving closer to the side of the building. About halfway down, the corral cut them off.

"Now what?" Callahan said.

She could hear him panting. Funny the way he'd tried to tell her he was almost well, Rio reflected, when he so obviously wasn't. Not up to running, at any rate.

"We're nearly there. Be quiet and follow me."

He huffed, clearly not used to taking orders from someone like her.

Before the barn had been built, there'd been an open shed with the corral circling around it. In the years since, the barn, first erected as an addition to the shed, had grown larger. Later, no longer needed, the shed had been allowed to fall in on itself with the corral now attached at the ends to the barn.

Rio ducked between the corral rails and took the shotgun from Callahan. "Can you get through?"

She hoped so. Noises were coming from outside the hotel now. Men were yelling. Someone, probably Marciano, called, "Spread out. He has to be here somewhere."

"What about the woman?" one of them asked.

"We'll deal with her later." Marciano again, definitely the one in charge.

Callahan looked at her. "I'll get through," he said, and he did. "Now what?"

He straightened and took the shotgun from her again.

"We're almost there. Try not to leave any sign we came this way." She led him to where the remains of the shed leaned haphazardly against the barn wall. A tree had grown in the middle of the wreckage, shooting up through what had been the shed roof. A sprawl of extremely thorny blackberry bushes guarded what had been its front

Rio walked right up to where the bushes circled around the tree. Then, pressing herself tightly against the back of the barn, with all due care she edged into what turned out to be an opening between the bushes and the barn wall and disappeared inside.

"What the—" Callahan said.

Her voice slightly muffled, she said, "Pass me your bag and the shotgun. If the opening is too narrow, you may need to get on your knees and crawl. The opening is bit wider at the bottom."

But not, apparently, quite wide enough for his shoulders to pass without getting caught up on a thorn or two. Rio heard him curse under his breath and hiss with pain.

The darkness inside the revealed cavity was deep enough for even Boo's white fur to show only dimly.

Callahan sat on the ground right beside the opening and panting, pressed his back against the barn wall. "What the hell is this?"

"A place nobody knows about that's going to keep us safe." She trusted. There was nowhere else for them to go.

"Pass me the shotgun," he said after a minute, "and don't let go of your dog."

"I don't intend to." Rio thrust the gun toward him. He was muttering something about the blackberry thorns being worse than getting stabbed by the knife. She didn't think he meant it.

Although she wasn't the one making any sound, he whispered, "Couple of them coming this way. Keep Boo quiet. You too."

She heard them now. City men, they didn't like

tramping around a barn and a horse corral in the dark. It was easy to tell when they reached the manure pile.

One of them cursed. "These shoes was new. I bought 'em special for the trip out here. Boss said we'd be inna hotel, not walking around some danged animal yard. Now they're gonna smell like horse crap."

The other laughed. "Breakin' them in right, eh? Anyways, there's plenty of horse manure in San Francisco. I dunno how you'd miss it."

"Well, I coulda. I'd stay outta the middle of the road. Least the boss coulda done was supply us with a lantern. Or even torches."

"Torches, hell. Give us each one of them new hand-held battery lights."

"Them? They're heavy as hell."

"How do you know?"

The other didn't answer. By this time, they'd reached the corral fence. "Lookit. That spotted horse is headed this way," the complainer said. "I ain't walkin' through its yard. Come on. There ain't anywheres for someone to hide here, anyways. We'll circle around the pen."

"It ain't a pen," the other corrected. "It's a corral. When out here in the boondocks, you gotta use the right words."

"Yeah? How'd you get so damn smart?"

There were sounds of them walking away still wrangling, the fellow with new shoes frequently raising his voice. Rio couldn't help thinking his reaction, should he have gotten caught in the blackberry thicket, might have been amusing. She wasn't feeling especially charitable to her hotel guests at the moment and wouldn't mind seeing them bleed.

The two soon moved beyond Rio and Callahan's hiding place, and she let herself relax. She knew he did as well.

He set the shotgun aside.

"How'd you know about this place?" he asked, for safety's sake, still whispering. Those men may have chosen the easy way to search, but that didn't mean all of the six would. They still needed to be cautious.

"This has been my hiding place from the time I was eight. Although the tree was a sapling then, and the blackberries hadn't spread even half as much." Rio allowed Boo to escape her grip, but he didn't try to get past Callahan. Instead, he set to sniffing as he examined the perimeter of the small space.

"You needed a place to hide?" Callahan asked. "Why?"

"I did if I didn't want hurt."

"Who wanted to hurt you?"

"My half brother. Sometimes my father. It doesn't matter now. They're both dead. But at least this is still a good bolt hole."

He went quiet, as if digesting her reply, then said, "Huh. As long as you can fit inside. Good thing you haven't put on weight."

Not many minutes later, she wondered how accurate that was. A bolt hole until it turned into a trap, maybe.

She and Quinn Callahan, with Boo sprawled across Rio's lap, sat silently. They were, she figured, in for a long wait. She had no idea when Marciano and his men would give up the hunt. Sooner rather than later, she hoped. After which, she wanted to get back to the hotel. She hated the necessity to abandon it, if only briefly.

What if these men decided to vandalize it? What if they decided to burn it?

Made nervous by all the what ifs and might be's filling her mind, she shifted uncomfortably. Boo, disturbed by the motion, gave a little "Woof" in his sleep.

And somebody, sounding as if he were right on the other side of the barn wall, said, "What was that? Did you hear something?"

Rio jumped. Quinn touched her arm in warning.

"No," somebody else said. "What did it sound like?"

"I don't know. An animal maybe. Right outside."

The somebody else snorted. "Look where we are, Bert. Surrounded by woods and a lake. Probably *is* an animal, and you'd better hope it ain't a skunk."

The first man grunted. "I'm gonna tell the boss."

"Tell him what? Anyway, you'll have to wait until he and Edgar get back."

"Get back?"

"Yeah, they followed the path through the woods them girls who work here took. He's gonna see if the Salo gal is with them. Her and Callahan both."

Rio's heart just about froze. Enough so she knew when Callahan turned to look at her. Not that he could see any better in the dark than she could. Right now she was grateful. She didn't want him to see what she knew must be a look of terror on her face. If anything happened to the Golz family because of problems at the hotel, she'd never forgive herself.

And here she was, trapped and afraid to so much as move.

Time dragged. The almost total darkness made her feel as if she were blind. Lost and blind.

After a while, she heard the men give up their search of the barn and go away. Quinn Callahan, who sat between her and the hideout's entrance and blocking her way, had gone to sleep. She heard him breathing, soft and regular. A good thing, she supposed, in case they had to make another run for safety. He'd need all the strength he could muster.

After what might have been thirty minutes—or even two hours with time lost in the darkness—off toward the hotel, she heard one of Marciano's men greeting him. "Hallo, boss," he said. "Any sign of them?"

Their voices carried on the still night air.

"Nothing." Marciano sounded disgruntled. "I got close enough to look in their windows. They got a big family and every one of them looked to be sleeping like my grandma when she drinks too much wine. She's a powerful sleeper and so are they."

"Then where are the girl and Callahan?"

Marciano, sounding a bit like Rio imagined an angry grizzly bear might, replied, "That's what I'm trying to find out."

She heard a funny snapping sound—his fingers?— and he said, "Did anybody check the boats? Are any of them gone? If they are, we've been wasting our time. They'll have taken cover by now and we'll never find them tonight."

There was silence.

"Well?" he demanded.

"I dunno."

"Well find out." The grizzly not only growled, he sounded furious. "Meanwhile, what's that behind the barn? Looks like a shed. Could be a place to hide. Anybody search there?"

"Conti and Nasato. Conti said it's nothing. Just a bunch of fallen-in boards with bushes around it."

"Those two." Marciano didn't seem impressed. "Worthless, the pair of them. I'd better check."

Rio's breath caught. *Don't let him look. Please don't let him look.*

She became aware that Callahan had awakened and had the thought he might be holding his breath too. She let hers escape, slowly, softly.

Her plea went unanswered. Made of sterner stuff than his men and undeterred by the manure pile, the fence, or even all four of the hotel's curious horses who'd come to the fence, Marciano started their way. Rio leaned past Callahan to watch through the narrow opening into the space. He leaned forward too, their faces nearly touching.

Until they were.

And neither made the effort to draw apart.

Rio lost track of Marciano. Conscious only of Quinn Callahan's cheek touching hers, the bristles of his whiskers softened as they grew over the last few days, and the confused thought that if she jerked away, he'd think her an overly prissy silly miss. It was enough to hold her there as if glued. She had no idea why he stayed in touch. Maybe he...well, she didn't know.

Vaguely, she heard Marciano cursing as he crawled through the boards of the corral, then a slap as he chased a horse away. The sound of his feet crushing pine cones as he neared warned them against making a move or a sound. Rio thought maybe she quit breathing.

"Stay still," Callahan murmured, so low it might've been a breeze in the tree branches over their heads.

So she didn't move. And he didn't either.

"Find any sign, boss?" the fellow who stayed outside the corral yelled.

"Not yet." Marciano had gotten very close by now and Rio was praying Boo didn't suddenly decide to make a fuss. She could see Marciano now, quite clearly, the quarter moon outlining him against the dark sky.

Quinn Callahan must have too, as she sensed his sudden small jerk of breath. She even saw as the man's hand came down, reaching to poke into the pile of fallen boards and thick bushes.

She held ready to grab Boo's muzzle if he tried to bark.

Until, with a harsh cry, he stumbled back, flinging his hand about as if to throw off the pain. "Ow. Ouch. Sonofa—" He seemed to be doing some kind of dance. "Why the hell didn't you tell me these bushes have thorns?"

He sounded enraged, maybe as if he suspected his men of playing a trick on him.

"Thorns?" the other man said. "What—"

"I'm bleeding." Marciano changed his mind about the search. "Ain't anybody hiding here, that's for damn sure. Unless they got elephant hide instead of skin. And I don't believe that girl does."

He headed back to slither between the boards. "I don't know where she got to that fast, but she must've figured about the search. We scared her off. Might've been a mistake." Easy to tell he didn't like admitting that.

The two met up on the path again, voices still loud enough to hear without straining. "I figure Callahan must be dead, boss. We haven't seen him since Toad says he killed him."

Toad? Did they call that ugly little man Toad? Evidently the girls weren't the only ones who saw the resemblance.

"Yeah?" Marciano was saying, his voice finally fading as the two moved toward the hotel. "Then where's his body?"

Chastened, the other man said, "I don't know. We've looked everywhere. Maybe somebody dumped him in the lake."

Rio started to say something. Afterward, she didn't remember what. Because just then she turned her head at the same time Quinn Callahan turned his. He kissed her, thoroughly kissed her, and yes, she found it very, very pleasant.

So she kissed him back.

———

HOW THE HELL, Quinn thought, *had that happened?*

Not a complaint, since the kiss had been beyond what he might have expected from this hardworking, matter-of-fact young woman. Turned out she was nothing like her brother. Or half brother, as she made sure to point out at the least mention of his name. The only resemblance between them he could see was their pale-blond hair, and it went better on her than him. Her quite beautiful brown eyes made for an arresting contrast.

When he'd gotten to Painter's Bay, he figured everything would go according to plan. His hostess welcomed him. Gave him a preferred room. Surprised him with excellent food and, to his amusement, had a friendly little dust-mop dog that followed her everywhere.

Plus, the tiny hotel was located in a pretty spot. Although he'd always prefer flatter land and, except when in the city, wide open plains. The heavily timbered mountains sort of closed in on him.

Not to mention he'd discovered, almost to his demise, the woods were more apt to conceal his enemies and allow them to sneak up on him than to give him shelter. He hadn't thought any of the others might beat him here. It appeared they'd all had the same idea—and they all wanted to be the one to get at Evan Salo first. Just like him.

Only Curran and his knife-wielding friend were prepared to go to any ends to make sure they won the toss.

Rio, along with the hotel bartender, had saved his life.

And, he thought now as he leaned against a weather-beaten old barn wall only feet from a towering manure pile while sitting in the dirt, she was saving it again. Not from Curran this time, but a bigger bunch. The San Francisco contingent. He recognized Luca Marciano's name. He was the leader of a gang equally as dangerous as Curran, only with more men. Worse, Quinn understood they were a faction of the San Francisco Black Hand.

He sighed. He'd taken the job and intended to see it through, regardless of a pair of soft lips, tentative at first, though eager and quick to learn.

How the hell had that kiss happened? One and done, he decided. He couldn't let it happen again.

Ten

S ometime during the night, the lights in the hotel
got extinguished. Rio was unaware of just when,
as she had, though not on purpose, managed to
drop off to sleep. She didn't know how long she slept
propped against the barn wall—except long enough for
her neck to get stiff. Not long enough to be rested, she
knew, astonished that she'd slept at all sitting here in the
musty-smelling dirt surrounded by vegetation. Quinn
Callahan still slept, with Boo curled between them.

"Call me Quinn," he'd said after the kiss. "I think
we've gone beyond mister and miss."

She thought they had too. Inwardly, Rio called the
going beyond point The Kiss. With capitals. It had
been...well, she didn't quite know.

"And I'm Rio," she said, agreement implied, and all
too aware she'd sounded breathless.

"I know."

So that much was out of the way.

Rio wasn't entirely sure why she'd awakened when
she did, but even as her eyes opened, Boo sat up, his

ears pricked and alert. He jumped across Quinn and out of the shelter before Rio could stop him, trotting away as if he had an important destination in mind.

Presently, someone spoke, calling his name.

Wash Ames. It could be no one else. Rio recognized his voice even at a distance.

Stealth being the watchword, she crawled past Quinn without waking him. The sky, she discovered once outside, was turning color, with dawn only moments away. More cautious than her dog, she edged beyond the bushes and, staying close to the barn wall, got to where she could see around the corner to the hotel.

Wash indeed. To her vast surprise, he wasn't alone.

Boo, jumping up and down like one of those Australian kangaroos Eino had endlessly gone on about when he'd been a kid, seemed to be the focus of Wash's attention. Not only his, but the group of men around him. Men who worked for him. Some from the sawmill too, because not all the men were Chinese. They were easily identified from the hats they wore. And she spotted Mr. Turner, standing with Wash with what looked like a shotgun cradled in his arms. The sawmill men carried their hunting rifles. The Chinese, Rio felt certain, had knives though she didn't see any brandished about.

Relieved beyond measure, she ran toward them, not even thinking of her legs for perhaps the first time since she'd been shot.

Inclined to throw her arms around Wash, she managed to refrain. He'd be embarrassed. She'd be embarrassed. Besides, Mr. Turner spotted her first and stepped forward.

"Couldn't sleep last night," he said, his usual dour expression changed into something more hangdog. "I got to thinking about them men at the hotel, Miss Rio, and that set me to worrying you might be in deeper trouble than you was letting on. Worst of all, I figured you might've told me a little fib and planned to see them folks out on your own. So an hour or so ago I got up and went to fetch Wash. Figured he'd know what to do."

The set of Wash's mouth was grim. "What is this all about, Rio? What are you and Boo doing outside at this time of the night." He eyed her critically, looked up at the sky and changed night to morning. "Looks like you've been playing in the dirt, if you'll pardon me for saying so. Are you hurt? Turner told me you've had some trouble with your hotel guests. That it got bad enough last night you felt called to send your helpers home early. So bad,"—the emphasis came down hard—"he thought it worthwhile getting me and the men up to see what's what."

Rio couldn't decide to scold Mr. Turner or to thank him. It depended on what happened next.

"I'm fine," she said. "They haven't touched me, Wash. But I have been staying out of their sight." She wouldn't mention her own special hideout. Or who accompanied her.

"These people. Chances are, Rio, they're here for a purpose beyond just making trouble. And not one that bodes well for you." His frown would've curdled milk. "Why are they going around terrorizing local people? Doesn't make sense."

"I don't know why. When they checked in, I believed they all were just ordinary travelers."

"Looks like some other purpose to me."

114

"Yes. It does. I don't know who they are or why they're here. But they're dangerous. I know that."

He took her arm and led her away from the men, leaving them to mill around muttering to each other, the whites and the Chinese separated by race. Or maybe some competition between sawmill men and loggers. Wash walked her down the path maybe thirty yards and stopped under a tree.

He leaned close, keeping his voice low. "What's been happening? When we last talked, you said your grand opening was a great success and all your rooms were full."

"That much is true." She swallowed hard on weak tears. Somehow, Wash learning how the situation had gone wrong made it all worse. Her ambitious plans derailed. Thinking back, she didn't understand why this was happening either. There didn't seem to be any reason. Except for Quinn Callahan. Quinn who had kissed her, there in the dark. Who hadn't told her why someone wanted to kill him. Wanted him dead badly enough to apparently send a whole hotel full of men to do the job.

How could she tell Wash any of that? It wasn't her story to tell—unless she repeated the same story she'd told Mr. Turner.

Buck up, she told herself. She'd have to try and talk Wash around to what she wanted to do next.

"I'd taken a reservation from a gentleman before the hotel reopening, if you remember," she started.

Wash nodded. "Last I heard, he hadn't arrived, and you were relieved."

That's right. She'd forgotten to tell him the guest had finally showed up. It hadn't seemed important.

"Yes, well, he turned up after all. He was here overnight. The next day, he went out in the evening—"

"Why? Why'd he go out?"

Something in the way she'd spoken must've struck him.

"I don't know. For a walk after supper? Does it matter? When it came time to close up, I thought he'd returned and gone to his room, but when Mr. Turner left to go home, within a few minutes, he came back and told me he'd found the guest. He'd been stabbed and was unconscious in the woods. You know Mr. Turner takes the shortcut to his cabin."

"Uh-uh? What did you do?"

She thought Mr. Turner might have told him this part since he didn't seem surprised.

"I went with him to see if I could help. We managed to get Mr. Callahan to the hotel. He awakened and said he was all right, that he didn't need a doctor, just a bandage. Which I supplied. He rested in his room a couple days and then left. I don't think anyone knew he was there." Certain her face gave her away, she finished that part of the story. She hated lying to Wash, of all people.

He was peering through the gloom at her, most certainly more questions on his tongue.

She guessed right.

"Did he say who stabbed him?"

"I asked. He said he didn't know. He said he never got a good look at the man in the dark."

Wash continued to study her. "Did you tell anyone what had happened?"

She shrugged, deciding on the spot not to bring Dr. Clement into the story. "Who is there to tell? Besides, I didn't think it was up to me. I'm not the one who got hurt. We need a sheriff, Wash, or at least a town marshal for Painter's Bay, and we need him now. Not only because of Mr. Callahan getting stabbed, but because of these hotel guests who've harassed the Golz girls, who've made trouble for me, and who may have ransacked my hotel last night. I don't know yet. I stayed away all night. I think they'd had too much to drink, and me being here alone I...the thing is—"

She broke off, then went determinedly on. "The thing is, I believe these men are here on Mr. Callahan's account. They seem to be searching for him."

Wash stared down at her. "Didn't you tell them he left?"

"They haven't asked, and I haven't volunteered."

"Huh. Maybe you should've. Save everybody from having to deal with a bunch of outlaws. If that's what they are."

To tell the truth, she was a little piqued. Was he blaming her for being booted out of bed in the middle of the night?

"Except there's nobody to back me up, is there?" she said, sharp and tart. "What this town needs is somebody honest and strong enough to uphold law and order."

Wash opened his mouth as if to speak, but Rio beat him to it.

"Somebody like you, Wash."

He was shaking his head before she even got the words out of her mouth. "Not me. I'm a logger, not a lawman. Right now, me and the men are going to spread out through the hotel and roust those *guests*..." The way he said it indicated he meant something entirely different than guests. "Yeah, roust those men out of their rooms and give them the boot. Then, I suppose a few of us will need to stick around today to make sure they stay gone. Maybe have a few men at the depot to make sure they get on the first train out. You'll have to pay the men extra. Can you do that?"

"I can do it." Or she could as long as her store of cash was still intact. Or, a better alternative, create a way to make it a business expense for the logging crew.

"Then let's get the men in place before they catch us at it. I'd as soon have surprise on our side."

Funny, Rio thought, how her own and Wash's thoughts meshed on the proper action to take. It was just their methods that were different.

Before they approached the hotel, they made plans. And remade, as Rio voiced her concerns. Somebody needed to waylay the Golz ladies and keep them out of danger. Rio wanted everyone accounted for before the trap was sprung. At least that way, if someone started spraying bullets around, not everybody would be in danger at the same time. A limit to the number of potential victims.

And, as she told Wash and to which, after a short argument he agreed, she had an idea of how to proceed. Plans made, they returned to the men.

Singling her bartender out from the group, Rio said, a smile trembling at the corners of her mouth, "Thank you, Mr. Turner. I'm grateful." And stepping close, she kissed him, a quick peck, on his gray-whiskered cheek.

The bartender blushed.

As soon as Rio entered the hotel, her footsteps light, quick, and silent, she knew the liquor in the bar would be sadly diminished. She smelled the potent fumes right away, a sure sign there'd been plenty of spillage. Hopefully, since the liquor salesman wouldn't be around again for a week, they hadn't drunk the place dry. She didn't want to short her regular customers.

Then it occurred to her she was being unduly optimistic. Any customers at all depended on what happened next.

Mr. Turner knew it as well, and the damage to his bar made him very cross indeed. "Worthless, no-good, thieving—" He broke off. "I reckon you could think of a few other names to call 'em."

"I could, Mr. Turner. But I'm trying to be a lady."

Her reply made him snort, and after all the years she'd known him, he said, "Just call me Turner. I ain't used to that mister stuff."

Rio took one look at him and said, "Turner it is." It was as if she'd just been elevated from little girl to adult. Or maybe passed a kind of test.

Along with Wash and a couple of the sawmill men, she and Turner made a quick inventory of the main floor.

"How is it?" Wash asked, looking around.

"Not as bad as I feared." Probably, she decided, because Marciano had kept at the search outside for so long and his men got tired. She paused to set a couple chairs upright that were laying on their sides and to mark where a glass had shattered on the floor. She'd have to get that swept up first thing so Boo didn't step in it and cut his paws. "They must've been too busy with their simpleminded outdoor search to bother tearing the main rooms up. Looks like they drank themselves into a stupor after they called off the search for Mr. Callahan —and me."

Wash grunted. "Still a mess though."

Rio, scanning the dining room and already feeling tired, knew that all too well. Dishes with dried-on custard from last night still littered the tables. Every lamp had been allowed to burn until the fuel was gone. All would need filled, their wicks trimmed and their chimneys washed, but that could wait. In the kitchen, more dirty dishes awaited attention. The pots and pans had gone unwashed, the stove top needed scraped where food had burned on, the odor lingering in the room. The floors needed swept and mopped, the laundry collected. And the boiler lit immediately, or nothing would ever get done.

And then there'd be a bit of cooking to do, that being part of her plan. It hadn't, after all, gone unnoticed that every one of the guests were healthy eaters and always ready for their breakfast. They'd be extra hungry this morning after their evening's endeavors.

Wash assigned one of his men to assist her. Chinese, of course, and an efficient helper. There was a language barrier to contend with, though at least he spoke some English. She set him to tidying the dining room. Wash went to the cellar and lit the boiler—coming back to report there were signs it had been searched—and she cleaned the stove before lighting the fire and starting the coffee. She figured everybody would need that. She most certainly did.

She and her helpers worked fast. They had some luck. The upper floor remained still.

Within half an hour, a tempting aroma issued from the kitchen. The smell of bacon wafted through the rooms, along with the potent scent of cinnamon, and of course, the coffee. Rio even set her Chinese helper to waving a towel to force the smells to the upper story.

With Wash's men arranged strategically out of sight, the time had come. Rio crept to the top of the stairs where she could see down the hall. A couple of the room doors had been left open, their occupants too drunk to bother with privacy. She already heard a few snores break off as men stirred, their noses reacting to the aromas arising from the kitchen below. Nothing smelled better than cinnamon coffee cake baking.

Even Marciano had evidently imbibed from the bar more heavily than prudent. His room at the top of the stairs, the largest of the five on this floor, was one with an open door. He sat up in bed allowing her a glimpse of dirty gray underwear. He was holding his head and glowering, his eyes bloodshot, his hands shaking.

"Breakfast in ten minutes," she shouted. "Come and get it."

"Stop that noise," he yelled, flinching at the effect of his own booming voice.

Rio, afraid he might reach for a gun, ducked out of sight. Wasting no time, she ran back down the stairs to the kitchen.

They were noisy up there. Loud footfalls, thumps and bumps, cursing. Lots and lots of cursing. Someone stumbled on the stairs. After a moment, the motion stopped.

What would Marciano do when they met face to face? He'd set his men to searching not only for Quinn but for her last night, seeming intent on making her a sacrifice to their whims. Would he have the same intention today?

Possible, she figured. Her mouth twisted. Thor

Donaldson, the former sheriff, might be dead and buried, but the jail in Painter's Bay remained. Residents, sanctioned by the law or not, if tried far enough, could make use of it. Vigilantism at its best.

As long as everything happened as it was supposed to.

Eleven

Rio set a couple tables in the dining room with utensils and cups. A carafe of coffee steamed in the center of each. Pitchers of hot cinnamon syrup wafted a tempting smell throughout the lower floor. An invitation to sit, if the situation warranted.

Maybe it would and maybe it wouldn't. She hoped it didn't get that far. Glancing over her shoulder, she spotted a fellow at the top of the stairs. Then, quite suddenly, a burly arm snaked around his neck and with a jerk, he disappeared silently from her sight.

She blinked. *Efficient.*

A door slammed upstairs. A minute later, someone else started down. The man who'd complained about getting his shoes dirty, she thought. There was something about the set of his shoulders she recognized. He reached the turn to his left to enter the dining room, until his mind changed and he went the other way, his new shoes scrabbling heel-first on the floor.

This was working—so far.

Marciano, dressed now in the same clothes he'd been wearing for the last several days, was next on the stairs. Two other men joined him before he started down. They were two whose names she hadn't heard and the quietest of his men, hard-eyed and bearing visible scars. One wore a funny little hat lacking a brim. She watched from the kitchen as they dropped into seats at the prepared table. Marciano stared around the empty room, frowning.

No, no. This wouldn't do.

Breathing slow and deep in an attempt to still the shake of her hands, Rio snatched up a plate with bacon on it and entered the dining room. She didn't speak. The men didn't either. She saw Marciano open his mouth, then close it again. He glared at her as if puzzled.

Feeling a little dizzy, she approached and put the plate on the table.

He grunted.

Satisfied she had their attention, she retreated. Halfway out of the room and walking a little faster now, Marciano called out to her before she could escape.

"You," he said, and she stopped, looking over her shoulder. "Where are the other girls?"

"At home, I expect. I told them not to come this morning. I didn't want them hurt."

His face shifted into a quasi-smile. A cruel smile, his thin lips twisting. "Hurt? Why would we hurt anybody?"

"I don't know." She faced him, regretting it immediately. "Why would you?"

She didn't expect an answer. Just as well since she didn't get one.

"So tell me, Miss Salo, where'd you get to last night? We..."—a wave of his hand indicated his men—"we got to wondering. We looked for you, thinking maybe somebody done you harm, but you weren't to be found. We looked for a long time."

"Did you?" As if she didn't know.

"We did. Couldn't find you though and after a while, we got tired of looking. Where were you?" The tone threatened and at the same time demanded a reply.

"Not here," she said. She spun around, intending to flee.

"Hold it," he roared.

The sheer volume, the menace in his voice stopped her again. She turned back.

A chair scraped across the floor. Marciano got to his feet, his hand inside his jacket where she knew he must have a gun.

One of his men muttered and Marciano, glancing around, nodded. The man, the greasy one who'd disliked the green worm, drew a pistol from under his coat.

"Where are the rest of my men?" he asked.

Rio shrugged. "I don't know. How could I? They're your men."

His eyes narrowed. "Where's Callahan? You know, don't you? He's not dead after all, is he? Curran said he was, but I'm betting he ain't."

"I don't know who you're talking about."

"No?" He glanced at one of the men. The one who'd drawn his gun. "Bring her to me, Edgar," he said, and the man took a step.

She reached under her apron for the pocket pistol

Wash had taken from a dead Chinaman last month and given to her. She pointed it at Marciano.

It was time. Time to run for all those abused legs of hers were worth. And trust the rest of the plan.

If they shot at her, Rio thought, she would duck low and scoot around the doorway into the kitchen. Provided they missed. If not, she'd no doubt be dead.

If they ran at her and she was still alive, she would fire into the mass of them, preferably at Marciano, but in reality, any of them in order to stop or slow them down.

"Gentlemen," she said, quite a lot louder than she usually spoke.

Oddly enough, Edgar had gone still.

"Gentlemen," she said again. "If you don't want shot, I suggest you place your weapons on the floor and kick them into the corner."

Three pairs of eyes stared at her, astonishment turning to disbelief turning to the amusement writ plain on their faces.

Then Marciano laughed although truly, he appeared far from jolly. "What did you say?"

She didn't answer.

"What?" he shouted, as if the volume of the word could make her obey.

Rio felt locked in place, as if her body was stuck to the floor and her mouth, though feeling quite numb, was the only part of her body that still moved. "You heard me. I'm asking you politely. Obey or bear the consequences." She sounded like some kind of fool. She knew it. They knew it.

"Consequences," Marciano said, snorting like an

enraged bull. His men seemed to take it as a joke to be laughed at. Until the one man still sitting, the one wearing the brimless hat, pulled a revolver from under his jacket and fired it at her. Careless in his hurry, he pulled the trigger too soon. The bullet gouged a hole through the wall into the kitchen at a level just about even with Rio's knees. She heard its passage like the drone of a bee.

Fury took over. Not again. They'd never shoot her legs out from under her again. She swore to it.

Her bullet didn't miss. She aimed for his chest and hit his shoulder. He went down howling and for an instant, all of them, even Marciano, stood as if frozen. Then Marciano started toward her, but instead of a gun, it was a knife he pulled from somewhere. A sharp-looking knife with a brightly gleaming blade.

That's when Wash appeared in the doorway from the lobby, his rifle at the ready and aimed at Marciano. At his shout, they all turned toward him. Then Turner popped up from behind the bar where he'd been crouching, his scattergun covering the men from a different angle. A couple of armed sawmill men appeared as if from nowhere, and a few Chinese filed in smiling and showing off their own well-sharpened knives.

They'd all taken their sweet time, in Rio's opinion.

It may have been the sight of the Chinese that did the trick. The tough guys from back east looked toward their boss and at his signal, their resistance wilted. But his eyes promised death.

Nothing there to allow her fear to fade. What now?

For the next hour, events passed in a blur. Men

called for Wash to oversee securing the prisoners, meanwhile passing congratulations to each other on the mostly silent captures before any lethal action developed. One of the sawmill men, the man with muscles like steel chains who'd choked Nasato at the top of the stairs, came in for admiration in particular.

Rio admitted to being one of his admirers. It turned out she had a few of her own. There were whispers about her prowess as a gunman, even as the man she'd shot continued to moan.

She ignored him, the local men, including the Chinese, ignored him, and so did his own compadres. One went so far as to tell him to quit his caterwauling. That he was giving them all a bad name.

Turner elected himself deputy to Rio, and when she went through the rooms with each of the men who'd stayed there, each with hands bound behind him and a rope binding his arms tight against his chest, he saved her blushes by packing their possessions while a Chinese guard stood by. One man was frantic to retrieve the collection of French postcards he'd hidden under the mattress.

Finally, the hotel cleared as the *guests* were sent off down the road under guard by Turner and the sawmill men. Bound for jail, there were complaints. Something about their rights, Bert's shouts louder than anyone else's. A moment later he was picking himself up out of the road and being prodded in the rear by a rifle.

But where were Wash and Marciano?

After a short search, she found them sitting at the vacated table in the dining room. Wash was drinking coffee and consuming bacon. Sullen, Marciano glowered.

Sighing, Rio sank onto a chair, glad to get off her feet. She had a good idea of what came next.

"Has he told you anything?" she asked Wash.

Wash shrugged. "Acts like he's forgot how to talk."

"Huh." She eyed Marciano, trying to read his expression. "Who do you work for, Mr. Marciano? Why are you here? Why my hotel?"

His gaze flicked toward her, then away. His upper lip curled. He stayed silent.

She wanted to slap him. Not, she figured, that it would hurt him particularly, or cause him to talk if he didn't want to. But it would make her feel better.

Or would it?

Almost casually, Wash reached out and snapped his fingers against Marciano's ear. The man jerked.

"Miss Salo asked you a question. Three questions. I suggest you answer." He paused. "And be civil about it."

Marciano snarled. "I don't answer to you. Nor to her."

"Not ordinarily," Wash agreed. "But we're in a different situation at present. Might be in your best interest to tell us what's going on. My patience is not limitless." His voice had risen. Now it dropped back down. "Our patience is not limitless."

If that didn't sound like it came from a man who'd make a good sheriff, Rio didn't know what would.

She looked at him and smiled a faint smile. "That's true. And mine has about run out."

Marciano turned his head, refusing to meet either of his inquisitor's eyes. "I got nothing to say."

"You will," Wash said, grim-faced. And to prove his point, reached for Marciano's ear again.

Marciano jerked his head back, but it didn't stop Wash. He grabbed hold of the ear and twisted. Twisted hard. Until Marciano screamed and Rio turned white. She had never, not ever, suspected Wash capable of anything like this.

"Wash," she whispered, and he let go.

"Something I learned in the Philippines," he said, and she remembered he'd been a young soldier just released from service when he came to Painter's Bay to work for her father.

"Simple questions," he said to Marciano. "The sooner you tell us what we need to know, the sooner you and the others can get on a train out of here."

"After you pay for the drink you consumed last night and the damages to my hotel," Rio said.

Wash nodded. "I'll take up a collection."

Rio gulped. "And never come back here."

"And never come back," Wash repeated, nodding his head. "I learned other punishments in the Philippines. I don't mind showing you what they are." He glanced at Rio. "But not for your eyes. They're not pretty."

Marciano was gasping, his face contorted. Whether from pain or fury, it was hard to tell. Probably both, Rio thought.

"Will it do any harm to tell us why all this has come about?" she asked. "This is my property. Was I always a target, or was it only Mr. Callahan? And why are you after Mr. Callahan?"

"What do you mean, your property?" He snorted. "Leave it to a woman to claim what don't belong to her. You're a thief, just like your brother."

"This most certainly is my property, deed and all,"

she declared stoutly, just before the rest of what he'd said struck home. "What do you mean, a thief like my brother? Anyway, my brother—my half brother that is— is dead." Which wasn't to say, she admitted to herself, that he hadn't been a thief when he was alive.

And, she warned herself, she hadn't seen a body.

"Since when?" Marciano snarled.

"Since when? You mean, since Eino died? Well...I don't know. I was told..." She looked at Wash, her dark eyes wide, then back at Marciano. "Are you saying Eino is not dead?"

He squinted at her. "Eino? What kind of name is that? I'm talking about Evan. Evan Salo, of Painter's Bay, Washington."

Wash shifted in his chair. "Sounds like something he'd do, Rio. Change his name. Eino isn't a common name. Not a name that draws respect at first glance. Too old country."

She couldn't deny it.

He shot another telling glance at Marciano. "Mind telling us what Eino/Evan stole? And why you think it'll take six men to take it back. I assume that's your intention." He watched Marciano. "Or is it?"

Marciano shrugged. "Looks like I might've made an error in judgment. I shoulda brought more men. Didn't expect a bunch of woodcutters to take a hand."

It wasn't a real reply.

"What did he steal?" Rio asked again.

"Twenty thousand dollars."

Maybe a little amused at their reaction, Marciano's gaze flicked back and forth between Rio and Wash.

Rio hadn't expected anything of that magnitude. Nor, she was sure, had Wash.

"But if Eino stole this money, why are you trying to kill Mr. Callahan?" Rio sounded quite plaintive.

Marciano stared at her. "Didn't say I was trying to kill him. Said I was looking for him."

She shook her head. That certainly hadn't been her impression seeing Quinn had been stabbed almost to the point of death. "None of this makes sense. I don't know why I should believe you about any of it. Eino or Mr. Callahan."

She stood up. "Enough. Take him away, Wash. I don't want to hear anymore."

"I'm not lying." Marciano sneered. "Maybe you'd better be watching out, girlie. Salo is headed this way. He'll be here any day now, if he ain't already. And where he goes, there's people out gunning for him no matter who else gets in the way. He's made some powerful enemies. Me and the boys, we won't be the only ones. Nor Callahan either."

Wash got up, lifting Marciano from the chair by his bound hands.

Marciano protesting the treatment, had more to say. None of it worth listening to, in Rio's opinion. But he'd left her with a lot to think about. Had he been lying? Or was everything he said the truth?

She had to admit, knowing Eino, it all made sense.

Which made her feel sick.

At the doorway, Wash turned to her. "I'll be back later. You gonna be all right? You aren't looking so pert."

She forced a smile. "No. I'm not feeling real pert."

He nodded. "I'll be back," he repeated, shoving Marciano out in front of him.

Rio collapsed into a chair at the kitchen worktable and put her head in her hands. Good Lord, she thought, was any of this real? The night hiding out with Quinn Callahan, a man who Marciano said was up to no good. Or had he said that? Now she couldn't think.

What kind of man had she kissed.

A man who was still hiding in a hole under some bushes, she remembered, suddenly horrified. Glancing around the yard, it struck her she hadn't seen Boo since all this trouble began either.

Summoning a burst of energy, she took off for the barn.

———

WASH FIGURED the cat right about halfway out of the bag after this.

He'd be just as glad when the damn tomcat finally revealed itself. One way or another, he figured somebody'd end up dead, but he was damned if it was gonna be him. And he'd do his best to see it wasn't Rio, either. Although with the cat in question, her death might be part of the overall plan.

Spite and jealousy could be strong motivators.

Pushing Marciano ahead of him along the shadowed trail around the point to town, the temptation was there to pull his gun and shoot the fellow. At least one part of his instructions would be out of the way.

Marciano, deliberately dawdling and earning himself another shove, snarled at him, adding to the temptation. "You're gonna be sorry for this, mister. You and that bartender. And that damn woman."

"Not as sorry as you. You got off easy this time. Come back and you'll find a more permanent end to the story."

The thug Rio had wounded kept up a constant complaint, slowing them all down. Impatience rode Wash at their slowness. He had an idea it would be no easy thing to get the six men onto the afternoon train out of Painter's Bay. How to get them to stay away might be another problem.

If it hadn't been for that gol-dang letter!

The letter had come, no return address on the day he and Rio were in Spokane for the probate hearing. It had been poked under his cabin door, a not unknown circumstance often used by someone wanting to buy logs or sell some timber when they couldn't reach him in person. Or even job hunters, though never by the Chinese. He'd been thrown by the signature on this letter and wondered at first if it was for real. The message convinced him. Made him furious too.

But he didn't see how he could deny the demand. He knew what would happen if he did. If he tried. It was the nature of the cat. His work of the last five years would go for nothing. He'd have to start somewhere else from scratch.

When Turner showed up this morning asking for help, the request actually made things easier for him. The latest under-door message had instructed him to clear out the hotel. He construed the message to mean the hotel guests—and he had an idea it'd meant Rio too though he was ignoring that part. He'd even been told what to do with the bodies.

Wash was no damn hired assassin but the demand made him into a target of those who were. So this, meaning events of the morning, might end up being no more than a delay.

Rio's plans had worked just fine as it turned out. And made him into something of a hero in her eyes.

Wash studied on the situation all the way into town. He wished he knew anything about this Callahan fellow Marciano kept going on about. Seemed everyone was worried about him.

Twelve

Quinn had left the shelter. Not that Rio blamed him. With the sun beating down on that side of the barn as well as the manure pile just around the corner, it smelled even more rank than it had last night. Not a place where anyone would choose to spend a lot of time. Or any, if they could help it. He had, she noted, taken his bag with him. She backed away, glad to be in the sunlight.

"Mr. Callahan," she called softly, then decided it sounded silly to call a man who'd kissed her mister. "Quinn? Where are you? It's safe to come out."

The horses ambled toward her from across the corral, the pinto she rode most often nickering a welcome. *Had they done the same with Quinn?* she wondered. And could he be as leery of horses as that man of Marciano's, meaning the horse that had scared him away?

"No," she answered herself. She'd seen him out here the morning before her court appearance. He'd been making friends with the horses, seeming to be at ease around them. Walking to the front of the barn, she called, "Quinn? Quinn Callahan?" into the opening. Nothing. Worry started gnawing at her. Had his wounds opened and begun bleeding again? Was he in trouble, lying unconscious somewhere? Or dead?

Returning to the hotel, she walked up onto the porch and called from there.

No answer.

Disturbed to find Boo missing as well, Rio determined a search necessary for the both of them. Where had the silly little mutt gotten to? Could it be... She went out onto the hotel's back porch, the only place she hadn't yet tried, and stood on the steps. "Boo," she cried, nice and loud, and with firm command. "Boo, come." Then she listened. And watched.

Quinn had walked the grounds around the hotel as well as the barn on that day, she remembered. And since Mr. Turner had found him in the woods, he'd no doubt probed through there as well. As if he, too, were looking for something. Or someone. She wondered if—

Boo burst out through the trees nearest the beach, close to the dock where the boats rocked at their moorings. He stopped halfway to the porch and barked, short and imperative.

"There you are. Come," she called. But he didn't.

Checking her pocket to make certain she hadn't set her pistol down somewhere—she hadn't—she went to meet Boo.

Arms akimbo, she said, "All right, where is he?"

Boo spun in several circles. Enough that he staggered when he stopped. He was wet, Rio discovered, as water sprayed from his coat. But he didn't smell of the lake. That meant he'd been paddling elsewhere. She was sure it meant Quinn had somehow found the spring. They pumped pure, clean drinking water from there and piped it to the hotel. The overrun made a lovely small pool in the woods. There was a small building around the pump itself, with a roof over the pool to keep debris from falling in. And a couple stumps made perfect stools on which to sit and enjoy the tranquility. Or to conceal oneself from people intent on gunning you down. Boo liked to paddle in the pool. If she had been an artist, Rio felt sure this would've been her favorite spot to set her easel.

"So," she said, following Boo as he sped off again. "Did you show him the spring?" Or had he already found it when he went exploring that first day?

Not that she blundered carelessly through the woods, but Rio didn't make any effort to sneak up on Quinn, either. Providing he'd taken shelter at the spring like she suspected.

As for Boo, pink tongue lolling, he trotted along ahead of her, happy as a clam at high water. As they neared the pool, he bounded forward.

Sure enough, Quinn was there. He smiled at her. "I wondered how long it would be before you found me," he said. "Sorry to make you walk, but I didn't want to take the chance of calling out. I heard a couple gunshots a while ago. Anybody hurt?"

"Only one of Mr. Marciano's friends." She didn't mention she'd been the one to shoot him.

"Did your friends gather up all of Marciano's men?"

He'd recognized them! And yet, he hadn't said anything last night. "Yes. They're being put aboard the train to Spokane this afternoon. You won't have to worry anymore about them trying to kill you."

He shook his head. "For a day or two maybe. Hard telling for sure but I expect they'll be back. That might depend on how much their boss pays them. Or he might send men no one here has seen. Whichever, next time they'll be a lot harder to spot when they come."

Rio's heart sank. "You think they will?"

He nodded. "Seems likely."

"Why? What have you done to make them want to kill you?" If she sounded angry, well, it's because she was.

Quinn's gray eyes studied her. "Didn't anybody tell you?"

"Of course not. Why would they?" Legs feeling as if they could hold her no longer, she plunked down on the stump next to him. "I'm a hotelkeeper and a chef. My guests don't confide in me. And I don't want them to."

"Don't you?" His eyes narrowed. "You sure?"

"Only when they intend on wreaking havoc on my hotel," she snapped. "I could use some warning then."

"I suppose you could," he said. He didn't add anything but gazed out over the pool as if pondering the mystery of the universe.

Her patience came to an end. "Why are you here, Mr. Callahan?" She was done with calling him Quinn. A kiss didn't make them partners. Nor even friends. It had been a heated moment, that's all. A respite from danger. "Are you wanted by the law and hiding out? Are those men bounty hunters? Have you taken something that doesn't belong to you? Killed somebody? Does someone want revenge?"

Sneaking her hand into the pocket where the pistol

weighed against her thigh, she grasped the butt and watched as his expression grew bleak.

"Is that what you think? And yet..." His voice dropped to almost a whisper. "And yet you let me kiss you. And you kissed me back."

Rio's face went hot. She had. And liked it too. At the time. "That's when I thought you were a victim. I should have known better, shouldn't I? Nobody has six men looking to kill him if he hasn't done something to deserve it." She knew it might be dangerous to say as much, but found she couldn't hold the words in. And why should she? She'd almost gotten shot. Again.

"Six men?" he said. "He sent six? I didn't know there were that many. Never got a chance to count them. Looks like he doesn't expect me to be the only one."

"What are you talking about? He who? The only one what?" Rio's voice rose with each question. So much so that Boo, who'd settled at her feet, got up, whined, and pawed anxiously at her knees. She lifted the little dog onto her lap and held him close. She was shaking inside.

"Well?" she said to Quinn. A challenge, but when she looked up at him, he was looking back at her with something that resembled pity.

"I know the judge has put through probate with you inheriting this place free and clear," he said, "but sweetheart, this may be biting off more than you can chew. Especially when he—when all of them—find out they can't legally collect anything from you."

Rio's dark eyes went wide. "What? Probate? How do you know about that?" She thought back. "Wait. I saw you, didn't I? In the courtroom, just for a second. It didn't strike me until just now. Why were you there?" Then louder, as if she thought maybe he'd gone deaf. "He who? Collect what? They who? What are you talking about?"

With a start, she remembered about the break-in at Mr. Brackman's law office, where someone had tried to find the paperwork that proved her ownership of the hotel. Paperwork that most surely would've been destroyed had the attorney not had the papers safe with him. Without those, there would've been no proof.

"Are you the one who tried to steal my mother's and my grandfather's wills from the attorney's office?"

His steely gaze sharpened. "Steal their wills? No. I didn't. This is the first I've heard of it."

"And the woman who was poking around in the deeds section at the courthouse? Who was that?"

"Woman? I don't know. Was she successful?"

"She may have seen my deed, but she didn't manage to take it."

But Rio knew when a fresh idea occurred to him. He had a tell shown by the way a crease formed beside each eye.

Quinn stood up and offered her a hand. "Correct me if I'm wrong, but I'm paid up for my room through the end of the week, right?"

Evidently, their talk was over. For the moment.

"Yes." And she added, "In theory."

That made his mouth twitch as if amused. "In theory?"

"Unless I throw you out. Refunding the remaining payment, of course."

His hand was still extended. "I'm hoping you won't. Throw me out, I mean."

"Why wouldn't I?" she asked bitterly, unaware of placing her hand in his.

Boo skipped off Rio's lap as Quinn drew her to her feet. "Because I'm going to tell you what I know of the situation here. And since I don't know everything, I'm afraid you've got stuff coming at you that may be hard to understand."

She stood rooted, the faint burble of the water in the pool, birds singing, Boo panting, all going unheeded. "What stuff?"

How could all this be happening? As if coming to terms with her father having murdered her mother—his intentions toward Rio following the same course—and knowing he'd almost gotten away with stealing her inheritance weren't enough to put any woman in a funk. As if being shot by her father's murderous partner in crime hadn't almost put an end to her life! And now this. Whatever *this* was.

"Tell me," she said.

Quinn tugged on her hand. "If I'm not mistaken, breakfast is included with my room. I'm starved. You must be too. How about we have something to eat, then I'll tell you what I know."

She glanced up at him. Quinn looked tired. Pale, too, as if his blood had yet to recover its normal flow. The night had been hard on a man who'd suffered the loss of so much blood only a matter of days before. She remembered young Win Ferris looking just like this.

Quinn moved stiffly and she supposed his wounds were hurting. As for her, she felt hollow. Maybe he was right. They should eat, fuel for what came next. He'd warned her that it wouldn't be good news. She had to know soon, but putting bad news off a little longer wouldn't hurt.

Rio gave in. "All right," she said. They moved off, both of them slow. Boo, on the other hand, being full of energy, bounded ahead.

The hotel seemed strangely quiet with everyone gone. Quinn, his gaze sharp, took in the smashed glass in the bar, a couple overturned chairs, the interrupted breakfast preparations in the kitchen.

He zeroed in on the new bullet hole in the wall. "How close was that to anyone?" he asked.

"Too close." She motioned him into a chair. "Sit down. You're pale. We'll eat here in the kitchen." Beckett Ferris, although paying for his room right on time, had never minded the kitchen. How would Quinn Callahan react?

The stove needed stirred up again, the pans reheated, the pancake batter whisked. Rio felt his eyes on her as she worked. Making up a story to assuage her? Or would he tell her the truth?

And how, she asked herself, would she even know which was which?

The time finally came when the food was eaten, the coffee drunk, the table cleared. Rio sat back down, folded her hands on the table, and said, "Now."

"Now." He nodded, then remained silent for several moments as if not quite knowing how to start. Then he did, most shattering news first.

"Your brother is on his way here. Frankly, I expected him before this."

"Half brother." She corrected him automatically before the import of the words struck. Dread coursed through her. "You're the second person today to tell me

143

Eino is on his way here. I'd been told he's dead." She'd hoped—and hadn't really believed it. "Although I didn't know whether the person who told me was truthful or not."

"A-no?" Quinn cocked his head. "He said his name is Evan. Evan Salo." He snorted. "I can see why he changed it."

Rio's smile flashed and was as quickly gone. "Father would have a fit."

"Would your father have a fit when he found out his son is on the run from some very dangerous men?"

"My father thinks...thought...anything Eino did was fine. Everyone around here knew he was a thief. A mean thief. My father would simply pay them back and tell them to keep their mouths shut."

She tapped her lips as if thinking. "I doubt he'd like too many on Eino's trail. Time lost dealing with them would mean money lost." She glanced at Quinn. "Is that why Eino is coming back? He doesn't know Father is dead and my half brother is expecting him to pay his debts?"

"Possible, but I think matters have gone too far for that to have helped. I know—" he broke off.

"You know what?"

He shrugged. "It might be best if you can plead ignorance. It's been what? Two years since you've seen him?"

"Just about, though he and our father wrote each other regularly for the first year. Then there were longer spaces between letters, then it became six months. Father was so worried. At the end, he kept calling out for Eino."

"He...Evan/Eino didn't write to you?"

She huffed. "No. Never. Nor did I want him to. Father kept me appraised of what he wanted me to know."

Her tone may have tipped him off that this hadn't been pleasant. "May I ask what that was?"

A fire seemed to light at the back of her eyes. "He told me over and over that when Eino arrived he would either kill me or send me away. That Eino would be rich and that he would rule the Salo empire." She paused. "Empire! But as it turns out, this hotel was never my father's to take or to give away. And anyone who thinks any differently will find out they are mistaken."

Rio had been trying hard to train herself not to think of the past. She'd as soon not been reminded. Why had Eino thought he needed to come back anyway? Why hadn't he truly been dead? Apparently there were some who might be willing to make it so.

"What did Eino do?" Rio asked, curiosity overcoming a certain reluctance. She wasn't at all certain she wanted to hear what he had to say. Would it agree with what Marciano had said? On the other hand, she blamed him for already getting Quinn stabbed, her hotel inhabited by a gang of hired thugs, and her friends and employees harassed. She guessed she'd be better off knowing everything at once than blundering around making more enemies.

Before Quinn had a chance to say more than, "He not only stole from his relatives but what was worse for him, got into trouble with some very bad people," all of which Rio already knew, voices sounded from outside.

The Golz ladies, en masse, had arrived, ready to work. They were laughing, incongruous considering what had gone on in the previous hours. When Rio looked out through the open door, she could see Blanche slashing at the weeds along the path with her whip.

For the first time, she wasn't glad to see them.

"This will have to wait," she said and Quinn nodded.

"Tonight," he promised, leaving Rio to wonder at the shiver that coursed through her.

Thirteen

Blanche Golz, every bit as sharp-eyed as her mother, spotted the signs of struggle in the dining room the moment she walked in. The glass on the floor, leftovers on the table, the overturned chairs. Gasping, she pointed to the bullet hole through the kitchen wall. Her blue eyes got big and her face flushed. Arms akimbo, she said, "What has been happening here? Rio, are you all right?"

"I'm good," Rio said. Truth to tell, mostly she felt embarrassed. "We had a bit of a set-to last night is all. I was afraid this might happen. It's why I sent you all home."

Blanche, after a first glance, continued to eye Quinn with a great deal of suspicion.

Eliza, however, greeted him with pleasure. "Mr. Callahan, you're back. I'm glad to see you."

"Thank you," he said, smiling at her. "I'm glad to be back." No explanation of where he'd been was forthcoming.

147

Eliza, nor any of the other Golz women, had any idea he'd been in the hotel the whole time. He'd adjured Rio to hold his presence secret and she'd done as he asked. It hadn't, Rio thought ruefully, always been easy.

Nodding to the ladies, he went off to his room and closed the door.

Lucky man. Rio, regretting the need to put off their discussion, supposed he'd have a nap, something she wouldn't mind for herself.

But that was not to be. They had business to tend to. Of necessity, Rio and Blanche settled at the table with Rio's grandfather's prized cookbook and put their heads together to plan the evening dinner, for which ten diners had already signed up. Rio hoped for several more drop-ins. And since tomorrow would be Friday with the restaurant's advertised fillet of beef, à la Wellington on the menu for the primary entrée, the two needed to confer. Blanche, not yet into the routine or the cooking methods, still required teaching.

The dinner hour was drawing in before it occurred to Rio that she hadn't heard from Wash or Turner. The train would've departed hours ago with their prisoners on board. Or should have. In spite of the generally quiet afternoon, she couldn't help worrying. Why hadn't Wash sent word? Had he and his men succeeded in ridding Painter's Bay of the invaders, or not?

One of the older town boys had rowed his small craft over earlier with items from the store and a refreshed list of people coming for dinner. Wash knew it was a standing agreement between the hotel and the store. He could've written a single reassuring sentence and sent it along.

Unless, she thought, something had gone wrong. But that would've made due notice even more necessary.

She, with Boo's help, was just showing a new guest to his room while assuring him of a horse to hire for a ride through the woods to one of the logging camps the next morning, when they heard voices raised downstairs. A woman, voice unknown and sharp. Lower, but only by a smidgeon, Blanche. The guest heard them too and cocked his head.

"Trouble?" he asked.

Rio did her best to quell the fear that spiraled through her. "I trust not." Despite the assurance, not being long on trust nowadays, she forced a smile.

With the guest safely stowed, she hesitated at the top of the stairs and listened. Someone, a man, had taken over the shouting. Today, of all days, she felt incapable of dealing with an angry man. The last twenty-four hours had been too much.

But this was her responsibility.

Taking a deep breath, she descended. Stopping at the bottom of the stairs where she had a view both to the lobby and to the kitchen, she saw Eliza standing behind the lobby desk. The girl faced toward Rio. Her eyelids were fluttering and her cheeks were very red. She looked on the verge of tears.

"I don't believe you," she was saying. "Miss Salo owns this hotel."

Rio sucked in a breath.

In the kitchen, Rio also could see Blanche hovering over a pot where she'd begun mixing the choux pastry for the crème-filled éclairs they planned for dessert. She held a large wooden spoon in what looked like a defensive position. The woman she faced was thin, dark-haired, and wore a forest green traveling suit.

Rio had the impression Blanche would sooner beat the woman with her spoon as the eggs into the flour and butter ball in the pan.

"Get out of my kitchen," Blanche said, voice raised and angry. She, too, was red in the face, but Blanche being Blanche, she eyed the other woman with a steely stare. It took a lot, Rio knew, to intimidate Blanche.

In fact, unsuccessful in her endeavor to do so, the woman backed off, which, unfortunately, didn't stop her mouth from flapping.

"You'll see. You're fired. I insist you leave. Go right now, or I'll have my husband throw you out." She had a harsh voice and a harsher scream.

Blanche's spoon raised. "I'd like to see him try it."

"Well, we know someone who can," the woman said.

Just then, Blanche looked up and saw Rio, an expression of relief spreading over her face.

Rio made a choice. She could tell Blanche would be all right for a few minutes; Eliza might not. Rio feared the younger girl was facing the threat of the husband, and from the sound of things, taking a verbal beating at the very least.

Behind the woman's back, she pointed into the lobby. Blanche, realizing her sister was in trouble, caught on instantly. She nodded.

The weight of her revolver touched her thigh as Rio hurried toward the lobby. She was glad of it too, grateful she hadn't had time to put it away after the morning's final kerfuffle.

The man, she saw, had his hands on Eliza, yanking at her in an attempt to pull her from behind the tall lobby desk where the girl had lodged herself. Rage suffused Rio and she broke into a run.

Before the man was even aware of her, she'd jammed the pistol barrel into his back. Jammed hard. "Let go of her before I shoot you like the cowardly thug you are." She waggled the gun, boring deeper to make sure he understood.

Eino Salo is on his way back here. She heard Quinn's voice saying those words as if he were whispering in her ear. And she had no doubt whatsoever that the man she was tempted to shoot on general principle was her half brother. She didn't have to see his face to know.

Eino let go of Eliza. At the same time, he flung himself around, whipping his arm out in expectation of clobbering her with his fist.

He was wrong.

All he did was fling himself off balance.

Apparently, Rio had reflexes that hadn't lost their memory of Eino's usual tactics. It was an act he'd tried on her before. She'd ended up with a lot of bruises and bloody gashes when she'd been young. Now she was older, faster, and ready for him.

She dodged, and instead of trying to get away, she stepped right up against him, the revolver pressed against his heart. The hammer was cocked. One little tug of her forefinger and it would fire.

He knew it. His eyes bulged with fury. And fear. "You. You little bitch. You're done here."

Rio stepped back, her nose wrinkling in disgust. He

smelled bad, she realized, as though he'd been sweating and hadn't bathed in several days. For all that, he wore an expensive suit and shoes of fine leather. A bowler hat that she felt sure had been custom made sat atop his blond hair.

The blond hair was the only resemblance they bore to each other. Rio had always longed for dark hair, like her mother and grandfather.

"Put that gun down, you crazy..." He shouted it. Then, even louder, "Garrity! Garrity? Where the hell are you?"

Rio had a sinking feeling. Who was he calling for? Not for the woman considering a name like Garrity.

It didn't take long for her to find out.

"Lady," a voice behind her said softly, "looks like you'd best back off."

She didn't. She looked at Eliza, whose complexion had gone from red to white, and whose teeth visibly chattered. "Eliza, I want you to go out the front door. Run for home and tell your father what is happening. Stay safe."

Knowing the Golz women, she should've known that wouldn't work. Made of stern stuff and no matter how terrified, Eliza shook her head. "Blanche?"

Rio smiled—sort of. "Stop and collect her first. She's in the kitchen and perfectly all right." It meant she'd have to hold this stance a while longer, but she'd manage. She'd have to. "Go."

Eliza ran, her footsteps across the lobby a light patter as she ran a crooked line around the man who'd spoken. He didn't try to stop her.

Prodding Eino with the barrel of her .32, Rio got

him turned far enough to see the person behind her. The aforementioned Garrity, she assumed.

A massively muscular man, tall, decidedly unhandsome. He wasn't carrying a gun, but then, she supposed, he didn't need to rely on one. Not against someone like her. Unlike her half brother, he didn't appear discomposed by her little .32. Given his size, it might take a howitzer to penetrate those muscles anyway.

"Well?" Eino said, impatient. "Do something. It's what I pay you for."

The big man's eyes narrowed and for an instant, Rio wondered how much loyalty he had to his employer. Or if he'd even been paid anything. As she remembered, Eino had a reputation for shorting the people who worked under him. Around here, most had been glad when he left.

She prodded Eino again. "He makes one move toward me, and I shoot you. Got it?"

Garrity glanced at his boss and lifted his hands in a helpless sort of gesture, silly in such a big man.

Putting on a show, Rio figured. Nothing to trust.

"You," she said to him, "sit down on the floor."

"The floor?" It was as if he'd never heard of such a word.

"Yes. The thing you're standing on. Now sit on it."

"What are you—" Eino sputtered, but she cut him off.

"And you, park yourself on the floor in front of the bar." She poked him in the chest when he started to protest, raising a glare that could've blistered paint. He obeyed, grunting as he folded his legs and sat. The men were a good ten feet apart, but in a line so that if she had to shoot one of them—and she'd made up her mind she wouldn't hesitate to do so—it would be easy to aim at either one. Now she stood with her back against the wall to the kitchen. Protection of a sort. The woman in the kitchen might be a wild card.

"You're making a big mistake," Eino snarled. "I'm taking over here now, today, and you're out. I don't care where you go, so don't bother trying to cajole me. And take these other stupid women with you. I'll hire my own crew."

He started to get up—until Rio fired a single shot into the floor an inch from his buttocks. He screamed at her, something crude.

"Sit," she said. The big man hadn't stirred, and wisely, Eino subsided.

"Shut up and listen." She drew a deep breath, noticed her gun shaking and tried to still her hand. "I'm only going to say this once."

Aware of people crowding into the doorway, she spotted Blanche wrenching the woman's arm behind her back and holding her immobile. One step from the bottom of the stairs, the newest overnight guest, drawn by the shot, gaped at the tableau. And behind them all, Quinn stood where none of them could see him. Tousle-haired and sleepy-eyed, he accompanied Eliza who, instead of running, had gone to fetch him. He'd strapped on his shoulder holster and revolver.

"Perhaps she..." —Rio pointed at the woman— "should have delayed a day or two when she ransacked Mr. Brackman's office and went through the files at the courthouse in Spokane. It would've saved this trouble. If she had, she could've told you that the hotel and the property it stands on has passed through probate and that I am the legal owner."

Eino cut in angrily, "That's not true. My father would never leave this place to you. A common whore's daughter."

Her mother had been an honest, hardworking wife and chef. Rio felt her lips trembling. How she hated this man, a feeling she didn't like holding within herself.

"This property was never his to leave to anyone. It did not belong to him. It belonged to my Serrano grandfather, then to my mother, now to me. And I'm not selling."

Eino sneered in triumph. "And I'm not buying. A husband inherits from his wife. And a son from his father. All I have to do it take it."

"Not when fifteen years ago Elias signed legal documents giving up all rights to the property." Rio sighed and decided to overlook his comment about taking it. "I'm sure the logging operation is yours to do with as you like. Which, knowing you, probably means running it into the ground."

"Logging! I'm no damn logger. I'll leave that kind of work to the Chinese just like Father did."

His father hadn't. He'd built the business up and gotten rich from it. Had her stupid half brother never realized?

"No, and you're no hotelier either. You haven't the work ethic. Or the personality."

Eino glared, sputtering hate. He seemed to have a lot of scorn for the concern that had financed his travels for the last couple years. Financed his whole life, to be accurate. And it was the land his father had selected to retain years ago. Not the hotel.

He seemed to have forgotten Elias had kept an iron

hand on the work right up until the last few months of his life.

Somehow, Rio got the idea that none of what she said was news to Eino. Nor to his wife, if he and the woman were even married. Rio had glanced at the woman when her half brother spewed his venom and called her mother a whore. The woman's mouth had puckered as if sucking on a sour lemon.

But that was neither here nor there. She just needed to get him out of here. Him and the woman and Garrity. And then for them to stay away.

"I'm not going to argue. The situation is settled, everything is legal and according to law. My own will is made and you, Eino, are not the beneficiary. There is no point in discussing this further."

"What did you call him?" The woman, her eyes bulging with anger, struggled hard enough against Blanche's strength that she succeeded in breaking free.

Everyone looked at her. Quinn, Rio noticed, with a slight smile. Eino shook his head and appeared furious. Aware of his name, the Golz girls gaped with every evidence of confusion.

"Call him?" Rio had to think. "I said his name. The one he got at birth."

This drew an outraged shriek, this time aimed at Eino.

"She called you some dumb name. A-no. If that's even a name. But it's what she said. You said your name is Evan."

Quinn had questioned that name too, Rio remembered. Even warned her that her brother might be using an alias nowadays. And here Eino was, stuttering as he tried to blame Rio for being the stupid one.

Enough of that. "No need to take my word for it, but you'll find his legal name is Eino if you care to look at the county records. Or ask anyone in town. They all know him." She waggled her gun, a sign for Eino to rise, which he did. Clumsy at it too, as he'd gained quite a bit of weight while he'd been gone.

Though favored and catered to by their father, the old man had always kept his son on the move so he'd been almost thin. Apparently he'd been living a life of sloth and ease of late.

"Gather your things and get out. All of you." Rio hadn't missed the stack of luggage piled at the desk. A trunk, a couple leather suitcases. A beat-up pair of saddlebags, a duffel bag, and something that could only have been a cosmetic case. Apparently, the woman needed enhancing.

Quinn drew his revolver as Garrity rose to his feet, and Blanche gave the woman a push.

The woman transferred her glare to Eino. "Are you going to let her do this?" She whirled on Garrity. "You. Take her, you stupid man. What are you waiting for?"

The big man shrugged. "Don't want shot."

"I told you to get her," the woman said, cold and harsh, but Garrity didn't move. "Evan! Do something."

"Shut up. You aren't helping. This is your fault anyway." Her half brother, Rio noted to herself, spoke to this woman just like Elias had spoken to her mother. She remembered clearly. Like father, like son. Vindictive and cruel. "Get the trunk," he told Garrity. "I'll get the bags. Flavia, get the rest."

"How will we get to town?" the woman wailed.

"Same way you got here, I expect. Take a boat," Rio said. "Leave it at the town dock." Preferably in one piece, she thought, although she didn't want to say so out loud for fear of putting ideas in their heads that might not already be there.

"We'll go for now," Eino snarled at her. "But this isn't over. You'll see. And you'll be sorry."

Rio didn't doubt him for a moment. And it went for both counts.

Fourteen

"Y ou should have seen her, Sister!" Eliza said as she and Blanche came together in a hug once the hotel lobby cleared of opponents and onlookers. "I thought he was going to pull my arms out of the sockets. He was hurting me and she scared him away. She...Rio...she was like a real live Valkyrie."

The front door, which Flavia had left open as she tugged the last of the luggage toward the dock, allowed snippets of the accusations and recriminations flying between the banished three to reach into the hotel. Most between Eino and the woman, as far as Rio could tell. Garrity wasn't saying anything. He just tossed the trunk (to Flavia's horrified screech) and the bags into the boat any which way, got in himself and took the oars.

The overnight guest, whom Rio had expected to ask for his money back, uttered, "Almighty!" in a flabber-gasted tone of voice, and figuring the excitement over, shook his head and calmly went back upstairs. Maybe he saw things like this all the time in other hotels where he stayed, but it was all new to Rio.

Quinn grinned at the Golz ladies. "A woman of myth."

"Yes," Eliza said. She'd already regained her color and most of her usual bouncing vitality. "She was fierce!"

Outside, the quarrelsome pair had gotten in the boat. Garrity pushed off, giving a mighty heave that set the small boat rocking. It appeared deliberate—and smart. The other two shut up and held on.

Only then did Rio take her revolver off cock and stow it in her skirt pocket. She didn't feel triumphant at all. Or fierce. She felt used, as if this had been a trial run for Eino to see if she'd be easy or hard to defeat. He'd given up too easily. And Garrity. He'd seemed some kind of bodyguard, but if so, he hadn't been worth his pay. Again too easy. She had no hope her half brother would give up. He'd just lurk in the shadows and bide his time.

Then there was the floor where Eino had been sitting. Her gaze fixed on where her bullet had gouged a furrow in the oak before coming to rest at the juncture of wall and floor. "My poor floor," she said, feeling near tears. "It's ruined."

Blanche steered Eliza over for both of them to take a look. Blanche examined the hole with a discerning eye. "Agh. That's not so much. Papa can fix that in a jiffy and nobody will be able to tell it happened. Don't worry, Rio. Please don't worry."

As if anybody believed she could actually stop.

"And now Eino knows the hotel is yours," Eliza added brightly, "he doesn't have any reason to come back."

"He'll be back." Rio knew he would. "He'll do

anything and everything to make my life miserable, just like he always has."

Quinn chose the moment to clear his throat. "What will he do? You have any idea?"

"Oh yes." Even though she knew her eyes had gone watery, she looked up at him. "Name calling, for one thing. Resurrecting and telling lies about me and my mother in an attempt to scare off my restaurant patrons. He used to do it all the time until our father finally noticed business would drop off every once in a while and wondered why. He actually told Eino to stop, that he was cutting into the profits. Oh, not that people hereabouts believed any of his lies, but he did scare some of them into staying away. Or maybe he just disgusted them."

Quinn frowned. "Hard to fight nasty rumors."

"Yes." She thought a moment before clamping her mouth and sighing. "The rumors may be the least of it. Eino has been known to use a gun. But his usual response is to hire thugs to intimidate, and if that doesn't work, to do actual harm. Mr. Garrity being the newest thug, I suppose. Eino did that with a homesteader who refused to let him court—if that's even what it could be called—his pretty young daughter. He had the man beaten badly enough he couldn't work for two months. Father paid the man's expenses and for his silence. But people knew."

Quinn's nostril flared. "Your brother is even worse than I've been told."

"Half brother," Rio said and added thoughtfully, "He's also been known to use fire."

Eliza heard this, though Rio had spoken softly. "You

think Eino would set the hotel on fire? Really?" the girl asked.

She nodded. "If it serves his purposes and he thinks he can get away with it. And remember, there's no lawman hereabout to stop him. It's another thing to watch for."

Blanche nodded. "Yes. I remember when Papa told us about Mr. Cutter's haystack just before Eino left. About how one of Mr. Cutter's haystacks burned and he had to sell several of his cattle before winter was over when he didn't have enough hay to see them all through."

"Ugh." Eliza made a face. "Everybody knew Eino did it."

The Golz ladies and Rio went back to work after a reviving cup of tea and a few oatmeal cookies with raisins in them.

In the afternoon, Quinn caught Rio as she was coming down the stairs carrying a giant armful of dirty bedding after cleaning and airing the rooms Marciano's men had occupied. He followed her out to the porch where she put the sheets in a basket to be picked up by the Chinese fellow who ran the laundry and asked her to walk with him.

Whatever he wanted to say, he evidently didn't want the girls to overhear. And if he didn't, Rio decided as she nodded and followed him out, she probably didn't either.

"It's about Eino, isn't it? I'm warning you, I've about had my fill of him for one day." She had been thinking about what he'd said earlier, about Eino being worse than he'd heard. Who had he been talking with? That's what she wanted to know.

He chuckled. "I'm not surprised." He pointed her toward the spring, where the air was fresh and cool.

Back on the porch, she heard the screen door slam open, then shut, and saw a small white blur come rushing to join them.

"Boo," she said, picking him up when he ran in front of her. "I've been wondering if you'd gotten over your fright yet. It's been one thing right after another, hasn't it? And I'm guilty of this last one."

Quinn deciphered what she was saying. "Is he afraid of guns?" he asked.

"Yes. Of the noise, anyway. A while back someone shot at us and Boo got a very painful sliver in his shoulder. He's so smart he put the two things together. Gunfire equals pain."

Quinn was impressed. "That is smart. Who did the shooting?"

"The sheriff," she replied dryly.

"Ah. Him again." Quinn paused, then said, "Your half brother, he seemed to think he'd be safe here at the hotel after Marciano's men left town. That's probably why he turned up only hours after they were gone. He wants to stay out of their sight and figured they wouldn't be back." His left eyebrow rose. "I'd say he's mistaken. My feeling is they'll be back."

They'd reached the spring, where the water burbled as it broke the surface. A faint breeze stirred the branches of the pine trees, spreading their scent along with a scatter of needles. Rio headed toward the stumps.

"So he just figured to walk in and take it from me." Rio's bitterness showed clearly. A new suspicion touched her. "How do you know what he thought,

Quinn?" she burst out. "Did he tell you? Or did Garrity or that woman?"

Questions she should've asked him before. And there were more. Why was he even here? Why had Toad tried to kill him? He must know a whole lot more than he'd admitted to her. Why had *he* remained out of Marciano and his men's sight? Most of all, just who did he work for?

She stopped and whirled around, realizing she'd left her pistol in the hotel after she got tired of it bumping against her thigh. What had she been thinking? She'd best go back for it—and never leave it far from her grasp again.

Boo wheezed, making her realize she'd squeezed him too hard. Poor little dog. A bad day for him too.

Quinn stopped too, looking down at her with what seemed to be surprise, except his gray eyes had turned metallic, the softer gray of clouds lost somewhere in this mess of distrust. "Is that what you think?"

"I don't know what to think." With a sense of horror, Rio heard her voice rising to a shout. A subdued shout, but with all the might of a thunderclap. "All I know is that my—and Eino's—father murdered my mother. Shot her in the head, put her in a cave and poured rocks and dirt down on her. But she, suspecting problems and fearing for herself and me, had already managed to ensure I inherited this hotel. I'm beginning to think she did me no favors."

She paused at Quinn's shocked expression.

"I also know my father and my half brother treated me like dirt beneath their feet from the time I was eight years old," she went on. "I know I worked harder than Father's Chinese coolies in this hotel all those years, then took care of the old beast until he died. I did that out of some kind of misplaced familial loyalty. And because I'm such a fool. Even though I didn't know I already owned this place, I intended to take it if I could. And God knows I earned it twice over."

Tears ran down her cheeks, though she paid them no mind. She wasn't crying. Not really. She was having a tantrum—and it felt good.

Before Quinn could speak, if he'd been so inclined, she had more to say.

"What I don't know is where Eino has been or what he's done. Oh, I know about the $20,000. But I don't know how he did it. Whether he killed somebody while he was at it. I do know it must have been bad. It's always bad, with him. But that was Marciano. I don't know anything about Marciano and his men except they're also very bad men and I'm well rid of them. If I'm rid of them. I don't know why you're here or why you were stabbed or who did it. I do know I'm scared."

"And angry," Quinn said.

"Yes. I'm angry." Rio rubbed her face in Boo's fur in an attempt to dry the tears and looked up at Quinn defiantly, almost as if daring him to laugh at her.

He didn't laugh. He just shook his head, stepped right up to her, and taking her by the shoulders, pulled her to him.

Rio blinked. "What..." she started to say, which he stifled by setting his mouth on hers and proceeding to kiss her. Thoroughly. With the curious effect of curling her insides into knots and twists and leaving her with an unfamiliar kind of need, even as she suspected what it was.

With a man who mystified her. Who worried her. Who she mistrusted.

All with Boo sandwiched between them.

Quinn broke it off when the dog struggled. "Little bugger," he said softly. "I'm beginning to think you're the only smart one around here." He led Rio to the nearest stump and pressed her down onto it. "I'm not your enemy, Rio, if that's what you're afraid of. I swear I'm not. We need to talk. I think I can relieve your mind."

He may have believed he did a good job explaining all her fears away. Rio, as she made her way back to the hotel twenty minutes later, wasn't so sure. She thought not. After all, now she'd learned there was a third player in the game. A player who commanded Toad.

————

WASH CAME AROUND JUST after the first surge of diners. His chin freshly shaved and his dark hair slicked back, he entered through the back and stopped in the kitchen. Blanche was refilling the soup tureen with beef consommé at the stove while Rio arranged various lettuces, green onions, and radishes on a dozen plates, drizzled them with some kind of yellow-colored dressing and scattered herbed croutons over the top.

Rio looked up as the screen door banged, a tense expression fading as she saw who it was.

"Wash," she said, smiling. "I was hoping you'd come for supper and let me know what happened with those men."

He seemed a little grumpy. "I'll take you up on the

offer. I missed supper in the mess hall." He meant the meal the Chinese cook made for the crew. Two months ago, the old cook had used a shack at the edge of the bay for their meals. But he'd been murdered and the new fellow insisted evil spirits occupied the place now. Wash intended to build a new mess hall during the winter but for the present, the men had fitted out a corner of the barracks. "Had to make sure those men got on the train this afternoon, which put me a whole day behind with my real job."

"And did you? Make certain, I mean. Was there any trouble?"

"Not much. They argued some. Didn't do them any good. To tell the truth, I think the men would've enjoyed a good old fist fight. Worst part is it put the work behind."

Her fault. "I'm sorry. Let me fix you a plate. Do you want chicken fricassee or Swiss steak?"

"I won't say no." He smiled at her. "I'll take the steak, please."

She'd been sure that would be his choice. He'd certainly earned her best effort. "Kitchen or dining room? she asked.

"Kitchen."

She'd guessed that too. "There just wasn't anybody else I could call on this morning. As I guess Mr. Turner knew." Rio filled a bowl with the soup and brought it to the table. "Sit."

He sat. "It's all right. You need somebody here, I think. A man. Or a stout woman, at a pinch. One who can handle that shotgun you keep on your porch." He eyed Blanche, smiled briefly, then seemed to relent even as he scowled back at Rio. "That feller—Marciwhatchamacall'im—you want to look out for him, Rio. He didn't take kindly to what happened this morning. Especially you being female and putting the whole bunch of them to shame."

"Do you think they'll be back?"

"I do. Some of them anyway. Keep your eyes peeled. You got your little gun handy?"

Rio patted her skirt pocket, hidden at present under her voluminous apron. "Yes. And Father's old revolver at the lobby desk. I'm aware those men are a danger." She kept her face hidden. "I've been warned to be on the lookout for retaliation."

Wash sent her a penetrating look. "Who warned you?"

She shouldn't have mentioned the warning, she realized. Best if Wash didn't get to wondering about Quinn's part in this—whatever this was. And whatever Quinn's part amounted to. Earlier, during their talk, he'd hinted.

She backpedaled. "Not warned, really. A guest just mentioned he'd heard Mr. Marciano has a reputation for violence. I don't know where he heard it."

That much wasn't untrue. The clues had certainly been there.

Had Turner told Wash about Quinn? Best if he hadn't. Or was it? She couldn't decide.

It was just that she didn't want Wash looking too closely at this *guest* and wondering why he'd felt called upon to taken a hand. She didn't want Quinn looking at Wash and thinking he might be in the way of what he wanted to accomplish either. Whatever that might be. Somehow, he'd managed not to say a word about it this afternoon.

It seemed safer to veer the conversation back to one she and Wash had had before. The question of hiring someone to keep lawbreakers from taking over this part of county. A strong town marshal might help, but someone with a bit more range and authority would do better.

"Have you thought anymore about trying to convince the county commissioners to hire someone to keep order until there's an election? Or taking the job yourself? After what happened here, it's easy to tell we need someone right now."

"We do, but not me. Some of us have talked of asking the commissioners for help. But it's not up to me, Rio. I'm nobody important. Shoot. I don't even own property."

"You're respected," she said. "And known to be honest and hardworking."

He snorted.

"Anyway, with Eino here, I think it would pay if we didn't wait for the fall election."

Though Wash had just seated himself at the kitchen table, he stood right back up, catching the chair before it toppled. Rio saw his knuckles turn white as he clenched the finials.

"Eino's here? Since when? Why didn't you say so." He spoke loudly enough Blanche, busy dishing up plates of chicken fricassee with some young asparagus spears alongside, looked up from placing them just so.

Quite the reaction. Rio's eyes blinked her surprise.

She waved at Blanche and shook her head. *I should be helping her*, she thought. But Wash came first. He deserved to know the worst, because if Eino decided to take the reins of the Salo logging operation, Wash would likely be out of a job.

Which, it occurred to her, might be the only way he could be persuaded to take on a deputy's duties. Or maybe running for sheriff.

THE LOWDOWN, lying, creeping, blowhard, four-flushing—

Wash gave up on tagging Eino Salo with words. There weren't any strong enough to fully describe him.

He'd sent Wash in to do his dirty work while he sneaked around playing it safe.

And here *he* was. Any way you looked at it he was in too deep to make himself look good. Try as he might, he saw only one way out.

By preference, Eino needed to end up dead, his mouth shut forever.

Fifteen

Exhausted after the previous sleepless night, then the kerfuffle with Marciano and his men followed by a full day of work, Rio should have been sleeping like a baby.

Should have. But wasn't.

She kept going over the meeting with Eino and Flavia.

In her own bed with Boo curled against her back, her open window allowed the chorus of crickets accompanied by a counter harmony of frogs to sweep over her. Normally the sound would put her to sleep within minutes.

Tonight it didn't.

And then, bam, the chorus went silent just like that.

Though her eyes had been shut, they flew open again, waiting for the night music to resume.

In vain. It didn't.

What she heard was the bump of a boat against the dock and the sound of oars rattling in the oarlocks as they were drawn in.

Somebody—a man—cursed, not loud, just enough to carry on the night air and in through her open window.

Somebody else—female—said, "Shut up," only her voice carried higher than the man's had. Probably not her intention.

Lying stiff in the bed, Rio's heart beat fast. Speak of the devil—metaphorically since she hadn't actually spoken, only thought—and he, or in this case she, appears. Flavia. The voice belonged to Eino's wife... woman...mistress...whatever position she claimed. Rio was sure of it. Which probably meant the man was Eino. Unless it was Garrity. Or maybe both. It might depend on what they had in mind.

She had an idea her half brother was never a good conspirator. Too unreliable. But considering he'd figure he had a score to settle with her, he'd want his revenge to be personal. Besides, he'd never been much of a hand with the oars—not that Garrity had either, or so she remembered from earlier.

She waited for the pair to pound on the door or ring the bell attached to the one in her room. It had always been her lot to get up in the middle of the night when late guests arrived at the hotel. Most assuredly neither Elias nor Eino allowed their sleep to be broken.

But the bell didn't ring, and nobody pounded on the door.

Where were they? What were they up to?

She lay tense and stiff, barely seeming to breathe.

Then she heard footsteps on the gravel path that went around the hotel until it led into the trees and thence to the barn. What on earth were they doing there?

Moving carefully to avoid awakening Boo, she slipped out of bed and went to the window.

There. Just a glimpse as with a flip of her skirt which had caught on a bush, the woman disappeared among the trees. They were definitely headed toward the barn.

Eino and Flavia, up to no good. She had no doubt of it.

Rio, aware of her half brother's history, was certain she knew what they had in mind too. She pulled on her shoes, picked up her revolver and, unmindful of wearing only her thin nightgown, ran down the stairs. She paused a moment in front of Quinn's door. Should she call to him? No. There was no time. She had to handle this. It was her job.

She took the same route as her unwelcome visitors, jogging at the verge of the path where grass cushioned any sound of her feet.

Passing the entrance to where she and Quinn had hidden behind the berry bushes last night, she spotted all four of the horses in the corral. Thank God none had been left in the barn. Their heads hung over the rails at the opposite side of the barn watching the intruders. Pointing out their whereabouts to her, actually. Always curious, they'd be interested in the people who disturbed their territory. But at least they were outside. Fire—if that's what this came to—wouldn't touch them.

And, she realized, it made sense for Eino to lead the way to the back where they'd be less likely to be seen. It was where the hay was brought into the barn. Out of sight from the hotel, they could take their time with whatever they were up to. Right now, she was glad the hay hadn't been delivered although she'd been worried about the weather. The barn, at present, stood nearly empty. A laugh on Eino.

Rio didn't bother following the pair. She needed to get to the back before they did damage. Yanking open the small barn door, she slipped inside and ran down the center aisle. The hay mow looming overheard always made the interior beastly dark. Right now, she was grateful for it. So far, they hadn't gotten inside, otherwise there'd be some spark to show them where to do the most damage.

Another thought struck her. Maybe they didn't plan on coming inside. Maybe they planned to start the fire outside.

Provided she didn't stop them.

The barn was a great deal larger than needed for four horses. Before the Salo logging crew's first barracks got turned into a hotel, at least two teams of draft horses had inhabited the barn as well as several riding horses. Elias's first wife had disliked living next to rough loggers and horses and insisted on building new barracks at the other end of the inlet, out of her sight. The old barracks were remade first into a home, then, when Edith passed, into the hotel. The barn was retained for personal mounts.

Nowadays, two of the horses presently in the corral were broken to harness for the buggy stored in an empty stall. All four could be hired out, but that rarely happened. The man staying overnight who'd asked to be supplied with transportation tomorrow—or was it today already?—was the exception.

Across the aisle at the back, another stall had been fitted out as a chicken coop. Whatever the midnight visitors were doing, the chickens had awakened and though still drowsy, were stirring. She could hear them rustling in their nests and clucking to each other, making her think Eino and Flavia must be just on the other side of the wall. The use of the stall for her chickens had occurred after Eino left. He wouldn't be aware of this new area of the barn.

He wouldn't care about the animals anyway. He never had. Even Elias had rebuked him for his treatment of his horse.

But he also wouldn't know the big door was no longer the only way in and out. A smaller door allowed entrance from the wire-enclosed pen that kept the chickens from coyotes or hawks or other predators. And also provided egress from the pen.

Silent as a stalking fox, Rio opened the coop and went in, shushing the birds as she passed among them. They were used to her and quickly settled. At the door to the pen, she paused and listened. Eino was talking. Still quiet, although he couldn't have been heard from inside the hotel from here anyway, even if he'd been loud.

"It's new," he said. "Sounds like a bunch of damn chickens to me."

"Where..." Flavia said, the rest of the question lost to the night.

The sound reassured her. They were far enough away she figured it possible to get outside without being seen.

Eino, an unimaginative man when you got down to it, was following the same process as with the other fires he'd started. Like Mr. Cutter's haystacks where he'd soaked some rags with kerosene, then lit them and tossed them into the hay. She'd been told the fire had been visible five miles away.

He'd been expecting a barn full of fresh dry hay here too, unaware of the heavy rains they'd had earlier in the spring that set all the crops back by two weeks.

Fierce anger burned through her again. He'd do anything to drive her away, including kill her animals. Kill her if he could get away with it, but only after he'd brought her low. Sometimes she thought hate was the only thing he'd learned from their father.

But maybe, the thought crossed her mind, she'd learned that lesson as well. And she didn't like it. Not in herself, and not in Eino.

Careful to hold the latch from clattering against the fence posts, Rio slipped through the pen. She could see them now. They were just beyond her, Flavia hissing at Eino like an angry snake as he bent over the padlocked chain holding the wide back door closed.

"You should've expected a padlock," she said. "This place is isolated. Easy for thieves."

Eino grunted. "Never locked the place before. Nothing worth stealing in the barn anyhow. It's her. She always was a scaredy cat."

He wasn't, Rio admitted, far off the mark. Just like right now when she really was afraid. Of them, of fire, of just about everything.

A ramp led up to where the barn sat on a thick cedar log foundation. Over the years wisps of hay had gathered under and around the ramp. Fodder for a fire. And though Eino didn't see it right off, Flavia did.

"Start the fire here. It will burn," she said. "Just like peat, I bet. You just have to get it going."

Eino grunted. "Yeah. All right. See if you can find

more loose hay. Or even some dry weeds. Anything that looks like it'll catch fast and burn hot. I'll start building what's here into a pile. Look around the pen. Might be something there."

"Me? No. It stinks." Plainly, Flavia didn't like the idea. "You do it. I'll ruin my hands."

"A worthwhile sacrifice." Eino made a show of stacking the debris under the ramp, then looked up at her. "Do it."

Rio ducked back as Flavia, huffing her disgust, headed her way. The woman was muttering in a foreign language of which Rio didn't understand a word. The tone, however, made Flavia's intent clear. She wanted nothing to do with the physical aspects of building a fire, although she just might enjoy lighting the match.

When Flavia, oblivious to her surroundings, walked right past Rio who'd crouched behind a large current bush growing just outside the chicken pen—the bright red berries were a favorite of the hens when they could reach them—Rio stifled a giggle.

Then Flavia, spotting a clump of hay caught in the blackberry bushes just beyond the chicken pen, reached down to gather the dry stuff in.

"Ow, ow!" Screeching like a flustered bird, Flavia stumbled back, shaking her hand and rubbing her forehead with the other.

The scream that followed, higher and louder than the old locomotive's whistle as it climbed the grade into town, woke every chicken and made the horses neigh. Credit was owed to a little help from behind as she lurched headlong into the berry bushes that had stymied Marciano's men the previous night.

Rio, with speed born of fear, resumed her position

behind the current bush half a second before Eino, his mouth gaping open rushed up.

"Shh, shh! Good God, woman, what are you doing? Be quiet."

"Somebody pushed me right into these bushes," Flavia wailed.

Flavia was sobbing and even in the dark, Rio could see blood, black against her pale face, streaking down to her chin.

"It hurts. It hurts, Evan." She waved the bloodiest hand at the bushes, inadvertently touching them again. The pained howls sounded anew.

"What are you talking about, pushed? There's no one here." He ignored her pained complaints and made a show of standing back and gazing around.

Rio huddled to make herself smaller, meanwhile thanking her lucky stars for planting the currents last year and having them grown double their normal size. The heavily fertilized soil around the chicken's pen got the credit.

"There is someone," Flavia cried. "I swear there is. I felt hands on my back. And he pushed me."

"For the love of God, be quiet, woman. They must be able to hear you in town." Eino ignored Flavia's pain and anger as if it didn't matter. "Next thing we know," he said, "you'll have my sister out of bed mad as fire. I'm told she ain't afraid to shoot that pistol she waved around this afternoon. And I don't mean into the floor."

His lack of consideration for the woman made Rio believe whatever they were to each other, it didn't include a love match.

Flavia continued to sob noisily. Finally, she stopped

and dug a handkerchief out of a pocket, dabbing gingerly at her face.

If it had been anyone else, Rio might have felt sorry for the woman. She knew blackberry thorns had an uncanny ability to stab deeply. They also hurt something fierce. The punctures were prone to infection too. Sometimes they even left scars. In this case, she didn't mind if they did.

Back at the hotel, the sound of the screen door slamming made the pair stop and stare at each other.

"It's her. Dammit." Eino's voice dropped. "Now you've done it."

"Me? Starting a fire is your idea. I said it wasn't smart. All it does is warn her we mean business. Anyway, she'd just one woman. Do what I say, and it'll be easy. Just shoot her."

Eino sighed. "That's not as much fun as..."

He broke off as back at the hotel, the door slammed again and a man called out, "Did you hear that?"

Another man, one closer to the barn, said, "I heard something."

Rio tensed. Flavia's wails had awakened both hotel guests. She hoped they stayed away.

"Somebody is coming," Eino said. "And I don't think it's her. Come on. We need to get out of here."

He turned and strode past where Rio crouched. He walked quickly, forgetting the kerosene-soaked rag on the ground by the ramp. "Hurry," he said over his shoulder. "We'll circle the barn and come down past the hotel on the trail. We can get to the boat dock from there and be gone before anyone sees us."

Flavia, seeing he'd leave her behind if she lagged too much, hurried to catch up.

When certain they wouldn't look back and see her, Rio stood, listening as they blundered through the trees to the trail.

There was no satisfaction in this night's undeclared war. She had stopped them this time—rather her blackberry bushes had—but they were bound to try again. She'd have to learn to sleep with one eye open, she thought wryly.

As for the slamming of the screen door and the voices? It could only have been two people, Quinn Callahan and Mr. Perry, the hotel guest who planned to visit the logging camp in the morning. And of the two, Rio was inclined to expect it would be Quinn who came to investigate. In fact, she was surprised the other fellow had inquired about the commotion considering the way he'd stayed in his room after the trouble this afternoon.

Not that she blamed him.

She set off to meet Quinn, who, on further reflection, she thought may have slammed the door on purpose, aiming for the exact result that had happened. The culprits were gone. No fire. No dead livestock. All safe.

For now.

A sudden thought struck and stopped her in her tracks. What if someone—meaning Mr. Perry in particular—saw her walking around outside in a state of *dishabille?* How mortifying, and not at all good for her reputation should it be noised about. Surely it wasn't too much to ask to get back to the hotel unseen.

She started walking again.

Except, it evidently *was* too much to ask.

Quinn barreled around the corner of the barn at the

same instant Rio turned the same corner. They slammed into each other with enough force she would've fallen but for the hands that caught her just before she toppled.

He eyed her, up and down and back again. "So," he said, "I'm guessing that wasn't you screaming."

He offended her by even considering such a thing.

"I vowed a long time ago never to let my half brother scare me again. So, no. I didn't scream. Blame Flavia. I don't know if she's his wife, but he didn't have much sympathy to spare when she went head-first into the blackberry bushes." She couldn't help smiling. Deciding further explanation unnecessary, she ducked around Quinn and marched on toward the hotel.

He turned and went with her. "Headfirst? Funny how your berry bushes keep saving the day. Hmm. I'm guessing she had a little help?"

Rio clamped her lips tight, but Quinn laughed. "She did, didn't she?"

She was saved from having to admit to any such antics when the other guest, evidently still holding a post on the porch, called out, "Hey, Callahan, what's happening?"

"He got woke up by all the turmoil too," Quinn whispered. "He's concerned. Said he thought somebody was being killed."

"I thought about it," Rio said.

Quinn broke off a laugh, calling to the guest, "I found her, Mr. Perry. All is well."

"Is it?" Mr. Perry returned, seeming doubtful.

"Yup. Seems the unruly couple from earlier were once again bent on causing mischief. But then the woman ran into a clump of thorn-filled bushes—to unfortunate results—and they changed their minds."

"Unfortunate for her, not for me," Rio added. She and Quinn were nearing the hotel now and no longer had to yell. Even so, Boo, closed inside her room, had heard all the chatter and was adding to it by barking his little head off.

"Oh, him—and her. I'm glad you refused them service, Miss Salo. Rude and unpleasant, both of them." Mr. Perry stood on the porch, peering in their direction.

Just at the edge of the trees, Rio stopped. She truly didn't want him to see her. He seemed the sort to disprove of a woman out at night clad only in a night-dress. He'd expect more modesty even in an emergency.

"Exactly," she said. "I wish for higher standards of behavior from hotel guests." Not mentioning people like Marciano or Curran or even, perhaps, Quinn Callahan.

Quinn sent her a look and winked.

"Well," Perry said, "Since the excitement is over, I'm going back to bed. Morning will be here before you know it." The screen door slammed behind him.

Sixteen

Mr. Perry had been correct. Morning did come early, even before the sun lit the sky over the mountains north of the lake with pink streamers. Rio believed her head had barely touched the pillow before she heard young Tommy Golz whistling as he arrived from the farm in time to saddle Mr. Perry a horse.

Groaning, she rolled over, keeping her eyes closed. Not that it did any good. Minutes, or maybe only seconds, later loud clumping footsteps sounded on the stairs.

Mr. Perry, ready for his expedition into the timber, and—

Rio shot upright. He'd be needing his breakfast. And no doubt have reason to complain of the laggard service he'd received at Painter's Bay Hotel. Dressing in record time, she flew down the stairs, Boo at her heels.

At least the stove, well-banked the night before, heated quickly and got the coffee going. Breakfast wouldn't be fancy at this hour of the morning. Sourdough hotcakes with maple syrup and a few black walnuts scattered over the top, a ham steak, a bowl of berries. Good enough.

But the bowl would not, she thought, smiling a little as she flipped the hotcakes, contain blackberries. Strawberries would have to do.

The guest had barely set off and Rio finally taken time to brush the tangles out of her hair when she spotted a boat bumping against the dock. Not a soft landing, but one made worse by the inept oarsman having to reverse direction in order to catch his line around a cleat set in the dock.

To Rio's surprise, the visitor was none other than Dr. Clement. More worrisome, even at a distance she could tell by his hunched posture he was anxious about something. And maybe more disturbing than anything, he wasn't carrying his medical bag when as a rule he took it with him everywhere.

She went to meet him, Boo bounding along ahead of her.

"What's wrong?" she called out while still on the path. "Is Molly all right? Has something happened?"

He looked tired, she saw, as if he'd been up all night. So what was he doing here?

"How did you know?" he said as he reached her, but then waved away the question as unimportant. "Molly is fine. And yes. Something has happened, which I'm sure concerns you. And maybe I should check on that fellow we treated last week."

Alarm darted through Rio like the zing of static electricity snapping off a blanket. "Something that concerns me? I don't understand. But I can assure you

Mr. Callahan is doing fine. Almost well, or so he said when he left."

"He's gone? Ah, good, good."

With Rio and Boo escorting him up the path to the hotel, the doctor gazed around and, curiously, sniffed the air.

She copied him, sniffing cautiously. Everything smelled fine to her. "What is it, Dr. Clement?" she asked. "What did you expect to find?"

"I thought—" He hesitated and waved what he'd meant to say aside. "Perhaps you can spare me a cup of coffee, my dear," he said and, mounting the porch, held the door for her to go inside.

At this, she smiled. "I can do better than that. I'm betting Molly isn't up yet and figure you've come away without your breakfast."

He gave a sigh that might have been relief. "You figure right. As a matter of fact...well, never mind. You may need to be sitting down when we talk."

Not a caution to relieve her mind, but certain to arouse her curiosity.

This seeming to be a visit between friends rather than professional, Rio got him situated at the kitchen table with a large mug of coffee and a pitcher of cream before busying herself at the stove. She slapped another ham steak into the cast iron skillet and began reheating the griddle for hotcakes when it occurred to her she was starving.

It seemed a good time to feed herself while she was at it. In minutes, they settled down at the table opposite each other.

The doctor dug in with a healthy appetite and a compliment. "You make the very best sourdough hotcakes of anyone I ever knew." He spoke with his mouth full. "Including your grandfather."

"Do I? I learned from him." Rio matched him bite for bite. "And my mother, who refined the recipe."

"And you've refined it even more."

At this, she laughed. "I think you're waxing nostalgic, Doctor." It felt as though the short laugh was the first time she'd had a truly pleasant thought since the probate hearing. Maybe longer. In fact, she couldn't remember when.

Soon she'd cleared the table and refilled the coffee cups. Gathering Boo onto her lap, she met Dr. Clement's eyes and said, "Now?"

He heaved a sigh. "Yes. Now."

But still he hesitated as if wondering how to begin. By this time, Rio was sure she knew what his news involved. Eino. It had to be. She decided to help him out.

"If you're here to tell me Eino is back, he's already let me know."

He gaped at her. "You've seen him? When?"

"Yesterday." Should she tell him about the meeting? Either the one in the day or the one in the dark? She decided to wait. Let him talk first.

"Yesterday? As early as that? Did he come here?"

She nodded and decided to impart just a little news. "He and his...wife."

"His wife?" He mulled this over for a moment. "But they didn't stay?"

Picking up her cup, she took a reviving sip of coffee. Not that it did nearly as much reviving as she could've used. "No." She paused. "I refused to let them stay."

"You did? May I ask why? I mean, beyond resentment for old hurts. I know you've plenty of bitterness to deal with."

"I do, but it wasn't about me or the old days. I'd been working upstairs, and when I came down, I found his wife in the kitchen badgering Blanche Golz—as if she had the right. Meanwhile, Eino was yelling at Eliza who was working at the front desk. Eino—although he prefers to be called Evan these days—said he was taking over and if they didn't do as he said, he would throw them out. While Blanche was holding her own with his wife, he actually set hands on Eliza. I stopped him."

The doctor made a clicking sound with his tongue. "You did? How?"

She lifted her head. "I drew my pistol and threatened to shoot him."

"He believed you?" Dr. Clement was smiling.

"Oh yes. He had that much sense, at least. Because I would have. I was ready to pull the trigger. So they, and a big muscular man with them who wisely refused to take a hand just then, all left. But Eino and Flavia came back during the night and tried to start the barn on fire. I put a stop to that, as well."

Dr. Clement had forgotten to drink his coffee. He stared at her as if undecided as to whether all this could be true. But then he surprised her.

"Ah, yes," he said. "From what I understand, fire has always been one of his favorite tricks."

"Tricks," she repeated, with so much emotion in the one word his mouth twitched and he shrugged.

"For lack of a better description," he said. "So let me tell you what else I've discovered. Something I think you probably don't know."

Clutching Boo as if to use him as a shield, Rio sank

back in her chair, her chin in the dog's warm fur. Stealing herself, she nodded. "Go ahead."

"I had a call during the night. Young Mrs. Leary—do you know her?"

"Not to say 'know.' I've heard of the Learys."

He nodded. "Well, as with so many first babies, the Leary's son decided to arrive last night along about midnight. By the time the process was finished and Mrs. Leary safely in the hands of her husband and her mother, I didn't get back to town until sometime around three. I'd just returned my horse to the livery and was taking a shortcut across the yard of Donaldson's old place when I saw them."

Rio winced at the mention of the sheriff. That's right. She remembered Thor Donaldson, her bitter enemy and the man who'd tried multiple times to kill her, had lived a couple houses down from the doctor.

She lifted her head, her eyes questioning.

"He...they...were going into the house, which has been standing empty. Apparently, he had a key, although the place has been locked up since Donaldson died. I did particularly notice the big man, as you mentioned. And the woman. They were all loaded down with baggage but were being quiet and secretive, like they didn't want anyone to know they were there. It seemed obvious they wanted to keep their presence a secret."

Rio snorted. "I don't suppose he does want anyone in town to know. I believe he's on the run from several factions. The big man is supposed to be a bodyguard." Where had they been, she wondered, after they left here in the afternoon? Hiding out in some small cove until dark?

"On the run?" Dr. Clement asked.

"He's trying to avoid detection, probably in hopes the people looking for him will move on and look for him elsewhere. You know he's always been a thief. Evidently he didn't change his way while he was gone. His problem is that these people want their money back."

Enlightenment dawned on the doctor's face. "I see. But why would he come to you?"

"He didn't come to me for help. He came to take possession of my hotel and use it for either shelter or leverage. Probably both. He intended to evict me at the least, at the most, to dispose of my body. I believe he'd prefer the latter. I have no idea what he's thinking, but he came here to hide. Or perhaps make a deal. If you remember, he's always been deluded as to his own importance."

"Rio," the doctor said gently, "you're very bitter. Are you sure—"

She merely stared at him.

"You are," he said and seemed to be pondering. "But why is he hiding in Donaldson's house now?"

"Because he's scared. He has at least three separate factions trying to retrieve what he took from them. Or maybe simply for revenge. Mind you, I'm guessing at some of this. But I know in one case, something called bearer bonds, whatever those are, are involved."

From his expression, the doctor knew what they were. "How dangerous are these groups," he asked. "Do you know?"

"Dangerous enough for Eino to be running scared. And to have hired the bodyguard. The bodyguard's name, by the way, is Garrity. I don't know if that's first or last."

Clement's mouth twisted. "Do you mind telling me how you know this?"

She set a struggling Boo who'd been wanting loose on the floor and beckoned Quinn to come on in. He'd been silently standing in the kitchen doorway listening behind the doctor's back for the last few minutes and it struck her as only practical.

Dr. Clement turned around. "Ah. Mr. Callahan. You do appear quite well. Miss Salo said you were gone." His expression asked a question.

"We thought it best to let people think so," Quinn said.

The doctor nodded. "I see."

Quinn, allowing Boo to herd him around, found himself a mug and poured coffee before pulling out a chair and sitting.

"I do heal fast," he said. "And you did a good job sewing me up. Besides, I had a good nurse." He winked at Rio.

Rio was unable to hide a blush as she said, calmly enough. "Mr. Callahan can explain Eino's trouble."

"You can?" The doctor's mouth puckered under his mustache. "You know, I suspected you were mixed in this somehow. Men don't usually get stabbed like you did unless there's something important afoot. Cut maybe," he added thoughtfully, "but not stabbed and sliced."

Quinn grinned a little, acknowledging the graphic assessment. "It so happens I'm one of these factions Miss Salo mentioned who is looking to take back what belongs to the people who hired me. Eino made his theft and moved on several weeks before they called on me. I've spent the last two months tracking him." He paused, then turned to Rio. "The man who stabbed me works for another group. He and a partner thought I was getting too close so decided to take me out of the equation. They want to be first at him. I suppose they figure if I'm able to reclaim my employer's property, that I'll take everything, not just what belongs to my client. That's what they'd do. They're after your half brother for revenge, as well. Seems he turned their crime boss in to the authorities and claimed a hefty reward for doing it. They want first crack at him."

Rio's eyes widened.

"The man you know as Toad did the stabbing. Audell Curran takes orders from his boss and passes them on to Toad. Toad, you see, is a fine, efficient killer, but not so good at covering his tracks. My survival was fifty percent luck and fifty percent tough on top of excellent doctoring."

"Curran?" Rio frowned. "He said his name was Smith."

Quinn huffed. "Not surprised."

The doctor, from all appearances, was having a hard time digesting all this information. "Toad?" he said on a note of wonder.

"Yes," Rio said. "It's an appropriate description. He has a similar appearance." Then to Quinn, "What about Marciano and his gang? Or is he on his own?"

"Marciano is a minor actor in a San Francisco-based Italian gang, though he'd like to play a larger part. I believe, but am not sure, they are connected to the Black Hand."

"The Black Hand?" Dr. Clement sat back, startled. "Oh my word!"

"I take it you've heard of them?" Quinn's left eyebrow lifted.

"I have. I subscribe to a San Francisco newspaper. I see mention of them every now and then."

This was all news to Rio. "What does the Black Hand do?"

"Extortion is their favored game," the doctor said. "Kidnapping. Things like that. The newspaper prints some of the letters their victims receive. Apparently they follow through on their threats."

She looked at Quinn who nodded.

"Death to those who don't pay up," he added. "Man, woman, or child."

Rio gulped. "Is Eino intending to trade me to them?"

Quinn studied her a moment, then said, "Possibly."

"Man!" Dr. Clement exploded, glaring at Quinn. "What are you trying to do? Scare Miss Salo to death?"

"No," Quinn replied just as hotly. "I'm trying to warn her, in hope of keeping her alive." He turned to face her. "I'd recommend having someone with you if you need to venture out. Especially after what happened yesterday. Somebody besides your dog."

She'd been scared for quite a while, Rio thought, and had been ever since Mr. Brackman told her about someone breaking into his office the night before the hearing. Only she hadn't been terrified then. Now she was. It had begun with Marciano claiming every available hotel room for his men, watching her, watching the door, sneaking around outside and seeming to wait for something—or someone. When Quinn turned up half dead, she'd guessed trouble likely to come for her, too, considering this all took place in her hotel. Only she'd thought the simple route of putting her newly revived hotel out of business had been the main objective. And she certainly hadn't realized there were two separate groups—three with Quinn—interested in catching up with Eino.

There'd been choices when it came to the cause. Donaldson told her Eino was dead, though there'd been no proof. And she'd never believed anything the sheriff said anyway. Her father, with his willing apprentice Eino, and the sheriff had been mixed up in opium smuggling for years. She'd thought perhaps this was a simple carryover from their partnership.

And theft...well, Eino had always been a thief, so word of his actions didn't surprise her. But what was she to do about it?

And why had Quinn been so reluctant to tell her all this? Would he ever, had Dr. Clement not come and started the information flowing? At least now she had a guess as to what she was up against.

Rio knew only one thing for sure. She was sick of thinking about the situation. Sick of Eino, the hotel, Quinn, and even Wash.

Wash, who'd been her steadfast friend for months but had, for no reason she could think of, seemed off the last couple times she'd seen him.

What next?

Seventeen

hat Rio came to call the siege—previous episodes of people sneaking through the woods after dark having frightened her away from wandering beyond the boat dock—began that night. No real surprise.

Wash, walking his regular path through the woods, came over after the disappointingly sparsely attended dinner hour to have a serious talk with Rio. He reported seeing men hanging about and, or so he said, he didn't think they were birdwatchers.

"Stay close to home," he'd warned her. "I don't know who these people are."

She could tell how serious he thought these men even before he spoke what with his face drawn up like an old man's. What else he, with a frown causing wrinkles between his blue eyes, had to say disturbed her a great deal more.

Though that turned out to be the least of it.

It all started with his light tap on the back porch door jamb, the door itself left open to allow the heat in the kitchen to dissipate. Running a restaurant kitchen was hot work, especially during the summer months what with the wood stove blazing away and steam rising from pots of boiling this or that. It surprised Rio that she'd so quickly forgotten the rising heat during the time the hotel had been closed.

Considering everything Quinn had said earlier, her first inclination had been to leave the door shut and locked. But Blanche, forced to wrap a band of cloth around her forehead to keep salty sweat from blinding her, had insisted it remain open. Nothing Rio could say about the danger changed her mind.

Blanche, waving her big wooden spoon about, said she knew just what to do if any rude folks bent on mayhem tried to get through that door.

They were waiting right outside, preparing for just the right time to come in and take over. Rio knew it. She could feel eyes watching, even though they hadn't—so far at least—bothered her customers. But she could feel their ill intent crawling under her skin like an itch she couldn't scratch.

Rio finally bent to Blanche's will and opened the door, thinking if anyone with nefarious intentions had really wanted they could have gotten inside already. Even so, when Wash tapped on the doorjamb, she jumped like a startled deer.

"My," Blanche said, having caught the action from the corner of her eye. "You are jumpy, Rio, aren't you?"

Rio didn't bother trying to deny it.

Wash came on in as she beckoned. He stood just inside, twirling his beat-up old work hat in his fingers, and gazing around like a stranger.

Just as if he hadn't been drinking coffee, eating, or

talking strategy regarding the logging operation in this same kitchen two or three times a week for the last several months. He'd even shot a man on her behalf. His curious behavior now made her even more nervous.

Rio frowned and cleared her throat. "Wash! I wasn't expecting you. Have you eaten? Can I get you a plate?"

He shook his head. "No, thanks. I came—" He started over. "About Eino. Did you know he was in cahoots with Donaldson before he left? Him and Elias both?"

"Yes. I knew. Something our dear father let slip before he passed." Rio's dark eyes narrowed. She'd forgotten she hadn't told him she knew about the skulduggery. She hadn't wanted anyone to know, especially when the leading players were all dead. Supposedly. Come to find out there was still Eino. But the present danger wasn't about that. Was it? And how had Wash found out at this late date?

Eino himself, of course. But why?

Wash's feet shuffled as if he'd like to take a backward step. Maybe even far enough to take him all the way through the woods to his cabin.

Rio was surprised by his reaction. Especially when he said, "Maybe you shouldn't have run him off yesterday."

Her brows lifted. "Oh?" She drew the question out. "Why not?"

His eyes kept shifting away instead of looking her in the face. "Well, I'm told this trouble happening around here is because he's got some bad people after him."

Told by whom? she wondered.

"They figured he'd show up here in Painter's Bay

and have been waiting around for him," he said. "Turns out that's who those men were that we put on the train."

Should she act surprised?

Wash was still talking. "Eino figures they'll be back. He says he can put all this right, but he'll need you to cooperate and give him the means for his plan to work. He's asked me to act as a go-between you and him."

"You've actually spoken to him?"

"Mostly, he talked to me," he said.

The part about bad men was nothing she hadn't already known. She considered Eino one of them. Their meetings so far proved that. Meanwhile, Rio could hardly speak when Wash, after a long hesitation, baldly put Eino's demand in front of her.

"And he says I should cooperate with him? What are you talking about? And why has he selected you as a...what did you call it...a go-between? Don't tell me that's why you're here."

Her astonishment echoed clearly. But not her anger —yet.

Over at the stove, Blanche had been dishing up the final order of the table d' hôte menu. The only item left was the beurre blanc sauce on the chicken and she stood with the spoon dripping as she unabashedly listened. She was giving Wash a death stare at the moment.

Wash swallowed, as if he might be having trouble getting out the words. "He knows you and me are friends. He figured you might listen to me."

Friends? And nothing more? After all they'd been through together? By sheer willpower, Rio kept her teeth from grinding.

"And since he's my boss now, apparently this is part

of my duties. Unless I want to go back to laboring alongside the Chinese," he said.

She sensed that had been the ultimatum Eino had given him. Looking down, she saw the edge of her skirt trembling in tandem with a most peculiar quivering in her still weak legs. She hadn't known it was possible to actually shake from the inside out like that.

She managed to hold her voice steady enough to talk. "Is that what he said? As if he's holding a gun to your head, eh? Exactly what does he mean by *cooperate*? And *give him the means*?"

"He just wants to stay in the hotel, is all. He got into town yesterday and hid out in Donaldson's old house for the night. But he thinks he'll be safer here, where there's more people around him. You know, you and the Golz family and any customers that show up."

Rio stared at him, aghast. "Listen to yourself, Wash! Do you think for one minute that I'd put any of these people at risk for someone like Eino? Or Evan, as I hear he prefers to be called nowadays. So says his wife, anyway. If she is his wife."

"Well, he is your brother. That must mean something."

She had the feeling of talking to a stranger.

"Half brother. And it does mean something. It means I won't allow him or his wife or the bodyguard on the premises. As he very well knows. I made that clear to him and to her when they tried to take over the hotel yesterday."

He frowned. "You mean you've already seen him?" He didn't mention the take over part.

"Yes. And that isn't what he said yesterday. Yesterday when he claimed he owned the hotel, his intention was to throw me and the Golz girls out, right then and there."

Behind her, Blanched nodded affirmation to Wash. "I heard him too, plain as day. So did Eliza. He set hands on her."

Rio's breath seemed to be caught somewhere at the bottom of her lungs, it felt so heavy. A moment passed before she could speak again. "I'm sorry he's threatening you, Wash. But do you know why these people are after him?"

"I'm not stupid, Rio. I figure he got sticky-fingered with something. Or maybe made unwanted advances to somebody's daughter. That's not my business."

What he was saying didn't even sound like the Wash she knew. Why was he even telling her this? He knew her history with her half brother and her father. He'd been a first-row witness to her father's treatment of her these last months.

"Not your business, maybe, but it is mine. Among other things, he stole from his mother's family when he went to visit them. He turned a crime figure in to the police for the reward money, which has the person's family vowing vengeance. He made off with thousands from an Italian extortion group connected to the Black Hand. They've vowed death, or rather, the return of their money and then death. Those are Marciano's gang, the very people we kicked out of my hotel yesterday."

Wash's mouth dropped open.

"If you, or he, think for one minute I'll allow any of them back, you are sadly mistaken."

"My job—" he said.

"Wash Ames, you know very well you can get

another job any old time. You've had several other companies try to steal you away from Salo Timber Products. You don't need to work for Eino." She stared at him, almost as if trying to will him into remaining her steadfast friend. "You know what he is."

He slumped down onto one of the kitchen chairs and stared at her. "Dammit, Rio, you know there's gonna be war, don't you? I knew you wouldn't do it, and I told him so." He thought a moment, then gave a half-hearted grin. "He threatened to shoot me if I didn't put this to you. Or sic the big fella with him onto me. He meant it too. I didn't see a woman like you're talking about. He must've left her behind."

"You can be sure he means to kill me, not just threaten," she snapped and heard Blanche gasp.

"I doubt he'd go that far," Wash said. "But in a way, some of what he said makes sense. Now, I don't know if you've been in town for a while."

It was a question. Rio shook her head. She'd sent Tommy Golz into town with purchase requests and messages, or sometimes with the grocer's boy when he delivered the hotel's standing order. Otherwise, she'd been working non-stop here at the hotel.

"When those men, Marciano's men, were here, stores got broken into at night, a few local men got egged into fights and were beaten up, some of the prettier girls were accosted on the street. People started locking their doors. Believe me, the folks of Painter's Bay got fed up fast."

"Are they blaming me?" If Rio sounded incredulous, it's because she was. "How could I know any of this? And why would my relationship to Eino mean anything for them? I will not be blamed for Eino's misdeeds. You see? We need a sheriff around here. Or at least a decent marshal. Somebody with guts enough to hold people like them accountable, and by that, I mean Eino right alongside Marciano and Curran. It's not my responsibility. In fact, I'd say it's the other way around. Apparently, I need protection."

Wash looked away. "Not blaming you, exactly," he admitted.

"Appears as if a man with guts isn't going to be easy to find around here," Blanche put in. She took the sauce in hand and poured a dollop over the chicken without looking up. In fact, she might have poured more than a single dollop.

Wash nodded. "She's right," he said to Rio, evidently not understanding the underlying meaning of Blanche's pronouncement. "And we need someone now, not later. Which brings me back to Eino."

But before that could happen, Quinn walked into the kitchen and made himself at home. While Wash stared at him as if puzzled and aggravated at the familiarity, Quinn pulled out a chair and sat beside Rio.

Actually, Rio thought, her head swiveling between the two, Quinn didn't look any friendlier than Wash. How much of Wash's go-between message had he heard? she wondered. From his expression, all of it. And from his expression, he wasn't impressed.

"This is the fella whose crew ran Marciano's gang out of town?" Quinn asked. There may have been an incredulous undertone to the question.

Rio frowned at him. He knew it was. He'd seen Wash, even if Wash hadn't seen him. What was he playing at?

Wash answered for himself. "Yeah, that's me. Washington Ames. Who are you?"

"Quinn Callahan," Quinn said. Neither man offered to shake hands.

Behind them, Blanche quietly smirked at the men's reaction to the other.

Rio didn't see anything amusing about their instant pugnacious attitude. "What about Eino?" she said, turning back to Wash. "You were saying?"

Wash glanced at Quinn. "This is private, between Miss Salo and me."

Before Quinn could speak, Rio shook her head. "You will find, Wash, that this is very much Mr. Callahan's business too."

Wash shot a glance between the two. "Why?"

Rio flicked her eyes to Quinn. "You tell him."

He raised a brow. "All of it? I've got to say, Rio, he sounds like he's leaning your half brother's way. I'm not so sure he can be trusted with anything you tell him."

She sighed. Truthfully, and five minutes ago this thought would never have occurred to her, she wasn't sure either. Not when he apparently wanted her to consider Eino's self-serving proposal.

"Wash?" Slowly, she turned to face him head-on, meeting his blue eyes and holding his gaze even though it tried to slide away from hers. "Tell me, why did Eino come to you? How did he get in touch? When did he get in touch?"

Rio sensed rather than saw Quinn tense beside her, but she didn't shift her gaze to look at him. That remained fixed on Wash.

No, some part of her was shouting. Wash wouldn't betray her. Not to Eino. Not after all they'd been through together. Finding her mother's bones. Him firing the shot that eventually killed the sheriff. Testifying for her at the probate hearing. *Not Wash!*

"He's my boss, Rio." Wash spoke softly, regretfully. "Yeah, I kind of got used to running things these last months, but when he showed up, that came to an end. He's the owner. As long as he's paying my wage, that puts me under obligation to him."

"That's what you think?" She sucked in a breath. Damn him. Legally, he was probably right. Morally? There were other choices he could have made. Braver choices.

"It didn't take him long to get with you, did it?" She grimaced. "Don't tell me he went into the woods to look you up wearing his nice suit and spit-shined shoes. Or did he send his bodyguard to invite you to a meeting? Or did you know he was coming before this?"

Wash's jaw clenched at the sharpness of her tone, enough to make Quinn glance at her with concern, as well.

"First I knew he was still alive is when I found a note under my cabin door the other day," Wash said, his voice level. "We met at night, after dark, at my cabin. He came by boat, him with the bodyguard doing the rowing. He found my cabin and knocked on the door just like any other man would do. He had his say. He told me he wants to stay at the hotel where he thinks he'll be safer." He looked around, almost as if he'd never seen the place before. "He might be right, as long as he and that wife stay out of the public spaces. At least this place is big enough you wouldn't be crowded."

In Rio's opinion, anywhere Eino stopped at became crowded. His outsized egotism overshadowed everyone else. And that went double for his wife, if wife she was. On short acquaintance, her temperament had not impressed.

But Wash wasn't finished. "Have you thought of this? Sooner or later, when there's no trace of him around, those men will leave. They can't stay here forever."

"Oh," she said, aware her face was hot as fire and must've been red as flames. How could Wash even suggest such a thing to her? "And what if Marciano's men bring reinforcements? You do know they're already back. What if they decide to take over the hotel? What if Eino decides to come out gun blazing? He's never had much control over his temper or his desires. I should know. I've been on the receiving end often enough."

Wash tried to say something but she cut him off.

"I don't know why you bothered to corral Marciano and his men and run them out of town in the first place. Why didn't you just let them take over and ruin me? Seems like that would've made more sense. Wasn't I just another complication?" If she sounded wounded—and bitter, oh so bitter—it's because she was.

"This is my hotel. I have the say on who stays here or not. And I'm saying he, his wife, or his bodyguard, are not." She was shouting, breathing hard, like she'd just swum all the way across the bay to town.

"Rio—"

"Go back and report to your boss. This discussion is over."

She stood up so fast her chair fell over. Rushing from the kitchen, she refused to look at any of them. Rio didn't want to know what they thought. Not Wash, not

Quinn, and not even Blanche, although if she had looked she would've seen Blanche silently clapping her hands together, applauding the action.

Seconds later her footsteps sounded going up the stairs, then Boo's toenails clicking on the wood as he followed her.

Blanche turned to stare at the men. Both men, but Wash in particular. Her upper lip curled. "Men. They'll turn on a woman faster than you can say *traitor*."

———

RIO HAD FALLEN asleep over her desk in the little made-over pantry she called an office having come downstairs when Wash had gone and Quinn, presumably, retired to his room. Boo, who had his own basket beside the desk to sleep in while she worked, awakened her with one of his soft *woofs,* more an outpouring of air than a bark.

It wasn't just Boo that disturbed her sleep though. There'd been something else. Some other sound that didn't belong in the silent hotel's empty spaces.

The lamp on the desk had sputtered, so only a pinpoint of light came from the wick. She raised her head, the arm it had rested on tingling and numb from the pressure. The paper under her hand rustled slightly. The sound she heard hadn't been that, though, she knew.

Sitting up, she moved the letter she'd written to Beckett Ferris aside and shook out her arm. Boo stared first at her, then toward the lobby, then back at her. Blessedly, he remained silent.

When her arm returned to normal, she picked up the revolver she'd moved from her pocket to the desktop and rose to her feet, cocking the little pistol. Then she pinched out the last of the light and waited for her eyes to fully accustom to the dark. Boo, a white blur at her feet, moved with her to the door open to the hall.

The sound she'd heard, though mostly subconsciously, had been the lock on the hotel's front door turning over. She hadn't heard the door open or close, at least not yet.

She and Boo crept down the hall, past the kitchen, past the entry to the dining room and the stairway, and had reached the nook that housed the bar when the front door swung open. She saw a man-shaped shadow pass through and pause as if scenting for danger.

Pushing Boo with her foot, she got them both into the lea of the nook. Reaching down, she placed her hand on the dog's head as the man started through the lobby toward them.

Rio couldn't risk peeking around the corner. She'd have to wait until he passed her. Her heart thudded in her chest.

Mind racing, she tried to think. Who had a key? She'd had the locks changed after Elias died and her legs had been shot out from under her. She and Anna Golz were the only ones who had a key, the other girls using Anna's when they came in extra early to work. They'd earned her complete trust in the weeks since the shooting. Besides, none of the Golz family would enter by the front door.

Whoever the man was, his feet shuffled across the floorboards as if skating, which must've annoyed Boo as he moved impatiently, causing his toenails to click.

The man stopped. The distinctive sound of a pistol's chamber rolling over seemed loud and obvious. No matter who he was, he had no business here and as proved by his firearm, meant harm.

After a few moments, while Rio remained immobile, he moved forward again. He went past her without noticing, pausing to peer into the empty dining room. Light from the room's wide window showed his body shape, an assurance it wasn't Eino or his bodyguard. It wasn't Wash, so familiar to her, either, and it wasn't Quinn, coming in from whatever he might've been doing. If he was outside at all. She was fairly sure he was asleep in his room.

Evidently satisfied, the intruder continued on, stopping now at the kitchen.

Rio'd had enough. She stepped out behind him, her pistol raised. She even had her mouth open to call to him when he suddenly turned.

He must've been expecting someone taller, because when he fired, the bullet zinged a foot over her head. Glass broke behind her. Forever after, she believed he'd scared her so badly her finger reflexively pulled the trigger on the pocket gun. The bullet, by pure accident, hit him squarely in the heart. He managed to pull the trigger one more time, but that bullet careened wildly somewhere into the dining room.

Though her ears rang, half the noise because of the shooting, half because her heartbeat went wild, she knew Boo barked and barked. She knew Quinn raced from his room wearing only his BVDs, or so she found when he lit a lamp. He was carrying a gun.

"Rio," he said, his gray eyes flashing and his face gone pale. "Are you—"

"He missed. I don't know how, but he missed." She began to laugh, aware of sounding unhinged but unable to stop. "Why do people keep shooting at me, Quinn? Why?"

Then, quite beyond her control, in an instant the laugh changed to sobs, dry and harsh.

"Was he alone?" Quinn stepped toward her. He didn't seem to know what to do, considering the state she was in.

She didn't answer. Couldn't.

"Who is he?" Quinn demanded.

So, as he held up the now-lit lamp, she looked. Not one of Marciano's men. Or not one of the men she'd seen, anyway. A complete stranger, but with an appearance close enough to be a relative of Marciano. A brother maybe, or even a son.

"Oh, hell," Quinn whispered, possibly to himself but loud enough she heard. "Vendetta."

Then he gathered her into his arms and held her until her tears stopped.

Eighteen

R io stared down at the man's body. There wasn't as much blood as she'd thought to see. Her pocket pistol was a .32 and the bullet hadn't gone all the way through his body. Having hit directly into the heart and stopping it instantly, most of the blood remained inside. Not nearly as much blood as her legs had pumped out, she knew. And certainly not as much as Quinn had bled when stabbed.

"Is he dead?" she asked Quinn.

"Yes." Even so, he took the .32 from her, setting the revolver aside as he knelt beside the man, and felt for a pulse. After a moment, he stood up again and shook his head. "Yes. Dead." He took a couple breaths. "What do you want to do with him?"

"Do with him?" She kept her eyes away from his... er...nighttime attire. But his chest was bare. She'd put her cheek against it.

"Want to row him into the middle of the lake and throw him in?"

Rio shuddered. "No. Yes. Maybe." She choked on a breath. "I don't know what to do."

Taking her hand, he led her away from the body and into the kitchen, calling sharply to Boo as well.

"Stay here. I'll get dressed. Build up the fire and make coffee. I think we could use a jolt. Put some brandy in it. Can you do that?"

She nodded. The clock on the shelf beside the stove said 1:13.

Thank God the hotel had been empty tonight, except for her and Quinn—and Boo. Upset by the gunfire, the little dog kept getting underfoot as she stuffed a couple chunks of wood in the stove's fire chamber, drew water into the family-sized pot instead of the restaurant urn, and put the coffee on to percolate. From the pantry, she retrieved the bottle of brandy she used to make a sauce to pour over cake and dumped a hefty amount into cups.

At last she gathered the dog into her arms. "You know, don't you?" she whispered into his fur. "I killed a man, Boo."

The memory came to her of shooting back at the sheriff, twice, as a matter of fact, and that neither time had reacted with her like this. And that man of Marciano's. She hadn't worried about him either. She'd known those men deserved it. And none of them, at the time, ended up dead. Somehow the knowledge had made everything different.

Quinn spoke from behind her. "He fired first, Rio. After he invaded your home. He's probably a hired killer who simply missed his mark this time. Don't waste your regrets on him."

"I don't regret doing it. I regret what I had to do."

She heard the echo of Wash's words to the judge when he'd spoken of shooting the sheriff at her hearing and tilted her chin. He'd regretted that, as well. "What did you mean, Quinn, when you said vendetta?"

He grimaced, his gray eyes turning hard. "You know what the word means?"

She drew a shaky breath. "I think so. It's an Italian word, isn't it? One that indicates a feud, or someone seeking revenge."

He nodded.

"I guess it also means you saw the same thing I did. This man's resemblance to Marciano. It's uncanny." Her shoulders drooped.

"Brothers, at a guess. Cousins maybe." Quinn eased her into a chair. "Sit," he said, "before you collapse. We need to figure what to do."

Rio kept her grasp on Boo, and the dog, bless him, let her. "I don't want to put his body in the lake. It just seems wrong."

"I wouldn't worry about it." He shrugged. "It's probably what he figured to do with you. And me, if he knew I'm here. That's why I suggested it."

"Really?"

"Do you have a better idea?" he asked.

"Maybe." Rio's own mother had been murdered, and her body remained hidden in a small cave for fourteen years, she reflected. Except by a fluke, it would've remained buried for all eternity. And had her father not confessed, actually bragged about his murderous act, they would never have known how she died.

"Bodies," she announced, "have a nasty habit of rising to the surface of the lake when gases build up inside them."

Quinn's expression first showed shock, then a kind of amusement as, avoiding his eyes, she went on. "I know of a place that might sidestep that danger. But we'll have to move fast. I'll need to be back here by daylight when Blanche and her sister arrive."

She put Boo on the floor. "Do you know how to saddle a horse?"

He seemed surprised at the question. "Sure. They do have horses where I'm from too, you know."

But he didn't say where that was.

"Then please go saddle the pinto for me, and put a packsaddle on the bay. I'll..." She swallowed hard. "I'll take care of things in here."

Grasping her intent, he shook his head. "I take it you have something in mind. You're not doing this alone, Rio. I'm going with you. He's too big for you to handle. I'll saddle two and the packhorse."

"You're still weak from the stabbing. The place I'm thinking of—"

He cut her off. "No argument. I'll manage."

The bullet hole in the dining room wall proved easy enough to hide. She simply exchanged a small picture for a larger one, thinking it would serve until she could remove the bullet and patch the hole later. If she was lucky, no one would notice the switch.

The glass in the front window was another matter. At least it was only one small pane, something she thought she could cobble together either a fix or an excuse. A bird flying into it, perhaps. It had happened before.

The body proved more difficult. She found an old quilt and some rope, intending to wrap and tie him. She'd bring the quilt back. The fewer things to point to the hotel, the better, even if it was only an old quilt found fifty years later. Managing to roll his body onto the quilt in the first place proved to be a feat that took all her strength. Last of all, she cleaned the floor where he'd fallen.

Quinn came back with the horses in tow just as she finished. The packsaddle had an axe and a shovel tied on behind. Providential of Quinn. She hadn't thought of it.

"I took a look around outside," he told her. "You'll be glad to know I didn't see anybody. My guess is this fellow came alone and ordered everyone else away. Plausible deniability in case questions were raised."

He eyed her preparations approvingly as he knelt beside the body. "What did you do with his gun?"

"He's wearing a holster. I put it back."

"Smart. We don't want anything to connect him to this place, even if it is a waste of a good gun."

Funny, she thought, that their ideas had meshed so closely.

"Did you check his pockets?" he asked. "Could be he has something to explain why he's here."

"I didn't check." She recoiled at the idea. "I'm quite sure we know his intentions," she added dryly. "Don't we?"

He didn't answer.

Quinn seemed to have experience in searching dead men. Loosening the ropes around the quilt, he checked shirt pockets and vest pockets. In an inside pocket of the man's jacket, he found a letter. It was from the Marciano—Luca—who'd stayed at the hotel, to this Marciano—Enzo—newly arrived from San Francisco with an invitation to join in the hunt for the boss's twenty thousand dollars. Enzo was apparently their number one assassin and pride a motivator in the quest.

Quinn refolded the letter and set it aside as soon as Rio read it. "No big surprise there."

"An assassin," Rio said in a weak whisper.

Enzo had carried quite a lot of money with him, tucked in a money belt. There were three gold coins in his pants pocket, one a twenty-dollar piece, and two fives. He had a small pack with some metal instruments that puzzled Rio. Quinn identified them as lock picks, which answered to how he'd gotten in. And last of all, he had a very sharp pocketknife, one that appeared specially made with a handle made of some shell.

Quinn said it was abalone, whatever that might be. Rio had no idea. Quinn informed her it was a sea creature and good to eat.

Enzo also had some lucifers in a metal tube, plus two cigars. And he wore a silver ring with a design etched in it.

Quinn hesitated at that. "Could be there's a couple things we should take and throw them in the lake."

Rio had been thinking along the same lines. "Yes. The ring and the knife. And the letter has to burn." She didn't wait. Getting up, she tossed the letter into the stove and watched it disintegrate in the flames.

He grinned at her. "You're plenty smart, aren't you? Do you agree we're not robbing his body?"

"Yes." She'd have had to be in far worse straits before she took the money.

So it was done, and with the help of ropes and one of the horses drawing on the end of it, they got the body lopped over the packsaddle and tied on.

Quietly, Rio led the way out of the hotel yard, still

leery of watchers. They saw no one. Heading deeper into the treed hillside, the horses plodded past the Golz farm and a couple stump ranches before they came to where an area of logged off timber marked the edge of the Salo Timber Products land.

An owl hooted from high on the hillside, a coyote called and another answered, both sounding as wrought up as young girls in the grip of hysteria. As for Quinn and Rio, they didn't talk, passing through the night like wraiths and allowing the warm air to dry the sweat of their exertions.

When past the last ranch, Rio kicked the pinto into a lope whenever possible, until they came at last to her intended destination.

The timber had been cut here last fall. Old piles of half-burned slash indicated this area would not be visited again for a long time; maybe even until the small standing trees grew to cutting size. The terrain was rough with nothing much to see.

In early April, Rio had brought lunch to Wash and some of his men who'd tended the fires, and even in the dark, with the sky open overhead, the place was as she remembered. Steep, with the hillside pelted with boulders. Logging here had been hard on horses and men. Pulling her horse to a stop, she pointed.

Quinn stopped right beside her, leaning forward to where she pointed. After a moment, he sat back. "What? Looks like a big tree fell over and the loggers neglected to retrieve it."

She nodded. "Exactly what I hoped you'd see. You or anyone else who might chance to come this way in the next twenty years."

He frowned and gigged his horse closer, studying

the setup a minute before shrugging. "I'm missing something, I'll bet."

She pulled the pinto in next to him and dismounted. "Yes. We're here. Get down and I'll show you. Bring the shovel."

Leading the way, she brought the axe. When they got directly under the tree, Quinn looked askance at the behemoth leaning over their heads. "Looks like this could fall on us any minute. Are you sure we should be here?"

Rio wasn't sure at all. She shared his unease. "No," she admitted. "But I'm sure Mr. Enzo Marciano should be. A poor wanderer who got lost and had an old rotten tree topple on him."

Quinn shook his head. "A poor wanderer with a bullet hole in him."

"Then let's hope nobody finds him for a long, long time."

"Luca will search."

"But I doubt Luca will find." She pointed to an area directly under the tree. "We need to dig just about there. Last fall, when they were logging this piece, there was a cavity in the outcropping. Probably an old bear den. Then this spring when I couldn't find it, Wash said the wind had toppled this tree over it. The cavity will still be there, just blocked now by dirt that spilled over when the roots pulled out of the ground."

Quinn nodded, understanding the layout. "So, I'll dig through the blockage. We'll shove the body into the open space and fill it back in."

"Yes. And then we'll pull the tree down to completely cover the area." She swallowed, remembering her mother's similar lonely burial place. "People have gone missing in these mountains before. Sometimes years pass before their bones are found, if ever. Generally, there's no way to know who the bones belong to unless they have a personal item on them."

"Like a match tube or pocketknife."

"Yes, something like that." *Or a wedding ring or earbobs*, Rio added to herself.

The dirt was soft and easily dug, having been sheltered by the tree. When Quinn deemed the space large enough, Rio drew the packhorse close and untied the body. Together, they pulled and pushed until they'd situated Enzo into the cavity. At the last moment, Rio pulled the dead man's gun from his holster and put it in his hand.

"Suicide?" Quinn said.

"Yes." Rio finished shoveling in what dirt she could. The area looked quite artistic when she finished, upon which she tossed a loop of the rope over the tree trunk and attached it to the horse's saddle. She went to his head to lead him forward.

The brown horse strained, but he was a saddle horse, not a draft animal. The tree didn't budge.

Worried now her plans might go awry, Rio went to add her weight to the rope, slapping the horse on his rump to get him moving. Quinn joined her to no avail.

"I'll see if I can attach one of the other horses." She looked up just in time to see Quinn jump high enough to grab hold of the tree. He hung there for a few seconds, then the tree moved, toppling slowly as Quinn jerked, the horse pulled, and gravity did its trick.

Quinn leaped aside just in time to avoid being crushed. Branches threshed and broke. The tip of the tree broke off, the heavier part of the trunk landing inches from where Quinn fell. The brown horse ran ahead for a few dozen yards until the trailing rope caught on a stump and pulled him to a stop.

Rio stood frozen, wide-eyed, her hands over her mouth as if to stifle a scream. After a few seconds, she collected herself and ran to him. "Quinn," she cried out. "Quinn."

More seconds passed, then he coughed, and inch by inch, sat up. He was holding his ribs and had a pained expression on his face. Panting, his mouth twisted, whether from amusement or the pain Rio couldn't tell.

"That didn't go quite like planned."

He was grinning, she decided. Sort of. "What were you thinking? You might've been killed!"

"Did the job, though," he said, just as if she hadn't spoken.

He continued to sit until finally, she asked, "Do you need help?"

He held one hand toward her. The other was still holding the spot she knew the deepest of his wounds was located.

Digging in her heels, she pulled him up, slow and gentle, until he made it to his feet and stood swaying.

"Are you bleeding?" she asked anxiously. "You may have pulled Dr. Clement's stitches out. He'll be so angry."

"I'm good," Quinn insisted. "Let's get out of here. Didn't you say we needed to be back by daylight? Don't know if we'll make it as it is."

He wasn't wrong. This time, Rio took charge of the packhorse's lead rope, and with the worry of jostling the body off somewhere along the way, they made faster time returning. As they passed the Golz place, she caught sight of smoke rising from the kitchen chimney and heard the sound of cow bells as the dairy herd came to the barn for the morning milking.

Back at the hotel, they barely had time to get the horses unsaddled and any sweat—evidence of use during the night—brushed away before Blanche and Maria could be heard teasing Tommy as they made their way to work.

They'd beaten daylight and the Golz family by a few short minutes.

ON THE OFF CHANCE ONE of the ladies would look in on her, Rio removed her filthy skirt and blouse, pulled a nightdress on over her head, and lay down on the bed. A little chilled in the morning coolness, she tugged up the blanket and closed her eyes.

She had a perfectly logical excuse for doing this. This way there'd be no question that she'd slept the night in her own bed. The bedding rumpled, her yesterday's clothing discarded—though how it had gotten so dirty might be questioned—her nightdress warm with use. And Boo, sleeping alongside her just like always. He'd been ecstatic when she got home and had tamed down just in time.

She'd rest here for just a little while. That's all. Then she'd get up and begin another day of work, no matter how exhausted she felt.

Three hours later she awakened to someone hammering on the door to her room.

"Rio," Blanche called out. "Rio? Are you all right?

You were going to guide me in making the Beef Wellington for tonight's dinner service."

A pause.

"Rio? Are you awake? Are you sick? Shall I come in?"

Boo crawled onto her chest and licked Rio's face.

"Rio, are you—"

"I'm fine. Sorry. I just overslept," Rio yelled.

Everything from the night before came flooding back the second she turned her head and heard a faint crunching sound. Raising onto an elbow, she found the crumbled remains of three or four pine needles on her pillow. Evidence of the night's adventure that must've been caught in her hair.

With an angry flip of her hand, she brushed them to the floor.

Lucky Quinn who got to sleep on. It was sometime past noon when he put in an appearance. The night hadn't been easy on him.

Nineteen

Two hotel rooms were taken by afternoon. An elderly couple from across the Canadian border in British Columbia for one. They intended to catch the train the next morning and head east across the states to visit a daughter. The second was a single man who wore a large revolver prominently displayed on his hip.

Rio admitted to wondering about him and his motives for the stay as he gazed around the lobby as if memorizing the location of every entrance and exit. Surreptitiously, she seized the club she now kept constantly at hand under the lobby desk A new precaution since Eino had manhandled Eliza. The fellow's actions almost made her refuse his patronage. Would have if she hadn't needed his payment in order to pay the bills.

But all proved well as he signed the register without undue complaint. She took his money with trembling hands, aware of a growing distrust of everyone.

She sat on a tall stool at the desk planning the table

d' hôte menu for the next week and doing her best not to interfere with Blanche as she went through the step-by-step process Rio had carefully written out for the Beef Wellington recipe. Blanche had the makings of an excellent chef, but she tended to learn things in her own way.

Sleepy eyes gazing down at a column of figures she'd already added three times—each time coming up with a different total—a shadow fell across the ledger page.

Raising her head, she blinked, doing her best to school her features into unconcern at the tight-jawed face looming above her. "What are you doing here?" she demanded. "I told you to leave and not come back."

If possible, the man facing her across the desk seemed even more uncomfortable than she. He snatched the bowler hat from his head, revealing a mass of unruly brown hair in sad need of cutting, then jammed the hat back on as if wondering why he'd removed it in the first place.

Of its own volition, Rio's hand reached to the shelf under the desk and took hold of the club. She would've preferred the .44 but the Golz girls had argued for the club.

He was breathing hard through his nose and staring at her like a hawk eyes a mouse.

"Mr. Garrity," she said, "I'm speaking to you."

The massively built man nodded and finally found his voice. "I know. I'm just trying to remember what I'm supposed to say." He smiled, a twitch of the lips easily missed if she hadn't been looking at him. "You know, I thought it then and I know it now, but you ain't homely at all. Matter of fact, you're a looker. How come Evan said—" He stopped. "That ain't what I meant to say. I'm starting over."

So saying, he proceeded to do so.

"It's about...you know who I'm talking about?"

She nodded. Did he think her as dull-witted as he seemed to be? Unless he was putting on a comic act and using her for practice. "I expect so. Get on with it."

"We been hiding out in somebody's empty house. Feller died, I heard, so I guess he don't have need of it."

Nothing she didn't know. "And?"

"And his woman, Flavia, she don't like it there. Not one bit. Says it's dirty. Says it's cold. Says it's unfair as Evan won't even let her light a lamp after dark. Says she can't even tell if her meat is cooked."

"Aw," Rio said. "Poor thing."

Garrity gave her a narrow-eyed look. "You wouldn't say something like that if you had to listen to her." He cleared his throat. "She ain't—"

He stopped again, seeming to have a difficult time when it came to speaking of Flavia. Well, Rio didn't blame him.

"What I'm trying to say—what she told me to say —is that you owe your brother the courtesy of him and her using his pa's old bedroom for as long as it takes."

Rio's eyes narrowed. "As long as it takes for what?"

Face reddening to the color of old bricks, Garrity said, "I wasn't supposed to say that last part. Slipped out. Pay it no mind."

Rio had no problem putting the comment into more definite terms. *As long as it takes to rob me blind. As long as it takes to run me out of the country. As long as it takes to see me dead.*

All three were probable answers to Eino—or Flavia's—instructions.

"Never mind. I know what she meant. And my answer is still no. I don't owe him anything. Period. However, when I cleaned out his room, I put all of his stuff in a trunk. It's sitting out on the front porch. You can tell him to hire a rig and haul it away. There's no need to enter the premises."

He frowned and said, "You ain't been listening." He stood before her as solid as a boulder embedded deep in the earth and probably as immovable as one. "Evan, he's got men looking for him. After they relieve him of his money, his and Flavia's, they plan on doing him harm. He just wants to live."

Rio snorted. "Relieve him of *his* money? From what I hear, everything dime he's got is what he stole from others. Having known him all my life, I'm sure I heard the truth. Whatever they do to him, he's probably got coming."

"Who told you that?"

"The people he stole from. Or rather, they showed me their method of dealing with the opposition. Gave me a good idea of how they solve their problems."

"Showed you?" A huge frown puckered his face.

"Yes." She preferred not to go into the details. "And when, or if, they learn Eino and that woman are sheltering in this hotel, they're more apt to burn it down around my ears than applaud me for being a good sister. Half sister, I mean." She hated to admit it, but her temper was on the rise. Why didn't this man shut up and go away? Didn't he see that she would have nothing to do with Eino and his thievery?

Just then, Marie poked her head around the corner

from the kitchen to the lobby and made urgent waving signs.

"Yes, Marie? What is it?" Rio answered to Marie's concern as Garrity turned around to look at the girl as well.

"Blanche needs you to come take a look at the pastry," Marie said. "She doesn't think it looks quite right and wonders if you know a way to salvage it."

A bald-faced lie, as Rio well knew. The pastry had been resting for a good half hour and had been perfect when Blanche rolled it out for the final chilling. It was obvious the girl had another problem. One that needed immediate attention and she didn't intend to let anyone but Rio hear it.

Turning to Garrity, Rio said, "This shouldn't take long, but feel free to be on your way. In fact, do leave. Please." She didn't realize she'd been gripping the club until she had to let it go to move away from the desk. Walking fast, she dodged around the man and fled.

Only it wasn't Marie waiting for her. Or Blanche. It was Quinn, as she'd half-expected, who drew her all the way out onto the porch, well out of sight and hearing of everyone.

"I've been thinking," he said. "Maybe you should do it. Let your brother—half brother—stay."

"What?" She stared up at him, wondering if she'd heard right. Had Quinn lost his mind, by any chance? Last she knew, he'd been as adamant as she in keeping Eino away from the hotel. He sure enough didn't want either Curran or Marciano to stick another knife in him. And neither did she.

"Let him stay. If you can keep his presence secret for even a day or two, we may be able to discover what he's done with the money. I figure it must be close by, otherwise he would've moved on by now. If we can find the money, we can see it dispersed back to its origins without anybody getting killed. You don't need to tell him that's your intention. As far as he—and Flavia—are concerned—"

Rio cut in. "Why should I? I don't owe him a thing. And I can't bear the sight of him. What you're asking curdles my blood."

Quinn flushed. "Can't say as I care for the fella, either. Don't forget it's because of him I got stabbed." He scoffed. "Nothing personal, according to Curran and Toad. They just want to take out anyone competing against them for the payoff. More for them that way. They'd take on Marciano's bunch if they figured they could get away with it."

She hadn't realized, although she'd certainly wondered, why Toad had tried to kill Quinn. Was it really this simple? They were afraid Quinn might claim all the money Eino had stolen if he found the money first. They no doubt wanted all witnesses to their shenanigans dead too. And by now, that must include Rio.

She didn't understand how these people thought, how they managed to thrive on violence although, she thought wryly, she probably should have. God only knows she'd lived with the results of their kind of skewed thinking for most of her life. To the point she'd had to resort to violence herself.

Glaring up at him, another question occurred to her. "You've never told me who you're working for, Mr. Callahan. One of these three possibilities, of course."

He gave a start when she used his surname.

"You told me about Marciano's Italian mob and about Curran's street gang. You've mentioned something about bearer bonds, but you haven't told me where you figure into this. Are you a bounty hunter? Or a lawman? Or did Eino grift you personally, by chance? Is that why you've been so careful to stay out of sight?"

Quinn's gray eyes surveyed her for a long moment. "I'm here because of the bearer bond problem. Since you asked, I'll tell you. I'm working for Salo's mother's people. The night before he left the White's home—for parts unknown and without telling his uncle—he robbed the safe and stole everything of value in it. That included $30,000 worth of bearer bonds, plus a good deal of cash his uncle had on hand. White had taken it from the bank in preparation for a deal on a piece of property."

Rio's eyes opened wide. "That much?"

"You didn't know your brother's relatives were wealthy?"

"I knew they weren't poor." She shook her head. When she spoke, her voice was small. "Why on earth did Eino come back here? Why didn't he flee to South America or Europe with all that money? Or maybe Australia? Why here?"

Quinn shrugged. "I don't know. Maybe because too many of us were close on his heels. Could be he knew he wouldn't be able to get to the coast and find a ship before we caught up with him. Or maybe—" He stopped. "Or maybe he sent some of his stash home for his father to keep and wanted to pick it up before he left."

"Is that what you think?"

He shrugged again. "It's a possibility."

Rio shook her head. "I don't think he sent it here. I think I would've known if Father had received something like that." But would she? Elias had only been totally bedridden and dependent on her for a month before he died.

Another idea occurred to her. An idea that made her gasp and provided an explanation to a question that had plagued her for weeks now and made her lose sleep. The reason that had almost cost her her life.

Made her look at Quinn with new eyes, too, as well as causing her to think about what he'd proposed. He might be right. With Eino staying at the hotel, there was a chance to recover stolen and misbegotten goods and put paid to her half brother's presence forever.

Meanwhile, Quinn didn't need to know all the thoughts racing through her mind. She made a quick decision, hoping she wouldn't live to regret it.

Putting on the most innocent expression she could manage, Rio looked into his eyes and said in a pouty tone of voice, "All right. If you think you can do whatever you have to do and make all these people go away, then I'll agree."

Swift relief passed over Quinn's face, smoothing the tension she'd noticed there.

"Good girl," he said, then grinned at her. "Just don't let on you know about any of this. You'll be safer."

And that advice, Rio thought, seemed a whole lot like locking the chicken coop after the fox got in.

She made to head back into the hotel. "I'll go tell Mr. Garrity." But then she turned and shook her finger at him. "But I don't like it. Not one bit."

"I know," he said soberly. "I don't either. Let's make sure everything goes to plan."

———

RIO, a bit to her dismay, found Garrity patiently waiting for her when she got back to the lobby.

"I'll tell him," Garrity said, grinning broadly at what he must've considered his effective argument having won Rio over. Even though she'd given him a set of orders to relay to Eino and Flavia, some of which included putting them in Elias's old room although he might have preferred the other larger room. But putting them opposite the bathroom on the second floor meant less chance of someone seeing them. She didn't want trouble simply because one of them got careless.

Neither Rio nor Garrity thought of discussing where he would stay. Not until, sweating like a team of Belgians dragging logs out of the forest, he'd carried all of Eino and Flavia's luggage from the dock where he'd tied the boat, thence up the stairs to their assigned room. This all took place later that night in near silence and the pitch dark after the Golz ladies had cleaned the kitchen and dining room and gone home. Blanche had still been blushing with pleasure over the compliments she'd received regarding her first successful Beef Wellington.

Three rooms were occupied, hopefully with their occupants sound asleep.

Rio, though swaying on her feet from weariness, remained alert enough to take one diverting item into consideration as Eino, as smug as if he'd just stolen Rio's birthright, followed Garrity on the last trip up the stairs. He and Flavia, having helped themselves to leftover beef and dessert while Garrity did the hard work, had never once let go of a pair of saddlebags and a gentleman's briefcase. He'd even stored the bags under his chair as he ate.

Like a jealous guard dog, she thought, watching with her lips clamped tight when Eino kicked at Boo as the dog, curious at the unaccustomed item, sniffed the bag.

Her half brother missed, of course, Boo being much faster and agile than Eino. Rio could tell Boo knew it was no game as his fluffy tail drooped. Something else she'd have to watch.

Leaving their dirty dishes for her to clean up, Flavia and Eino ascended the stairs as if they were royalty. Rio followed them, inserting her foot in the door when Eino would've closed it in her face.

"We haven't discussed payment," she said, well aware this would get a significant rise out of Eino. "And you do know Mr. Garrity's room will also be at the normal charge. You may not remember, but while the rooms include breakfast, dinner is the regular restaurant fee. Your dinner tonight will be on the house, this time only. Everything else will be at the normal fee."

Eino lifted a brow. "What do you mean, payment? I'm your brother. I'm not paying you."

"This is a business," she said. "I don't house or feed people for free. Especially criminals. If you want your presence kept secret, you'll pay."

Eino took instant umbrage. "Now listen here..."

"I'm not paying for Garrity," Flavia squeaked. "Talk to him. He'll have to pay his own way."

Rio shook her head. "That's between you and him. I'm sure Mr. Garrity told you my terms before you showed up here. Yet here you are. Tacit agreement to those terms, which includes normal payment for the two rooms."

Flavia was shaking her head until Eino took charge. "What the hell. We agree. Pay her, Flavia."

The woman whirled to glare at Rio. "All right, all right. It seems you win. As for now, get out. You'll have your money in the morning."

Rio dipped her head. "Very good. I'll hold you to that." She backed out of the room and closed the door behind her. This had been a mistake. She knew it. She shouldn't have let Quinn convince her it was the smartest thing to do.

"Keep your enemies where you can see them," he'd advised.

She would rather quell fires and shoot outlaws than have her half brother and his floozy under her roof. And it wasn't greed or the need for money that made her insist on payment. The argument depended solely on her knowledge of her half brother. Let him get away with one single trick and he'd take it as a sign to take everything.

———

AS IT TURNED OUT, Garrity had his own idea about taking a room. He didn't want one.

"Can't afford one," he said, shamefaced. "I'm pretty well broke. Salo, he ain't too good at keeping up with my wages. And her, she don't like me anyhow."

Rio understood the her in question to be Flavia.

"They agreed to pay," she said.

Garrity shook his head. "Doubt they will when

push comes to shove. I seen a cot out on the back porch. Or I can sleep over in them trees. In fact, I'd druther."

He meant the pines shading the path up from the dock to the porch. In truth, Rio had thought about placing a campground in there. A pretty spot, it was near the spring, though she planned to keep that part private as her special place.

"How about I put my bedroll there?" Garrity was saying. "This time of year I like sleeping outdoors. Don't like being closed up in some little room."

Rio wondered why he was working for Eino then, since he had always hated the outdoors. She knew other people like Garrity though. Cattlemen and the loggers who regularly slept under the stars as part of their job had mentioned it to her. Most said they couldn't breathe in a closed-in hotel room. But they sure did appreciate eating in her restaurant.

"All right," she agreed. "I'll have to charge you for meals though. I don't want you being careless with a campfire in the trees. If the fire got away, it could burn the hotel."

"Yes, ma'am. I won't build no fires 'cept in a pit," he agreed, so it was done.

Rio smiled to herself and wondered what Eino would think when—or if—he learned of the deal she and Mr. Garrity had made.

Twenty

"That is the rudest, most awful woman ever born. I don't know how anybody can get along with her." Maria made her opinion known in no uncertain terms as she peeked into Rio's office after delivering dinner to Eino and Flavia the next evening. It was late. The delivery of their meal had been the girl's last chore of the day.

"What happened?" Rio looked up from the letter she'd begun writing to Beckett yesterday and had just now had time to finish. She'd found it difficult to know what to say. The stronger the message the more likely he'd pay attention but she couldn't confess to shooting a man, not even in self-defense. And certainly not in a letter.

"She ordered me around like a slave. Then called me a name when I tried to clear the little table so I could lay out their food. She said I was snooping and that when she finally got some say around here she was going to tell everyone I'm a thief."

"Pay her no mind," Rio said. "She'll never get a say,

so you don't need to worry about her. She says nasty things to me too. And especially to poor Garrity who looks out for them."

Another thought struck. Maria was a pretty girl with her rounded figure, flashing smile, and blonde hair a much brighter golden than Rio's own pale mop. In contrast, Flavia came across as dark and dour. A likely reason, Eino being the sort of man he was, for the woman's animosity.

But Maria's final complaint surprised and amused her.

"Then she had the nerve to say the beef was cold and the gravy lumpy. Oh, and the dessert tasteless and that she isn't going to pay for undesirable food. But I'll bet they eat every bite. You just wait and see because Mr. Salo finally told her to shut up or he'd eat her portion. He already had his mouth full when I closed the door on them."

Rio had to smile. "Ignore her if you can, Maria. I'm sorry to put you through this. If we're lucky, they won't be here for long."

"The sooner they leave, the better," Maria said, and Rio couldn't have agreed more. It all depended on how long Marciano and his gang, and Curran and Toad were prepared to stay around before giving up on the job. If they ever did.

"I know. Thank you for your work today, Maria. And tell your sister, too. Just ignore Eino and Flavia and don't let anything they say affect you."

Maria huffed. "I'll try, but it's hard. Blanche does better."

Rio nodded. "Blanche knows her own worth, which is substantial to say the least. It's time you knew your worth, as well. Eliza too. I'm so lucky to have you working for me." She sounded like a seventy-year-old sage, she thought ruefully. But Maria seemed to take the praise to heart.

Both her employees called a more cheerful good-night to her as they left. That should've perked her up, but when Rio finally finished the letter to Beckett and read it over, she found the words had taken on a desperate note. The whole thing had gone from what she'd intended as a newsy letter in search of advice on how to handle her half brother to a plea for help.

"Pathetic," she said to herself. Or maybe to Boo, who lay at her feet waiting to go to bed. He pricked his ears. "I'm not sure if I should send this."

Nevertheless, she affixed a two-cent stamp to the envelope.

The dog following at her heels, Rio went around the hotel, locking the front door, checking the windows, and setting the latch on the porch. When satisfied, she returned to her office.

Earlier, after seeing, and hearing, Eino and Flavia already quarreling worse than cats and rats, the situation nearly sent her into a fit. Her pokey little room was next to theirs, which had been convenient when looking after her father, but appalled her now. What's more, she didn't trust the security of her possessions with them so handy to her room. She suspected one or the other of them would riffle her room as soon as they got the chance. It would be Flavia who made the search, she'd bet. And with her devious female mind, she might even discover where Rio had hidden Elias's money cache, along with some letters and papers that could mean ruin for certain people if they got into the wrong hands. And by that, she meant her half brother's.

Well, she wasn't going to let that happen. She packed up the money and documents, a fresh set of clothes for the morning, and her pillow. When Garrity had refused her offer to move the office cot to the porch, it had given her the idea to use it herself. Permanently. Not just occasionally as she'd been doing. This way she would be closer to hand if anyone tried to break in, and put some distance between herself and Eino. Plus, she could secure the money and documents where neither her brother nor his wife would ever think of looking.

In fact, she smiled to think of it now. It would be beneath their dignity.

Using the office to change into her nightgown, Rio claimed her pillow and a fresh blanket against the night's chill and settled in on the cot with Boo.

She slept.

And so did Boo.

For six hours, only to awaken in the darkest part of the night to the persistent sound of scratching on the porch door. The noise awakened first Boo, who stood up and growled and in his turn woke Rio. She, blinking and disoriented, sat up, tossing the blankets aside and getting to her feet all in one motion.

Wishing her nightgown wasn't quite so visible, she crept out to the porch, moving to the side of the door to where she could see out the window. Just then the scratching came again.

Boo barked this time. Not loud and only the once.

"Shh," she said, raising her head barely enough to see through the pane. Jerked back. Then eased forward again.

The shape of a large man took form. He had his back turned to her and seemed to be looking toward the woods where the path meandered between the hotel and the loggers camp at the other end of Painter's Bay.

Something in his stance indicated anxiety, as if he were getting ready either run or find cover.

Flipping the latch, Rio eased open the door. "Garrity," she whispered, "what is it?"

Idiot, the thought flashed into her mind. *Why aren't I carrying my gun?*

"Can I come in?" he asked. "You've got visitors coming through the woods. Two of them, I think."

Setting prudence aside, she opened the door wide enough for him to pass through. "Who?"

"Don't know for sure. Can guess."

She could too, and sighed. "Unless someone else has tracked Eino here, it must either be Marciano's gang or Curran and Toad."

"Or the tracker," Garrity said. "He's prolly the most dangerous to Evan."

"Dangerous?" Rio, caught looking outside in the direction Garrity indicated, froze. "The tracker?"

Garrity nodded. "Guess maybe you'd call him a bounty hunter. He finds people and stuff they stole and gets paid a reward."

It was like a heat wave rushed over Rio, making her hot but cold at the same time. Moving precisely, she closed the door, hooked the latch and ran the bolt. She took her time, hoping to school her features into careless curiosity. At last she turned. "Does this tracker have a name."

"Yeah." Garrity's voice rumbled. "Something Irish sounding."

"Ah." So he was definitely talking about Quinn. Quinn of an Irish sounding name like Callahan? If Garrity was on to him, so must Eino be. And probably Marciano and Curran.

Garrity had said tracker equaled bounty hunter. Dare she hope it might mean Quinn not only wasn't her enemy, but someone actually out to do the right thing while recovering his client's possessions? Did it mean he truly was on her side?

Or did it not?

When this was over, what would he do regarding Enzo Marciano?

Instead of lying down and crying, Rio gathered up Boo, and with all the dignity she could muster, muttered something about it being almost dawn and time to get the new day underway. That she guessed as long as he and her other unwanted guests stayed out of sight, it probably didn't matter if somebody watched the place. So saying, she left Garrity to see what he could see and headed back to the office.

Walking on tiptoe past the only guest room on the ground floor, she was unprepared for an arm reaching out and dragging her into the room before she could do more than say, "Irk."

"I heard you talking. Who came knocking at this time of night?" Quinn scowled down at her. He wore britches over his union suit Rio was glad to see, but eyed her with what appeared to be disapproval.

His lamp, lit but with the wick a mere pinpoint of light, used a bare foot to shove the braided rug into the crack between floor and door. It kept both sound and light from being apparent in the hall, she realized.

Rio's mouth clamped. She set Boo down and nodded toward the rug. "Is that an old tracker's trick?"

He ignored her question though his eyes flickered at her use of the word 'tracker.' "What's going on?" he demanded. "Who were you talking to? And what are you doing walking around in your nightdress? Lord, woman, don't you know that thing is..." He hesitated. "It might give a man the wrong impression?"

Rio took one infuriated breath. Then another, and another. And one more. Reaching around him for the knob, she made to wrench the door open. Quinn leaned his back against it. Thwarted and effectively captive, she glared at him. A scorching glare fit to set a man on fire.

"This is my damn house." Her ess's came out in a hiss. "I'll walk around in a nightgown if I damn well please. And I'll talk to whoever I please. Get out of my way."

His jaw tightened. "Who...were...you...talking to?"

"My man friend. Nobody. None of your business." She goaded him on purpose. "You don't tell me your business. Why should I tell you mine?"

Gritting his teeth, he caught her by the arms and dragged her up close. "Because I'm trying to keep you alive."

"You are? Why?"

He glared down at her. "I'm beginning to wonder." Then, "Why not?"

An impasse, she thought, and silly all around. Boo, disturbed by what he sensed in their voices, whined.

"Then thank you," she said, and knew how ungracious she sounded.

Surprising her, Quinn laughed. "You're welcome."

Maybe sensing an advantage, he pressed on. "Seems as if you're a dangerous woman to be around. I figured it might be helpful in doing that if I knew who showed up here at this time of night. If I knew his intentions. And why you aren't tucked up safe in your bed."

His hold had lessened, but he didn't let her go. Not until she shuddered, her bare arms making gooseflesh under his hands. He stepped to the side, out of the way if she decided to leave.

Her feet shuffled, bare toes curling on the cool floor, then stood still again.

"Garrity," she said abruptly. "I was talking to Mr. Garrity."

The lamp flickered, making it harder to read Quinn's expression. "Garrity? What's he doing roaming around in the night? Shouldn't he be keeping his attention on your half brother?"

Although he'd asked a question, it struck her as more rhetorical than an actual expectation of knowledge. She answered anyway.

"Flavia refused to pay for his room and evidently, he hasn't been paid his wages for a while. He asked if he could spread his blankets in the woods. I said yes. I was sleeping on the porch. He came and scratched on the door when he heard someone prowling around a while ago. Boo heard him and awakened me." She reached down to pet the dog, all to the good since it gave her a moment to think.

"Who? Who'd Garrity hear?"

"He didn't know but he thought he should tell me someone was out there. He also asked to stay inside until morning, so he's on the porch for now."

He studied her. "You trust him? He's Evan's man."

Rio wrinkled her nose at his use of Eino's preferred name. "I trust him in this instance."

"Ummm." Not a word, but agreement nonetheless. He went to sit on the chair and pull on his boots, grimacing at the pull on his stitches.

Rio, certain Dr. Clement had never intended this kind of workout for them, shook her head. "What are you doing?"

"I'm going to see if I can spot whoever spooked Garrity. Let me out the front. I don't want him to know I'm around."

She didn't try to argue. Quinn would just go ahead with whatever he had planned anyway.

Silently, they went through the hotel to the front, passing down the dark hall and the eerily echoing lobby. Duly cooperative, Rio went outside first, sniffing the air and listening for anything that shouldn't be there. Or things that should be but weren't. Like the usual presence of crickets, and an owl that lived in a fragrant cedar tree. Both were silent in the hour before dawn. Even the morning breeze refused to stir in the trees, which made the gentle lap of waves on the shore sound louder than normal.

Inside again, she shook her head. "He's right. I didn't see him, but someone is out there. You be careful, Quinn Callahan, you hear?"

He leaned toward her, then stood erect again. "Lock up behind me," he said and was gone before she could say, "I will."

She made her way to the office in the dark, using Boo's white fur as a guide. Knowing there was no use trying to sleep any longer—not with Quinn out stalking whoever had invaded her woods—she dressed quickly, wrapped a coverall apron over her skirt and waist, and went to the kitchen. She stoked the fire, put coffee on to boil, and began her morning routine.

Mix the flapjack batter, slice the ham as a change from bacon, bring butter from the icebox to warm and soften, slice and fry some apples. She found herself hoping more folks came around for breakfast. Anything to prevent her from worrying about Quinn.

Quinn, who sometimes made her so angry.

――――

YOUNG TOMMY GOLZ, whom Rio hired to take care of the horses, ply the rowboats back and forth between the hotel and the town upon demand, and generally do the things Rio never had time for, looked to be bursting at the seams when he rapped on the porch door a few minutes before the restaurant was due to open for business.

Two customers were already waiting on the seats out front and Rio had spied a boat with a quartet of fishermen headed for the dock.

Which meant Tommy had appeared at just the right time with a basket of new-laid eggs for the morning breakfast.

Arrived with news too, that being the cause of his excitement.

"Miss Salo, something strange is going on down at the barn." Tommy's face, flushed with importance at being the bearer of this news, had his mouth open talking before she could even unlatch the door and say, "Good morning."

Rio's first thought was of fire, considering her experience of only a few days ago, but soon discovered differently. "Something going on? Like what?" She knew better than to ignore anything a Golz told her, even a young one like Tommy.

She hadn't doubted Garrity when he spoke of men prowling the woods, and here was another witness.

"A man. He was poking around in the tack room when I got to work this morning. I thought at first he must be somebody staying here, but then when I asked what he wanted, he hemmed and hawed and acted so fishy I knew he must be a thief." He snorted. "'Specially as I caught him sifting through the grain barrel like he'd lost a gold nugget in there. And I could see he'd been in the hayloft and even sat in the buggy."

Rio blinked. "Really!"

"Yeah. Dusted off the seat with his backside. And he carried a lever-action rifle with one of those telescope things on it." Tommy took a breath. "He scared me, Miss Salo. So I dodged away and hid around back of the manure pile. Pretty soon he came out, looked around, and all the sudden he run off into the woods."

"Did he threaten you with the rifle?"

Tommy's mouth pursed. "Well, not directly, but ma'am, I didn't like the look of him, all dark and frowning and being where he had no business being. And he kind of came toward me like he—" He stopped. "Well, I don't know. That's when I ran. But I came back and done my chores when I seen he was gone."

"I'm glad you ran, Tommy. I'm relieved he didn't hurt you. I suppose he was just looking for anything he might sell."

Tommy cocked an eyebrow. "In the grain barrel?"

He had a point. Rio shrugged. "You never know

what some of these vagrants might think." Only she didn't think he was a vagrant. All dark and frowning, Tommy described him. Just like at least two of Marciano's men, if she remembered correctly. And he wouldn't have been looking for anything to steal—at least she didn't think so. More likely, on orders from Luca Marciano, he'd been looking either for money or for Enzo. Either his person or his body.

In the grain barrel? She shuddered.

"Be sure to tell me if you see any other strangers going where they shouldn't," she told the boy. "And try not to get too close to them. It's best to be cautious." She didn't mention the rifle. Tommy being a country boy, he'd know to be aware.

And so would she. She'd warn Garrity and Quinn. And Wash, too, although if the men had started out from that direction, he might already know about them.

Rio's heart gave a lurch. She didn't want to think of Wash betraying her. Of all people, not Wash.

Twenty-One

Rio had no trouble handling both cooking of the breakfast meals and the serving of them. Not even when another three men rowed across the bay and strode along the gravel path to the hotel. They were gawking at the tidy hotel grounds as if looking for faults right up until they walked into the dining room. She knew one man. The banker, Mr. Masterson, accompanied by two strangers. He seemed to be the host, smiling when one of the men mentioned something about the trip across water to "The quaint little building. Pretty location though." And that it seemed a lot of trouble for what no doubt would be ordinary scrambled eggs and rubbery pancakes.

"You will find the food equal to the finest city restaurants," Masterson said. However, even from several yards away, Rio could see a trace of apprehension on his face.

Put on her mettle, she determined on perfect food and perfect service, so she barely noticed when, hurrying between the kitchen and dining room, she spotted Quinn's room door close behind him.

Back safe.

It was after the three men had eaten and she went about the dining room refilling coffee cups that she overheard one of the men speaking. Stopped at the next table, she paused to listen.

"...the Salo property..." His words came across loud and clear. The other fellow, eldest of the bunch as his graying mustache attested, shook his head in a sharp remonstrative movement.

Curiosity aroused, Rio stepped into the bar niche out of their sight and listened.

"He approached us about six weeks ago," the gray mustache man said, explaining something to Mr. Masterson. "He mentioned a forthcoming circumstance that would precipitate a fast sale. Everything you've told us so far leads me to believe he was telling the truth."

Mr. Masterson nodded. "Yes. He was, as far as anyone knew at the time. But he is no longer with us, and new facts have come to light."

The younger man scowled. "No longer with us? What happened? Did he look for a different deal? Perhaps one more expeditious?"

"No," Masterson said. "I mean he's dead."

He who? A series of men's names rose in Rio's mind. Who were they talking about in the same breath as they spoke of Salo property? Which of the men who were connected in some way to the Salos and were now dead? First there'd been the timber cruiser. Then the Chinese cook. Her father. And last, the late sheriff who'd been crooked as the spring out of a clock. And now Enzo Marciano—but the banker couldn't know about him. No one could. Not ever.

And Eino. But he most definitely was not dead. Not, perhaps, that the banker knew that.

Silence fell at the table.

Rio peeked from the niche in time to see the youngest of the men, the one with pomaded dark hair and already showing a tendency toward corpulence, spread a generous spoonful of strawberry jam on his toast.

"There must be some way around these blockages," he said. "One way or another."

Masterson swallowed the last of his coffee and shifted uneasily in his chair. "Some of this is best spoken of in private."

Cutlery clattering, mustache man slapped his hand on the table. "Then why are we here? Why bring us all this way if..."

His voice lowered and faded although Rio heard Masterson say, "I wanted you to see for yourselves, because indeed, I do think the problems can be overcome."

See what? The question burned in Rio's mind. *What problems?*

"Then we should avail ourselves of the privacy of your office," gray mustache said, belched in a genteel manner, and rose to his feet. "Carver, you're junior in this business. I believe it would do you good to man the oars across the bay."

Turned out Carver was the chubby fellow, Rio discovered, seeing the dismay on his face before she slipped from the niche and hurriedly made her way across the room to wait by the cash register. In the flurry of other guests leaving, Masterson and his guests didn't seem to notice, and she was glad of it.

She needed to talk to Quinn. And to Wash. She needed to tell them about what sounded remarkably like a plot, and not one to her advantage.

But not the men together. Most definitely not.

By afternoon, Rio knew she needed to hire more people if she were to make a success of the hotel. Tending to the threats surrounding her took a great deal of time. She needed someone to clean the rooms, first of all. Another to clear tables and wash dishes. Yet another to take care of the boats and keep the grounds.

But she couldn't. Not with Eino here, his presence like the manure pile out back of the barn and drawing ever more flies. A miasma unseen but smelled.

Win Ferris, she thought, Beckett's young brother, had been a great helper until he had to go when Beckett left to continue his job tracking the opium smugglers plaguing the northwest.

Beckett—what would he think when he got her letter. Would he even reply? Would Win? She'd gotten a couple notes from him, but nothing directly from Beckett.

Two hours before dinner service, Blanche and Eliza arrived, which finally left Rio with enough time to finish cleaning the rooms, bathe, and change into fresh clothes. At times she'd thought of expanding the hotel, but on days like this knew she had all she could handle.

The dining room had every table filled at the first dinner seating. A menu of chicken rice soup, pork chops glazed with an orange sauce, creamy mashed potatoes, sautéed mushrooms, fresh green peas and a dessert of a creamy vanilla pudding and strawberry macarons. All perfectly arranged on the plate, of course, and garnished with appropriate greenery.

The second seating left one table empty. The third gave customers more time for conversation, and Rio with a chance to deliver dinner for Eino and Flavia to their room on a tray.

Eino, for it had been he who cleared a space on the small table brought special to Elias's old room, eyed the settings as Rio removed the domes from over the plates. Judiciously, he nodded as if surprised. "I see your standards haven't dropped. If anything, they've gone up."

Rio didn't care what he thought. She simply nodded as Flavia seated herself.

"As long as you haven't added anything that shouldn't be there." Flavia's upper lip curled. "Like belladonna. Or arsenic."

Rio couldn't help herself. "Oh, hemlock would be my choice."

Flavia's head jerked up.

"My half sister's idea of a joke," Eino assured her. "She'd never allow a word like poison be associated with her cooking."

He was right.

Although she hadn't intended to speak with Eino about what she'd overheard this morning, when he talked to her almost as if she were human, Rio decided to take the chance.

"Do you remember Eldon Masterson, the banker?" she asked.

Eino, busy slurping soup, almost dropped his spoon as he shot Flavia a glance. "Yes. I haven't been gone that long."

"He came for breakfast this morning." She waited a

beat. "He had two out-of-towners with him. Men wearing suits—suits as well tailored as yours, Eino—and each with an air of importance."

Slowly, Eino said, "Did he?"

"He did. They weren't at all cautious in what they said. Nor were they particularly quiet."

Flavia's eyes were bright. "Something that excited you, from the way you're acting."

"Excited?" Rio's brow crinkled. "I don't think that's quite the right word for what I feel."

Busily cutting his pork chop, Eino took his time before looking back at her. "So what is the right word?" He pushed aside the mushrooms and started in on his potatoes.

"Interested might fit. So might curious."

Flavia set down her knife and fork while Eino resumed eating. "I'm sure you're dying to tell us what you heard."

"Not dying, still wondering if I should tell you at all. Or it could be you already know." Turning away from Flavia, Rio eyed her half brother. "Edifying. That's a good word too, because I finally understood why you came back here even after stealing all that money. I didn't understand at first. It didn't make sense, what with three different factions trying to catch up with you. And each one trying to get to you before the other one does."

Although Quinn had had a chance and hadn't taken it. Not yet anyway.

Eino blanched. It took more than an implied warning to thwart his appetite though, as he started in on his pudding and munched a macaron.

"Did you think I hired Garrity for the fun of it?" he

asked. "Speaking of Garrity, where is he? Next door watching my door, I trust."

Rio nearly choked. Let him think so. She wasn't going to tell tales on the bodyguard. After all, he'd done her a good turn in warning her of the prowler.

"I don't know where he is," she said.

"Tell him I want to talk to him," Eino said. "I've got new orders."

"I'm not your messenger. I expect he'll check in when the crowd clears."

"Crowd?" Eino's expression showed doubt. "There's a crowd?"

Flavia had had enough of hearing about Garrity or hotel business. "What did you suddenly understand?" she demanded. "What are you talking about?"

Rio ignored her and turned her level gaze on Eino. "It's not going to work with the bankers, you know. Not now. They're looking at the wrong piece of the pie at the moment. You don't need to be here. Safer by far if you leave. Hal Majors is your local attorney, isn't he? He can handle matters by long distance."

"What's she talking about, Evan?" Flavia turned to Eino, who stared at Rio as if he'd like to strangle her. "What piece of the pie?"

"Nothing," he snapped. "She doesn't...she can't—Nothing."

Rio smiled, just a little, to show she knew more than he thought she did, and that he didn't scare her. "By the way, there's another word that might describe me. Furious. Think about it."

Spinning on her heel and outwardly ignoring the pull in her legs, she moved to the door. "Put the dishes on the tray and leave it outside the door when you finish eating," she said over her shoulder.

The noise of a heated argument began as soon as she closed the door on Eino and Flavia. She could hear their raised voices through the thick wood, though not the individual words.

More trouble awaited her downstairs. Trouble that halted her before she made it all the way down. From her vantage point, she saw the dining room had emptied, the tables cleared, and only one light left burning. From the kitchen came the clatter of dishes and women talking as the Golz ladies finished cleaning up for the night.

Then she noticed the man sitting in the near dark at the table tucked close to the bar. He rose when he saw her coming. "There you are," he said. "I've been waiting for you."

She didn't ask why. She knew why. A queer dizziness spread over her, hands and even her feet felt weak as she stopped. Her hand crept toward the pocket of her skirt and settled on the butt of her .32.

"Mr. Marciano." Her voice held steady, an effort that took concentration. "You shouldn't be here in Painter's Bay, and especially not in my hotel. It is not a wise idea. You're not welcome here. The door is that way." She pointed.

"You ran from me last time. You'll run this time too, but not until I'm done with you."

God help me. The terse little prayer flashed, but even so, she pulled the small revolver from her pocket and held it at her side. She'd taken care of one Marciano by herself. She could take care of this one as well. If she had to.

"What do you want with me? You have to understand this: I have nothing to do with my half brother. Don't you know we loathe each other? Always have and always will."

"He'll come back for this." Marciano waved a hand as he took a step toward her, even as she stood as if frozen on the stair.

"This hotel is mine," she said. "Free and clear under the laws of inheritance. You may check that at the county courthouse. He has no claim on it. Whatever his debt to you, it has nothing to do with me. I won't defend him. If you catch him, do what you will. Just stay off my property."

He laughed. "Says you."

"Says I," she agreed. "Leave now."

Marciano shook his head. "No. I'm not done here. I'll take care of Evan Salo soon enough. But for now, I'm looking for someone other than your brother."

"Half brother."

He nodded almost as if he understood the correction. "I've got relatives too. A cousin. The day before yesterday he got in touch with me. We talked. He told me he was coming here. That he'd make his own search." Marciano bared his teeth. "He's good at that sort of thing. He said he'd be back by morning."

Rio's fingers clenched on her pistol's grip. She wasn't sure she'd even be able to squeeze the trigger when the time came. If it came.

She didn't say anything.

"But he wasn't." Marciano watched her like a robin watches a worm, head cocked, ready to pull her from the ground and suck her down his gullet.

Her shrug could've indicated either that she didn't care or didn't know. "I can't help you."

He eyed her, suspicion plain. "I could beat it out of you. I ain't opposed to slapping a woman around."

She forced a smile. "But I am opposed to being slapped around. I could tell that about you, Mr. Marciano, from the first time I saw you. But I don't know what you're asking. If you're asking if your— cousin, you said?—is here, the answer is no. No one is here except me, you, and my overnight hotel guests."

"Was he?"

Rio shook her head in a pitying kind of way. "I wouldn't know. I suppose he could've had a drink at the bar or a meal. I can tell you I haven't had an introduction to anyone saying he's related to you. Nor has anyone signed the register with the Marciano name." She frowned. "If his name is Marciano."

He looked doubtful. There was honesty in her reply.

There was also a lie.

Rio could tell when he decided to make his last move. He raised his hand and drew it back, a gold ring on his middle finger, gleaming in the lamplight. Made of a rough-cut nugget, the ring was likely to cause damage when it came in contact with a face.

Her face.

"Not a good idea, Mr. Marciano." Almost of its own accord, her pistol leveled on his chest. It didn't waver. "I'm prepared to defend myself."

Slowly, his hand dropped to his side. "All right."

"All right?"

"I believe you. He ain't here." His swarthy cheeks suddenly flushed an unwholesome burgundy color.

"Christ. What am I gonna tell my uncle?" Oddly, he collapsed onto his chair.

Is he asking me? Rio wondered. Most surely not, and yet, in that moment her guilty conscience got the best of her. She crossed the final step to stand opposite him.

"I'm sorry I can't help you," she said and knew that in a way, she truly was sorry.

Moving behind the bar, Rio uncorked a bottle bearing not the best, but not the worst label in the selection, poured a shot of whiskey and set it before him. He looked down at it for a moment, tipped it to his mouth, and swallowed it down. Then, nodding to her, he got up and left.

Rio's breath shot from her lungs, leaving her weak. Still she stood, motionless and solid, in case he looked back.

He didn't.

Twenty-Two

As far as Rio could tell, over the next few days Marciano did call his men in from the woods around the hotel. At least, she saw no sign of them, and Quinn said that's because they weren't there. Apparently, Marciano had taken Rio at her word—for now, at least—when she told him Enzo wasn't there. How long that would last remained up in the air but for now, Luca Marciano's search moved farther afield.

Quinn went out at night, ghosting through the woods taking pains to avoid Garrity's small campsite. He reported to Rio in the early mornings before daylight and the hotel staff arrived. It was always quiet then, hotel guests still abed. Wash's logging crew headed out even earlier into the timber, and the sawmill workers' start time was still an hour or so away.

It seemed to Rio that Wash deliberately stayed away. Notable because he'd always found time to check in with her when they conferred in running the business as her father grew too feeble.

One of Quinn's reports included his findings when

he happened on one of Garrity's campsites. It turned out Garrity changed places every night. Quinn examined Garrity's camp one evening when Eino kept the man on watch until late. In the morning, just as the sky had changed to a steely gray that seemed to portend rain, holding back a yawn, he told Rio about having followed the big man to his chosen spot.

"Did you know he set up this camp only a couple hundred yards from the hotel?"

Rio shook her head. "He hasn't ever given an exact location. Just that he's not far away and a loud scream will bring him running." She smiled a little. Garrity, a big lummox she considered not too bright had grown on her. Ever since their understanding he'd treated her with utmost respect. She thought it might be because Eino didn't.

"A loud scream, eh? That sounds about right. His camp doesn't amount to much. A battered tin can he uses to boil coffee and a frying pan he must've found in somebody's trash. I've never seen such a careful camper using such a bitty fire. All he has otherwise is a tarp and a single blanket, an extra shirt and pair of socks."

"You were quite thorough in searching his camp, I guess." Despite herself, she felt some sympathy for the man.

"Yes. To all appearances, he's a simple man." Quinn made a face. "But not a man to discount in a fight, whether he's for you or against you."

Rio nodded. She'd formed the same kind of opinion.

On the very next day, circumstances changed.

Quinn, first checking to make sure she was alone, came to meet her as soon as he heard her stirring in the kitchen. He was dressed entirely in dark colors and Rio found it easy to see how he escaped notice at night. Anyway, his attire wasn't what drew her attention. That honor belonged to the taut expression on his face.

Looking up from pumping water into the coffee pot, she set the pot on the stove plate just now getting hot. Metal clanged. "What happened? Are you all right."

He cast a cautious look around before nodding. "I am. Bad news though. I was seen."

"Seen?" She went still. "By whom?"

"Toad."

"Toad?" Her dark eyes rounded. "Oh." The short word escaped on a breath.

"Damn it all." He sounded fretful. As well he might considering the damage Toad had inflicted on him previously.

"Did he spot you here at the hotel?" It struck Rio that if the small, lethal man had, everyone in the place might be in jeopardy.

"Not that I know of. While we were in the woods. Probably easy to guess I'm here, though, just like before."

She had to agree. "How—" she started before his head jerked around and he looked out the window. Putting a finger to his lips, he slipped behind the kitchen door and pulled it in behind him.

She blinked as Garrity shuffled onto the porch and rapped lightly.

Lightly for him, at least, as she didn't think the sound would carry to the upper floor where three guests plus Eino and Flavia were presumably still sleeping.

She took a fortifying breath. "Come in, Garrity," she said. "You're up early. I'm surprised to see you."

She was very conscious of Quinn standing behind

the door. Thank goodness he'd been alert enough to spot Garrity in time to hide.

"Morning, Miss Salo," he said. He raised his head, his nose sniffing much like Boo when he smelled bacon, as the coffee began bubbling. "Something happened last night I figured I'd better tell you about first thing. Looks like we might have some trouble heading this way."

Did he think this was news? she wondered. She'd gotten kind of used to it.

His expression remained unworried by the idea. Maybe even a little excited.

"Trouble? For me or you or for my half brother?"

"All of us, I guess." He grinned. Oh, yes. Excited.

"What is it?" Rio's mind raced. "Sit down, Garrity. Coffee will be ready in a jiffy."

"Yes, ma'am." He moved softly for all his size, the chair creaking as he sat. This put him with his back turned to Quinn's shelter.

A very good thing since Boo, trotting into the kitchen from his morning inspection of the lower floor, ambled over to stick his nose into the opening and greet Quinn.

"Boo," Rio called. "Let's find you some scraps."

"You'll want to keep that little fella close," Garrity said.

As she'd been doing ever since Quinn had been stabbed. "What's happened?" She rummaged in the icebox, finding some bits of steak for Boo suitable to use as a diversion.

Sighing, she sat across from Garrity where she could hold his attention. Bad news on its way. She knew it.

"That's what I come to tell you about." He settled

into his chair as if trying to get comfortable. "I done a patrol round about one o'clock. Didn't see nothing. Or hear it either, so I rolled up in my blanket and went to sleep."

Rio nodded.

"Slept for maybe two hours when something, I ain't sure what, waked me up. Thought I was dreaming at first. Got an eye open and I seen a whole bunch of little rocks had fallen on me. Guess one clunked me alongside the head. It's what got my attention." He held up a hand. "I figure you're gonna say that was just my imagination, but nope. Sure enough, I seen a whole circle of them pebble-sized rocks around my head when I got my wits about me."

Quinn's work, no doubt. Rio jumped from her chair and hurried to pour coffee. "Go on." She sat again.

"Alla sudden this little man came barreling out of the woods. He had a knife in each hand and looked as if his intention was to cut me into steaks. Ma'am, he was over me like stink on...um..."

He trailed off and Rio frowned. Stink on what? "But he didn't, I see. Cut you into steaks, I mean."

Relieved, Garrity took a big swallow of the scalding hot coffee and grinned. "No, ma'am." He waved the cup. "Good coffee."

Rio tried a sip, finding it plenty strong and too hot. Unlike Garrity, she'd have to let hers cool a trifle.

"No, ma'am, he didn't get that close to me. A near thing, though. I managed to throw him off. Throwed him good, I mean, right into some brambles. Discouraged him and he ran off. I knew who he was though. A crooked little bastard who'd as soon make mincemeat of you as not. I wasn't lying about the steaks. He likes cutting people. Thing is, he knows me too. And he knows I been working for Mr. Salo. Pretty sure he can guess if I'm here, so is Salo."

"Who is it?" Rio asked, just as if she didn't already know.

"Why, it's that little fella that partners with Audell Curran. Thing is, Miss Salo, I been walking around. Met up with some folks from town yesterday evening, and from what they're saying, I got it in my head that I-talian fella, Marciano, is back. Got all his men with him too."

Rio feigned a startled gasp. Not a lie, in fact. Had Marciano abandoned his search for his cousin already and come back to hold the hotel in siege? "What do you suppose *he* has in mind?"

Garrity stared at her. "Ma'am, I don't know if he has anything in mind beyond grabbing the boss. He comes around here again, you better watch your step."

She nodded. "Thank you for the warning. And letting me know about the other. Mr. Curran's partner."

"Uh-huh." Garrity stood, the chair squeaking relief at being rid of his weight. "About the boss—" He evidently changed his mind about saying more about Eino because he just shook his head and took his leave. Fortunately, he was looking over his shoulder to remind her about keeping Boo close and didn't see the door wriggle, then one of Quinn's fingers catch it from opening wider.

The porch's screen door slammed behind him.

Quinn emerged from concealment, his mouth open to speak until Rio breathed, "Wait."

She should've been able to hear Garrity's shoes crunching on the gravel path. For long seconds, she heard nothing. She'd just taken a step toward the porch to see why when she heard Garrity finally move away, striding swiftly into the growing daylight.

"All right," she said after a moment. "He's gone. Do you think he somehow sensed you?"

Quinn huffed. "Maybe. I said he's a simple man. I didn't say stupid. Or unaware. He does have a certain reputation as a bodyguard, you know."

She hadn't really thought about it. It made sense though.

"Your helpers will be here any minute. We'd best finish this up." Quinn moved to where he could see out to the path the Golz women always used. "Did you know your brother spent some time outside last night?"

"Half brother," she said automatically. "No. I didn't hear him go out. I slept in the office last night. Must've slept harder than I thought."

Quinn smiled a little. "Lady, I don't know when you sleep at all. Don't worry about him getting past you. He's not too bad at sneaking himself." He turned thoughtful. "I'd be surprised if his woman knows. I've got a hunch he keeps his business close."

Rio agreed. "That's true. He's always been secretive, even with Father. Of course, Father was like that too. I sometimes wondered if his left hand knew what his right was doing." An old cliché, she knew, but apt.

"Eino took a different route than he usually does, last night. More direct," Quinn said. "He didn't stay out for long, nor go far."

Different route? Was Quinn saying Eino had been getting past her routinely? "Did you follow him?"

"Yes. That's how Toad managed to spot me. Fortunately, on the way back. I don't think he saw Eino."

"Where did Eino go?"

"There's a cabin just this side of the loggers' barracks. I don't know its purpose. It had a padlock on the door, and he had the key."

That had to be the old cook shack. "Padlocked?" Rio remembered something Wash had said about locking the place up after the sheriff murdered the cook, Li Bai, in there. Apparently, he'd followed through. "And Eino had the key?"

"He did. I don't know what he was doing in there. The building stayed dark inside."

"There's only one window," Rio said. "At the back. You might not have been able to see light in the shack. Li Bai, the cook, used to open the door when he had meals ready." She pondered a moment. "I need to get in there and see if I can tell what he was doing."

"Do you have a key?"

Her face fell. "No." But she probably knew where one was.

Quinn smiled at her. "That's all right. I can pick the lock."

She huffed. "Don't bother. I'll manage. I wonder if he stashed his loot in there."

"Good question," Quinn said softly. "In which case, he may be getting ready to make a dash for the border."

"With or without Flavia, do you suppose?"

"Going by the way they fight, my guess is without. She probably doesn't know it though."

Rio grinned. "Or he might try for Australia," she said, thinking back. "I remember he was always going on about seeing Australia, kangaroos, and crocodiles. It always made his father so angry. He wanted Eino to follow his example. To stay here and become a logger and businessman. And a smuggler on the side," she added thoughtfully.

"What did your father think about him being away from here so long? Two years, wasn't it?"

She nodded. "I think he was happy Eino stayed in the United States. At least until Eino quit writing. Then he got angry, when he wasn't worrying."

And every time Elias got angry, he took it out on her, as if his son's defection was her fault. Rio got hot just thinking of the abuse she'd suffered at her father's hands. His cruel words. His lack of love, which at one time, when she'd been a child, she'd craved.

"Rio?"

Quinn's low voice drew her out of those memories. "The ladies are coming. We'll have to talk later. Set a time to search the shack."

She heard them now, Blanche and Eliza talking back and forth, their cheerful voices carrying as they neared. She nodded. "Go."

Only an hour later, the situation changed again. Rio, with Boo on her heels as she swept crumbs from the dining room floor into a neat pile, looked up at the dog's sharp bark—a warning if Rio had ever heard one— to see a face peering in the window. A sharp-nosed face, with a thick black mustache and a flat kind of beanie on his head.

He was all too familiar; one of the men who'd been searching around the barn the night she and Quinn hid behind the blackberry bushes. The one who'd complained so vigorously of the bush's thorns.

He must have spotted her, for the jumping stopped. He moved on.

Rio patted her pocket, felt the weight of her

revolver there, and without thinking to set the broom aside, strode out through the lobby and around the side of the building with it in her hand. He was still there, all right, only he'd moved to the kitchen window and was trying to see in through it. This window was farther off the ground, which meant he was trampling a part of her herb garden as he leapt about.

Anger flooded through her. She'd just put a stop to that right now.

Twenty-Three

R io vaulted from the porch like one of those
Viking women the Golz girls had compared her
to and rushed toward the would-be spy. Boo,
following as she stormed outside, ran with her.

The man's beanie made a slow slide from his head
as he jumped up and down like a giant demented
rabbit. Oblivious to her approach, he paused long
enough to retrieve the hat. When he straightened, Rio
stood right behind him.

"You," she jerked out, poking him in the ribs with
her broom handle. "You've trampled my herbs, you
idiot."

He spun around, his beady little eyes squinting at
her. "What the hell?"

"My herb garden, you stupid, stupid man. Go away
and stay away. Now."

He stared at her, his face reddening as he absorbed
the import of her diatribe. "Who you calling stupid,
woman? Herbs? What's that? This bunch of weeds?"

Deliberately, he ground a size eleven foot into a patch of thyme.

His lack of remorse infuriated her, but not as much as the destruction of one of her cherished herb plants.

"Leave, I said." Rio shook her broom at him, thinking she probably ought to have dropped the broom and drawn her pistol.

In fact, she knew it when his eyes squinted in anger and he swatted at the broom, missed, then made another attempt at grabbing it out of her hands.

No time for the pistol now.

With a hard twist she wrenched the broom away from him only, to his utter surprise—and her own as well— instantly reversing the action, jabbing the stout, bristly end into his face. Just as quickly she pulled back and switched ends before he could scrub the dirt out of his eyes. This time, using the end like a sword, she thrust the sturdy wooden handle into his chest, then, harder, into his gut.

"Move it. Scat." She jabbed him again. Boo, gleeful at the tussle, grabbed the fellow's pant leg and gave it a sharp tug. Sharp enough for the cheap fabric to tear horizontally, leaving a gaping flap.

The man—she remembered the name Conti— cursed and lunged for her. "You asked for it, woman." Fist clenched, he aimed a boxer's punch at her.

Rio had a good grasp on the broom's handle, a strong one made of hickory. There was no give to her when she belted him again, this time alongside his head.

He reeled backward, clutching the affected appendage and cursing fit to turn the air blue.

By this time, guests who'd come downstairs looking for breakfast were drawn outside by the noise. And the barking, Boo's contribution to the turmoil being notable. Blanche and Eliza had come around from the other end of the hotel, Eliza's eyes wide at the sight of Rio doing battle. Meanwhile, Garrity lumbered from the woods in a half-run, his expression anxious. And the man who'd been partnering with Conti showed up as well, hanging back as if preferring to remain invisible.

Only Quinn, Eino, and Flavia stayed holed up inside the hotel.

"What the devil is going on here?" A thin fellow sporting a British accent rushed toward them from the dock where he'd been tying up his boat. He stared down a markedly important nose at Marciano's man and said, "Do be quiet, sir. You're disturbing the fish with your noise."

Conti glared at him and rubbed his head.

"Well? Explain yourself."

Conti didn't speak.

Quite possibly, Rio was the only one who noticed his hand inching toward the gun she knew he concealed beneath his jacket. Garrity was hustling up behind Conti, but with the man's back turned, he might not even know a gun was about to come into play.

Garrity could be shot. Her guests might be shot. She might be shot!

Rio stepped forward. "Sir," she said to him. "Take your hand away from that gun."

He showed his teeth at her in what may have been either a grin or a grimace and shoved his hand inside his jacket.

He'd left her without a choice. Rio set her feet, aimed the broom handle at his forearm, and put all her weight behind the blow she delivered. With a crack, the hickory broke in two. Conti's arm may have as well. Certainly his screech seemed to indicate so.

Putting a period to the disturbance, his gun plummeted to the ground at his feet.

One of Rio's guests, a lady of some years wearing old-fashioned bloomers and a canvas vest adorned with hooks and shiny lures for her scheduled fishing excursion, looked on in horror. "My dear Miss Salo, that man was going to shoot you."

Numbly, Rio nodded. "Looks to have been his intention."

The lady's husband was frowning. "Is that why you were striking him with that...that broom? Is he a guest?"

Rio's rage soared again, though she tried her best to bank it down and hide the signs from her guests. "No. He's not a guest. He's a known criminal. Not only was he spying on me through the hotel windows, but—" She stopped and eyed her mangled herb patch. "He's trampled my garden."

One of the guests started away, muttering about "a lot of furor over some green stuff."

The bloomer-wearing lady commiserated. "A shame about your herbs. Thyme, isn't it? A real shame."

One had caught on her outcry of Conti being a criminal. "Checking to see what's worth stealing, I suppose. Well done, young lady."

Garrity had corralled Conti, telling him to hush up his caterwauling and hit the road. Shouting threats, Conti did, unwilling but at Garrity's strong *suggestion*, leaving his revolver on the ground. His companion faded away without ever saying a word.

Shaking in her shoes now the excitement appeared

past, Rio was near enough to hear Garrity mutter an unexpected word to himself. "Escalate."

Thoughtfully, she picked up Conti's revolver with no intention on handing it back to him. She'd give the weapon to Blanche, she decided. When she got over being surprised Garrity even knew a word like escalate.

RIO HAD no intention of waiting for Quinn to pick the padlock barring entrance to the cook shack. Not if, as she felt certain, the lock was at her half brother's instigation. After giving careful thought to old habits, she believed she knew a way in. And if she was right, she also believed there might be a way out of this whole affair that would satisfy each of the factions making a mess of her business.

Well, maybe not Eino and Flavia, a thought that made her smile to herself. Blatantly enough, as it turned out, that Blanche commented on her expression as they stood together later in the morning prepping for the evening dinner. Roast lamb tonight, Rio had decided. She wouldn't eat it, but that didn't mean she was unable to cook it.

"What's got you tickled?" Blanche demanded, hands on hips and a suspicious quirk of her eyebrows.

Rio waved the query away. "Nothing much, but maybe..."

Blanche waited. "Maybe what?" she urged.

Rio just shrugged.

No. Probably Eino and Flavia wouldn't like her solution, but the others, Marciano for the Italian gangsters, and Curran and Toad, for the criminal reward money, they might be satisfied. And so, she imagined, would Quinn.

Later, in the quiet hour before the evening rush, Rio found herself with enough free time to take the path through the woods to the shack. She carried an old fishing creel by a leather strap, the creel itself redolent of fish although the receptacle was empty. Boo bounded along ahead, flushing a few birds from the bushes, chasing rabbits and innumerable bushy-tailed squirrels. Once, a young doe sprang in front of them in a startling display of athleticism before dashing deeper into the cool shadowed woods.

Rio called her dog away from giving chase, and wonder of wonders, Boo obeyed.

It had been weeks since she walked this path, she reflected, pausing a moment to pick some green leaves from a spreading plant of wild mint. More than two months since her father died and a full six weeks since she'd been shot. Today it struck her that she walked without a limp, her stride quick and sure.

Out of the blue, she heard herself humming a tune she'd made up years ago. Not that the song lasted long as just before she took a breath to hit the high note, a man materialized out of the bushes right in front of her.

Toad stood there, his popping eyes not moving from her.

Rio stopped short, her song gone on a gasp. Hoping her fear didn't show, and watching closely for a knife, she said, "Please move aside, Mr...." Well, she didn't know any name for him but Toad. "Sir," she said instead. "You're blocking my way."

"*Huut*," he replied, exactly as his namesake creature might. "Time you and me and the boss had a talk."

"Is it? I can't imagine what we have to talk about." To her ears, that sounded like a fine reply. Her voice didn't even shake—much. "You have no business on the Salo property. Please leave."

Her words had no effect. Toad folded his arms across his chest and stayed in the middle of the path.

At least he wasn't reaching for his knife.

Boo, who'd been ready to take on Conti this morning, must've sensed danger from this man, as he cowered and did his best to hide under her skirt. Meanwhile, Rio's inner self was saying, over and over, "Oh, no. Oh, no. No, no, NO."

A noise like the huffing of a winded buffalo blundering through the bushes alongside the path warned of more company. The tips of the bushes waved and broke marking the buffalo's progress.

Toad shook his head, likely, Rio thought, at the contrast with his own almost invisible approach.

Sure enough, with a final swipe of his arm to push aside a low branch of the fir standing in his way, Curran lurched onto the path. His eyes were flashing. "Damn uncivilized backward country ain't even got any decent streets or alleys. Can't hardly get from here to there without poking your eyes out." He went into a spasm of coughing strong enough to bend him over.

Toad reached into a pocket and, although Rio expected the knife to show, came out with a silver flask. He offered it to his boss and when uncorked, she smelled brandy.

In a way, Curran's appearance greatly relieved Rio. Toad frightened her more when on his own than he did when with his boss. Thankfully, the little man's attention had gone from eyeing her like a frog does a fly to

watching Curran. Figuring the movement went unnoticed, she sneaked the pistol from her pocket and held
the creel in front of it.

Curran took two big gulps of the brandy before
handing back the flask and drawing a large, well-used
handkerchief from his jacket pocket, wiped his lips.
There was a smear of blood coloring the fabric as he put
the kerchief away. After a moment, he caught his breath
and said, "Your brother. Where is he? I got business
with him."

"Half brother, you mean?"

Curran snorted. "I don't care what he is to you. I
want to know where Evan Salo is."

Hah. Another who knew her half brother by his
assumed name.

"Him and me," Curran was saying, "we got a score
to settle. And believe you me, no puny little woman,
sister or half sister, is gonna save him from me. I'm
justified!"

Rio blinked. Plain talk, for certain. Fine. She'd do
some plain talking too. "I don't know where he is. Why
should I? And his name is Eino, not Evan. I have no
interest in your quarrel with him. Whether he kills you
or you kill him, I don't care." The truth. She was
amazed to find herself saying so in such an emphatic
manner. "My only concern is keeping my hotel out of
the mix. He and I may have shared the same father, but
I am my mother's child. Eino's father murdered my
mother. I have no loyalty to either of them."

Curran stared at her a long moment, his breath
rasping. "What do you think?" he asked Toad.

"She ain't lying."

Nice, Rio thought, the sarcasm rising strong, to have

earned Toad's approval. But then Curran settled a disapproving eye on Toad and asked, "Which part?"

"Eh?"

"I'll wager she's lying about something. Which part?"

Toad's eyes bulged, and he turned to stare at Rio. First Rio, then at Boo, just now emerging from behind her. "Want me to find out?"

Curran coughed and said, "Yeah. I want you to find out."

Almost casually, Toad reached behind his neck and drew out a sharp-looking knife. He sent an awful grin in Rio's direction, but instead of threatening her, he reached down and grabbed Boo by his scruff before the dog could even growl. The blade was already descending when Rio kicked the knife out of his hand.

A strong kick, one that sent the knife flying into the weeds beside the trail and Toad looking after it in shock.

"Hey!" he yelped.

His fingers were bleeding, Rio saw with satisfaction, cut with his own knife. In his stunned hesitation, Boo fought his way out of the little man's grasp, managing to give him a good nip in the struggle.

Meanwhile, Rio had her .32 pointed at Curran's hollow-looking belly. A necessary precaution since he'd been in the act of reaching under his jacket for the gun she spotted there.

She shook her head at him, and he, bowing to reality, spread his arms wide to show compliance. She backed up a few steps, thinking a bit of distance between them wise.

"You," she said at Toad who, not surprisingly, had started after his knife. "Leave it."

He ignored her.

So she fired. Purely by accident the bullet glanced off the knife blade and went whizzing off God knows where. Rio certainly didn't.

Toad cried out in anger while Curran gaped at her. "If you missed, woman, you mighta killed him. Hell, you mighta killed me with the ricochet."

"But I didn't miss." Hah. Claiming prowess she didn't have. "And I will kill you if I ever see the pair of you around here again." Firm and cold, but the thought occurred that she could have killed herself had the ricocheting bullet gone the other way. She wasn't sorry she'd taken the shot though. A very wise man had told her that in a tough spot, you shouldn't make threats you weren't prepared to follow through on.

The wise man had been Beckett Ferris and he'd given her the advice just before he left.

Rio's hands had begun shaking, enough so that she took her finger off the trigger. The problem confronting her at the moment seemed to be one of what she should do with the pair now she had them. She didn't feel safe just turning them loose to wander through the woods.

"Where are you staying?" she demanded.

"Who, me?"

She sighed impatiently. "Who do you think I'm talking to? The wood lice crawling on your collar?"

Eyes showing alarm, Curran squirmed. "Lice on my collar?"

"Hmm," she said. She'd lied about the wood lice. There were none. They were nothing more than roly poly bugs anyhow. Not lice at all and harmless to boot.

Maybe, if she was lucky, he'd be so appalled by the idea he'd leave without any more argument. Or threats.

"How did you get here? Walk around the point on the trail? Hire a horse or a buggy in town? Hire a boat—or steal one?"

Curran continued to brush at his collar.

"Boat," Toad said after a while when Rio had begun to wonder if they'd all gone mute.

She nodded. "Good. Then you can leave the same way you came, and I'm warning you, don't come back."

"My knife." Toad watched her, his protrudent eyes full of hate.

"My knife now." She made a slight gesture with her revolver. Nothing fancy that might give him time to make a move. Just enough to warn she meant business.

"Let's go," Curran said, turning toward the woods, which forced Toad to grab his coat and pull him in the right direction. "You got lots more knives." They started off, Rio and Boo following a safe distance behind.

At a split in the trail where a smaller, lesser-used path led down the lake, Curran turned back to her. "I'll be back." He glanced at his partner. "We'll be back. Count on it."

"Best if you don't." But she had no doubt he would. "I'll be ready."

From the familiar trail she watched them slowly make their way down to the lakeshore where, now she knew where they were going, she spotted a small boat. A green one, barely visible in the shaded water, which meant it belonged to Buel Reading. He owned a saloon on the outskirts of Painter's Bay. A dive, one of the places where opium had been rampant before Beckett Ferris closed the trade down. A rough place, she'd heard, no doubt suitable for bad people like Curran and Toad. And Reading had a couple rooms he let people stay in, she remembered—for a fee. Usually, or so she'd overheard men say, there was a woman involved.

Rio kept up the watch until they'd gotten halfway across the bay, Toad at the oars. Not that she was surprised as from the sound of Curran's cough, the man suffered from tuberculosis. He probably wouldn't have the wind to row a boat.

With the interruption, time ran short to finish her business at the cook shack. She'd have to hurry. Still, she'd come this far and hated to stop midway. Events were crowding in. She might not have the opportunity again.

"C'mon, Boo," she said, and as the dog came to heel, picked up her pace.

Twenty-Four

As Rio had expected, the compound was deserted when she cut through the woods to the back of the cook shack. Over at the sawmill, the regular crew had gone home but she could hear someone pounding metal on metal. Just the maintenance fellow who sharpened the saws, she assured herself. The man who kept the chains running, the equipment greased, and sawdust cleared from the pit beneath the saws.

Rio only knew his first name, Abe, and knew the scream of saws cutting through logs and clatter of chains within the mill had made him mostly deaf. He'd be paying attention to his work, not his surroundings where he expected to be alone.

Ducking around the end of the shack, she knew from the noise he was busy inside the open-ended building that housed the mill.

The door, just as Quinn had told her, bore a shiny brass padlock. A big new one, not easily cut even with hefty bolt cutters. Which suited Rio since she didn't have bolt cutters anyway. What she did have was knowledge of where Elias—and then Eino—had always secured a key, whether to the hotel, the barracks, or, in this case, the cook shack.

With another glance around, Rio knelt in front of the steps leading into the shack. Each step was made of a two-inch thick red fir plank. At the second of the three steps, she measured off what she thought was the center and reached her hand under the step until she touched a metal hook affixed at the back. Attached to the hook was, as she'd expected, a key.

A key that unlocked the padlock. In seconds, she had the door open and replaced the key where she found it. In only a few more seconds, she and Boo had slipped inside.

No wonder Quinn hadn't been able to see anything when he tried to look through the window. The room was dark as an unlit cellar and someone had hung a cloth over the one window, sealing the interior to the outside.

Rio's nose wrinkled. The place smelled of mold and mice. Evidently the food remaining in stores hadn't been cleaned out after Li Bai was murdered. With items left to rot, rodents had found a way in and deposited their bit to the scene. Rio didn't envy any cook who took over the job—if another ever did. It might depend on who ended up running the place. Eino, or Wash. Or even someone else as it might be sold to some bigger corporation. Possibly those men who'd accompanied the banker to breakfast.

But that wasn't her concern. A small barn lantern sat on the table. Working by feel in the dark room, she struck a match and lit the wick.

Nothing much had been done but lock the place up, she soon discovered. Old dry blood still stained the floor where Li Bai had died. The remains of broken chairs were gathered and placed beside the stove. A dirty rag hung from the handle of the oven door.

And nothing, no matter how closed up a building might be, could keep dust from gathering.

Rio took a close look around, holding her lantern above the telltale marks of two people imprinted on the dirty floor. She almost laughed out loud. Although it appeared an effort had been made to wipe out the traces of their presence, whoever had done the sweeping hadn't been very thorough. The narrow heel of a woman's shoe, the tread of a man's shoe sole revealing the brand of an expensive shoe. Eino and Flavia, without a doubt.

On the kitchen shelves, disturbance in the dust showed where someone's curiosity had led him—or her —to check in jars and canisters for anything valuable. Flavia's work, Rio imagined, as the woman searched for any money or opium Li Bai might have stashed and been overlooked.

Not likely. Li Bai had been careful with his money and drugs. As part of the smuggling ring, he'd had to keep careful track of his inventory or risk repercussions.

But there were only so many hiding places in the building, as most of the floor space had been the mess hall for the loggers when they were staying in the barracks. That meant a long and plain rough-built table and a mix of chairs and stools. Only in the cooking and stores area of the single room was there a possibility to find what Rio was looking for. And she knew exactly where.

The cooking area had been formed for efficiency, as she remembered, with Li Bai doing the situating himself with her father's help. Odd, that, when she thought about it. But the setup turned out handier in some ways than the kitchen at the hotel. Across one wall was a low cupboard with a hanging cabinet above it. Next to that was a dry sink, and while there was no running water, at least the wastewater could be drained away via a pipe into a graveled hole twenty feet from the shack.

Next to the sink was another low cupboard, wider than the first one, and another hanging above that. Next came the stove, just far enough away as to prevent the danger of a fire. Between the two was a stack of firewood.

Rio couldn't help smirking a bit. Freshly chopped blocks of wood, the cuts still oozing amber beads of sap and smelling strongly of pine, lay ready to burn. She shook her head.

In moments she'd moved the wood and opened the hatch into the side of the cupboard where a six-inch cavity had been blocked off from the rest. Her father had always had a penchant for hidden compartments. The one in the armoire in his room came to mind. Without the considerable amount of money she'd found there starting the hotel restaurant might have been impossible.

The one she found here seemed entirely in keeping with his others, and it made sense Eino would know about it.

Within the cavity, she found a pair of saddlebags, one of them quite heavy, along with one of those slim cases, she'd forgotten what they were called, but she'd seen business people carrying them. Pulling them all from the cavity, she undid latches and straps. And found exactly what she expected.

Money and documents. A lot of it. A whole lot.

Behind her, Boo gave a little whine.

Rio sat back on her heels and looked at her dog. "What should I do?"

But Boo just cocked his head and stared at her. Rio shook herself as a wave of apprehension and dread swept over her. Take it or leave it? She didn't know what was right.

There were so many ways the situation might play out. Leave it there for Eino and let him run with it? Separate out those bearer bonds and the White's cash for Quinn and settle one—the only legitimate recovery, in her opinion—then leave the rest to Eino? Or in an anonymous fashion, portion out what Marciano and Curran were owed, and hope they'd be satisfied and leave? Or would they consider retribution necessary? In that case—well, any case really—what would Eino do? He'd know she'd been the one who found his stash. Her? Or Flavia?

Who frightened her the most?

Marciano? Curran and Toad? Eino? Quinn?

Decide.

After a while, she did, then closed the hatch and restacked the wood just as she'd found it. More careful than Eino and Flavia, she wiped out every trace that she'd been here, including her footprints and Boo's paw prints.

She blew out her lantern and checked carefully before stepping outside. The sound of repair work continued unabated, Abe as oblivious as ever.

"Let's go, Boo," she whispered and, sagging a little with weariness and the weight of the creel, hurried to return to the hotel. Not counting the stop they made at the barn while she caught her breath, that is.

———

PEOPLE WERE LINED up on the front porch for the first dinner seating. Rio heard them talking as she sped down the path between the barn and the hotel hoping no one spotted her. Boo bounced alongside her, appearing every bit as glad to be home as she was.

Out on the lake, a boat pulled up to the dock, a small wake drifting behind it. A fairly large boat, the one supplied by the livery stable in town with two young men at the oars. Every seat was taken, mostly by men who'd be visiting Turner at the bar as they waited to be seated for dinner.

There'd be a full house tonight, she thought. A profitable evening. And poor Blanche must be panicking, wondering where she was and what was keeping her.

A correct assumption. Blanche's greeting, hands on hips, face red and sweaty, carried a sharp note. "Where have you been? I was beginning to think that brother of yours sneaked out and killed you."

"I know. I'm sorry. I got waylaid."

Blanche's expression changed. "Waylaid? Who by? Are you hurt?"

"No." Rio tried to smile and wished she could tell Blanche everything. "Not hurt, just scared. The redoubtable Mr. Curran and his nasty little partner Toad stopped me on the path. Then Boo took a dislike to Toad and Toad acted like he was going to stab him. I had to use my gun."

Blanche gawked. "I thought I heard a shot a while ago! Did you shoot him?"

Rio shook her head. "No. A warning shot only. I don't really want to shoot anyone." *Anyone else*, a part of her mind amended. "Even after I saw them going away across the lake, it took me a while to recover my wits. I don't mind saying they left me shaking in my boots." No more than the truth, though a somewhat incomplete accounting.

"So they're gone?"

"Yes. At least, I trust so." But Blanche's query raised chills on the back of her neck again. Yes, they'd left, but would they be back?

"Well,"—Blanche turned practical again—"there's nothing like hard work to bring you out of that state. If we hurry, maybe we can get that mint sauce you mentioned fixed before the lamb goes out. You did get the mint, didn't you?"

"I did." It was a trifle bedraggled and crushed but at least Rio'd remembered to grab a handful from a clump that grew wild along the trail.

Rio donned her apron and the two women set to work.

SHEEP RANCHERS FROM HOTTER, drier areas of the state had begun driving their livestock to higher mountain pastures. Hence the supply of lamb for Rio's dinner menu. The only thing to surprise her was the number of people more used to beef or poultry who had enjoyed the roast lamb with mint sauce, choosing it over the alternate entrée of baked ham with spiced raisin compote.

Blanche and Marie had gone home some time ago. With the kitchen cleaned and set in order for the morning, Rio sat for a moment on the porch steps, letting herself rest after the hard work. Evening noises filled the night and she was glad of the dark around her.

After a few minutes, she rose from the steps and latched the back porch door. She took her time, making her way through the mostly dark building to the front. All her guests were tucked up in their rooms and if not asleep, at least quiet. Rio wished she were as well. Asleep, that is. And maybe Boo wished the same, for although he accompanied her, he lagged at her heels

She'd begun to insert the key when she heard feet thudding onto the front porch. Someone said, "Dang. Place is dark. She'll be asleep."

"No she won't. There's still a light on," said someone else.

She frowned, aware of an increase in her heartbeat.

The first man replied, not loud enough for her to hear. But she didn't miss the way Boo's floppy little ears seemed to prick.

Friend or foe?

Boo pranced in place, then scratched at the door. *Friend*, he was saying.

"Boo?" the person outside said.

Boo gave a happy little "arf," a reaction that decided Rio her dog knew. This was someone he trusted—and so did she. She threw open the door. Boo ran out and jumped on the fellow who stood there grinning at her.

Another man stood behind the first. He wasn't grinning. In fact, he looked just a little wary.

"Win!" Joy flooded through her as she looked from one to the other. "Beckett!"

Win Ferris held out his hand to shake but she pushed it aside and hugged him instead. "Win, I'm so glad to see you."

Win hugged her back before, overcome with a young man's shyness, he backed away. "I'm hungry. Is there anything to eat?"

She couldn't help laughing. "Win, this is a hotel. Of course there's something to eat. Go on through to the kitchen and look in the icebox. But be quiet. Everyone is asleep." She hoped.

So far, the second man hadn't said a word.

Win paused long enough to pick up his duffel bag in one hand and a squirming Boo with the other. "C'mon, pup. Yeah, I'm glad to see you too."

Knowing the way well, he headed for the kitchen and Rio turned to face the other man. He stood leaning against the doorjamb, studying her with a troubled intensity.

"Win got your letter a few days ago," he said after a moment. "He showed it to me. Got me worried. Got us both worried."

Rio knew she blushed. Had she said too much? Showed too much? At the last moment she'd sent the letter to Win instead of Beckett. "I was sorry I sent it afterward. But he'd asked how the hotel was doing and...and..."

He nodded. "I know." After a pause, he said, "Was your invitation just for my brother or did it include me?"

"Of course it included you." And in a burst of honesty, she stood back and said, "It was meant for you."

At that, his expression changed. Grew more intense. He stepped fully into the lobby, set down his own duffel and slow and easy, gathered her into his arms.

"Oh." It was as if she had been cold and now was hot.

His head lowered, his dark, dark eyes holding hers. Then his lips slowly, gently, touched her own. Eyes closing, she lost herself in his kiss. Truly, a shower of stars surrounded her. His kiss deepened, grew harder, more insistent, and when at last he drew away, she discovered her arms were wrapped around his neck and she was pressing her body against him like...well, she wasn't exactly sure like what.

"Well." His breath came deep. "Well. I can't say as I expected a welcome quite so...welcoming."

Rio trembled. What had she done? What must he think of her? "No. I...I'm sorry." Afraid to look at him, she backed away, needing the space.

She'd kissed Wash. She'd kissed Quinn. Both had been nice. But this? They'd been nothing like this.

"Don't be sorry. I'm sure not." Beckett followed, catching at her hand. "Don't run away."

She stopped, tried to think what to say. "I'm not running away."

He smiled. A smile that held her in place. "That's my girl."

Rio, unsure of what he meant by that, didn't know whether to laugh or to cry. She decided on normalcy.

"Are you hungry? We'd best get to the kitchen before Win eats everything in sight."

But at this, his smile faded. "You're not afraid of me, are you, Rio?"

Of him? No. Never. Afraid of what she felt for him? Maybe.

She shook her head. "Of course not."

After a moment, he nodded. "Sure, I'm hungry too. The café in town was closed when we got off the train. We caught a freight out of St. Regis this afternoon, so nobody knows we're here. Is that what you meant when you wrote to Win about needing outside law enforcement and keeping it quiet? So these characters you wrote about can be taken by surprise?"

"Yes," she said, then added anxiously, "I know this isn't your problem. I know I shouldn't have told you. I'm just so afraid something awful is going to happen." It had already, but she'd never reveal that—not to anyone. It would remain between her and Quinn. Forever. "And the county has done nothing to fill the sheriff's position, not even assign a deputy to fill in."

Beckett shrugged. "I'm a federal officer, but also a private citizen. I can take a hand without being elected to any position—and make a citizen's arrest if that's what it takes. Anyone can, if they have the guts. I'll need to witness a crime. Do you think it may come to that?"

She moved toward the kitchen. "I don't know. Maybe. Can the discovery of stolen bearer bonds make a case? Or stolen money?"

"Bearer bonds?" This stopped him again. "Depends."

Win appeared in the hallway, a slice of the lamb

tucked into a bread roll in his hand. "Are you coming, Beck? Rio's got all kinds of food in here. All of it mighty tasty."

"Coming," Beckett said. He started moving again but was looking at her in a puzzled sort of way.

"Let me warm something for you," she hurried to say. "You must be in need of a hot meal."

Win answered. "If he ain't, I am." He eyed the last bite of roll in his fist. "Although this is good any old way."

After filling the stomachs of her newest guests— more like a homecoming than a hotel check-in—it was late. Too late for the conversation they needed to have. The Ferris men started toward their old room before she stopped them.

"That one already has an occupant." And right now she wished there wasn't. "There's an empty room upstairs. I'll show you."

It was her old room, although she didn't say so. Tomorrow would be soon enough to fill Beckett in on events. And hopefully, to put Win to work.

For the first time in days, weight seemed to fall from Rio's shoulders.

She smiled on the way back downstairs. Just wait until Beckett and Win met Eino, she thought.

Her half brother just might discover he'd come up with a more unmovable force than either Marciano or Curran. After all, neither of them had the power to put him in prison. Beckett could start him on his way.

Twenty-Five

R io may have believed with Beckett—and Win's —arrival that she'd sleep like a baby. Lord knows she needed it after so many nights of broken rest where she knew people were sneaking around the hotel. But that didn't happen. Right on schedule, she rolled over in her cot and sat up, sure she'd heard people talking. Quiet as could be, she got and padded barefoot from the office to the porch, holding her .32 at her side. Standing by the window, she held her breath and counted off seconds. Right up until she heard footsteps crunch in the gravel path that led around the hotel. Whoever the footsteps belonged to was walking softly. Softer than Garrity ever could. But not as soft as Quinn might. Which was, she reflected, a good thing when one came down to it. She had a little warning.

This was what she'd been waiting for. Fearing for. She could feel it in her bones.

Rio wasn't the only one who heard the movement

outside. Boo joined her, his nose pointed toward the window. He gave a small "ruff."

"I know," she whispered. "Good boy."

She edged closer to the window, staying far enough back an intruder would have to stretch to see her. From the side, she peered out. A man stood on the path, almost directly opposite the porch window. He wasn't looking inside but seemed to be concentrating on something at the hotel corner. He wore dark clothing and had an object, indiscernible at this distance, in his hand. Something bulky.

Another sound drew her attention. She saw another figure stumble over the drainpipe that led down from the roof and carried rainwater away from the side of the building. There was a clatter as the tin rattled against the siding.

He—or she—also carried a bulky object that clunked against the hotel as he caught his balance.

One of them, she thought it was the man by her window, made *psst* sound, probably to warn the other to be quieter. But then she saw the flare of a match, and the bulky thing he held instantly caught fire. Soaked in kerosene at a guess. He threw it flying at the window where she stood.

She gasped, staggering back as the glass shattered in front of her. She felt the sting of small shards, then had no time to worry about that.

A burning torch landed almost at her feet. Her bare feet. Without pausing to think, she grabbed a handful of the towels she and the Golz women had used to clean up after the dinner service and set to soak in a bucket of water. Dropping them over the torch, she beat at the flames with her hands, crying out at the heat.

Boo barked, loud and long as another blazing torch followed the first. Grabbing more of the towels from the bucket, she smothered that one too.

One of the men said. "Damn. They went out."

The other said, "Look. It's her. I see her moving."

"Get her," said the first, "and get that damn noisy dog too." Immediately, a shot came buzzing past her, breaking the rest of the glass from the window frame as it went.

The men still stood on the path, one of them taking aim for another pot shot. Rio remembered her own pistol then but couldn't find it. Flailing around in the dark, she found it on the bench by the bucket and picked it up. Almost of its own volition, the .32 raised, pointed, and the trigger obeyed the squeeze.

The man outside dropped his pistol. He bellowed anger and clutched at his arm before he turned to run. All Rio could think was that she'd almost missed him.

By then Quinn was there, and although he'd taken enough seconds to pull on his britches, his chest and feet were bare. He ran right past her, breaking the latch as he yanked open the door. He jumped the steps in full pursuit of the two fleeing would-be arsonists.

"Don't shoot me when I get back," he called over his shoulder.

"I won't," she said, but she didn't think he heard.

Footsteps heralded the arrival of the upstairs occupants. First, of course, came Beckett, pounding down the stairs with Win hard on his heels. Then the couple from a town on the coast, there for the fishing on Painter's Bay. And last, two travelers, rubbing sleep from their eyes.

"What's happening," the woman half of the couple

cried out. She wore a rather grungy robe over her night-gown. "Is it a robbery? What's all the shooting?"

"V...Vandals," Rio said. "They've run off now."

Blood made a dark spot on the pale granite gravel of the path. A gun lay abandoned in the middle of the blood.

She took an old barn coat off a hook beside the door and drew it on over her nightdress, taking care to hide the pistol in the pocket.

Someone rounded up a couple lamps and lit them, unfortunately revealing the burn marks in the porch floor.

"They tried to set the place on fire?" the woman gasped. "With us inside? But why?"

"I don't know," Rio said, but she did. Oh yes, she did. Another item to chalk up to Eino. Who, she was glad to see, didn't bother to put in an appearance.

It was almost funny, she was thinking as Beckett took charge, reassuring the guests and saying they might as well go back to bed as the excitement seemed to be over. Funny, because

Beckett didn't have to wait until morning to be clued in to a crime. He was getting a firsthand intro-duction.

"Who was that went after them?" he asked, then, before she could answer, said, "Don't move or you'll have glass between your toes." Orders got issued, mostly to his young brother. "Get a broom after this glass, Win."

After some discussion, the guests did as directed, trudging up the stairs and talking among themselves. Beckett drew Rio away from the porch and into the kitchen.

He indicated a chair and took one himself. "You're shaking," he said.

"Scared," she replied. Even Eino and Flavia trying to start the barn on fire hadn't frightened her like this. If she'd been asleep—if it weren't for Boo's warning—God only knows what might have happened. She became aware of the pain in her hand where she'd beat at the flames. A quick look showed blisters forming. Her right foot was bleeding, leaving a toe print on the floor every time she put her foot down.

"Who was that went after them?" Beckett asked again. "Not Wash." And this time, Rio knew she'd have to answer, even if Quinn wouldn't like it.

"No, not Wash." Something in her tone must've warned him that all was not well between them because he frowned.

"Tell me when you're ready," he said, knelt in front of her, and lifting her foot in one hand almost casually plucked a sliver of glass from her toe. Blood ran.

"Ow," she said, her look reproachful.

He grinned at her. "The more it bleeds, the cleaner the wound."

Rio had to concede the fact. Didn't stop the sting though. Worse, there were still her hands to deal with. She decided not to mention those although a surreptitious look showed only a couple actual blisters. The rest were simple reddened marks. Bad enough for a hard-working woman to deal with.

"Now," Beckett said just as Win peeked into the room after disposing of the broken glass outside in the trash heap and announcing he intended to get another hour of sleep. Beckett nodded.

"Thank you for your help, Win," Rio said.

Win just waved, and Beckett sat back in his chair. "Tell me."

So she did. She talked and talked about her inheritance. About Curran and Toad. About Marciano and his men, though no mention of Enzo Marciano. And most of all, she spoke of Eino.

At the end, he shook his head. "What a time you've been having."

"Understatement." She forced a smile.

"And Wash? What's going on with him. I can see there's something."

Rio didn't understand why he kept coming back to Wash. She was still trying to figure out why her old friend seemed to be backing Eino when he knew her half brother's crimes.

She told Beckett that too and wondered at the way he relaxed halfway through the narrative.

Sunlight struck the side of the old hotel, shining through the kitchen window before Quinn slipped into the room where they sat talking. Beckett tensed up again but not maybe, as much as Quinn.

Quinn had stopped in his room to don a shirt and shoes. He still carried his gun and eyed Beckett as if expecting yet another adversary.

Her dark eyes shifting between the men, Rio hurried with introductions. "Beckett Ferris, meet Quinn Callahan. Beckett is a customs agent working to corral opium smugglers in this part of the country," she told Quinn, and to Beckett, only fudging the truth a little, "And Quinn is a private detective working for the family Eino stole the bearer bonds and a lot of money from. He's hoping to recover the bonds and money and return it. He'd as soon not get the law involved as that might hold up the return."

Both men nodded, shook hands, and shifted their attention back to her.

"Did you see who those men were?" she asked Quinn, fairly sure she knew the answer.

"Some of Marciano's bunch. I found the guy you shot sitting beside the path to the sawmill. The other fellow kept going. I took the wounded fellow down to the dock and got him in a boat and over to Dr. Clement. That's what kept me out so long. The doctor promised to see his patient settled in the jailhouse when he got through with him. Said he thought the mortician would be fine with checking on him now and then."

Rio had to smile. It was true. Last she'd heard, Mr. Meadows was still seething over the way his mortuary had been invaded. That Marciano's man would answer to higher authority seemed certain.

"Maybe," she said, hesitant as she didn't know what they'd think, "we three can work together to satisfy everyone." Then, with a quirk to her mouth, "Everyone but Eino and Flavia, that is." She wasn't ready to admit to having retrieved Eino's stolen cache and hidden it herself. She wanted to make sure Eino didn't somehow escape justice first.

"What about Wash?" Beckett asked.

Rio sighed. "I just don't know."

"Then we'll work without him," Quinn said, and Beckett nodded.

"Callahan can fill me in. We'll come up with a plan and get together tonight after the hotel is quiet." Beckett took charge, which was fine with Rio.

Fine with Quinn, as well, going by his quick agreement. "As long as I can satisfy my client," he said. He looked utterly weary, reminding Rio it had only been a couple weeks since he was at death's door himself, and these nights of keeping watch were not helping his health.

The sound of the Golz ladies as they arrived for work reminded Rio of her duties and the realization she was still wearing a bloodstained nightgown and a barn coat. Jumping up, she winced as her toe hit the ground.

"Breakfast in an hour," she cried, and hied off to get dressed and put herself in working order.

———

THE EVENING RUSH OVER, Rio wearily made her way up to Eino's room with a heavy tray. They'd be fuming by now, she thought, he and Flavia, as their wait for supper had gone on longer than usual.

The tray needed both of her hands to carry, so Rio kicked lightly on the bottom of the door with the heel of her shoe, a tap, tap...tap tap tap. There was no answer.

Eino, punishing her by keeping her waiting outside the room, she figured. Just like him.

She kicked again. When she put her ear to the door, she heard movement. "Come on. It's just me," she said, hoping he—but no one else—would hear her.

A minute later, the door creaked open. Eino stood there rubbing sleep from his eyes, his shirt rumpled and blond whiskers sprouting along his jaw. "I gave up on you. Figured you'd decided to make us go hungry."

She'd been tempted. Crossing to the table, she set the tray down. "You can help yourselves, can't you?"

"I suppose," he said, shooting a puzzled look around the room. "Where's Flavia?"

Rio glanced around too. "How would I know? You're the one living with her."

"I was asleep." Eino's eyes narrowed. "She hasn't been downstairs?"

"Not that I know of." Though she started to shake her head, Rio changed her mind. "She better not have been. That was our deal. I have no idea whether Marciano or Curran might have hired someone I can't connect with them."

Air rushed in and out of Eino's nostrils as he huffed his unease. "Go see if she's in the bathroom. Hurry."

For a change, Rio had no inclination to argue. The bathroom was only a few steps across the hall. Knocking first on the door, when there was no response, she turned the knob. The room was empty.

"She's not in there," she said, reporting back. "Where would she go?"

Eino's heavy jaw clamped as he strode across the room. His curses got loud and bitter as he flung open the armoire's double doors and discovered the only things hanging there were several of his shirts and his spare banker's suit. The gowns that had filled the piece to the point the door couldn't close were gone. Eino's boots were toppled over on the bottom. In a fit of anger, he tipped the drawers out. The two that had been filled with Flavia's fripperies were empty.

Her half brother's face had become a violent red. "She's gone. The bitch has gone."

He must've been sleeping extremely hard not to have heard as she packed her things. Could be there'd been a little something added to his latest meal or drink of whiskey.

"I know where she is," he gritted. "She's run out on me. The conniving, lying bitch."

And if that wasn't a case of the gun blaming the bullet, Rio didn't know what was.

He'd been barefoot. Now he pulled on his shoes and took a revolver from the drawer in the bedside table. Almost as an afterthought, he went to the table on the other side of the bed and looked there. That drawer contained only a couple slips of paper. and what looked like face powder residue.

"She took her gun," he said, but as if he were speaking to himself, not Rio. "She's left me."

She stood back and said nothing. She suspected she knew where Flavia had gone, but she wasn't going to say so. What would Flavia do when she discovered the money gone from the stash? Would she be back? Would she dare?

Eino, having checked the loads in his gun, clicked the cylinder into place. He gestured at Rio. "See if anyone is in the hall. I'm going after her. And you're going with me."

"Me? No."

He pointed the gun at her. "You are. Move. Hurry."

She shook her head.

Startlingly fast, he lunged at her, grabbing her arm with his strong fingers digging into her muscles. It was, she discovered, exceedingly painful. A squeak escaped her mouth before she could stop it.

Eino laughed, igniting her rage.

He shook her, making the pain worse. "You think that's bad? I won't shoot you. But I will club you with the barrel of this gun. You see the sight on the barrel? Believe it when I tell you it can do plenty of damage to that pretty skin of yours if I strike you with it. Sure to leave scars." He laughed. "Won't any man look at you then. Guaranteed."

Shoving her away, he pushed her toward the door. "Go."

Rio didn't see she had much choice. Not at this moment. But her dear half brother didn't know she routinely carried a gun. Knew how to use it too. And she knew the path to the cook shack a whole lot better than he did. There might be a chance to slip away.

For the first time since this had begun, meaning Eino and his enemies all gathering at the hotel, she'd be glad to see one of them. They'd be aiming for him, not her, and she just didn't care what they did to him. Whatever they decided on, he had coming.

The hotel had gone eerily quiet, with an odd waiting quality to the atmosphere. Eino dug the pistol barrel in her ribs urging her down the hall to the stairs, then gestured for her to go first.

They went quickly, the carpet runner laid down the middle of the stairs muffling their footsteps. At the bottom, he said, "Out the back."

As if she didn't know.

They passed the darkened kitchen, then her office and Quinn's room, and entered the porch. She knew the way well, dark or not. Shadows seemed to grow in the corners before receding. Aware of Eino pointing his pistol first here, then there, she knew it all disturbed him. He knew his enemies. It struck her that he was every bit as afraid of what—or who—might be outside as she. And when a small object, a wood chip, a stone, a clothespin—she didn't know what—rolled and skittered between one of his feet, she heard his weapon cock and believed for a moment he intended to shoot her. If so, he refrained—for the moment.

She made it outside with him close behind, he using her body as a shield in case of gunfire.

He stopped to listen. "That way," he whispered and pushed her toward the path. "And be quiet."

Beckett. Quinn. Wash, if he was still her friend. She needed them. One of them. Any of them. She needed them now.

Where were they?

Eino clasped her wrist like an iron clamp, alternately yanking on her and pushing on her. The action made her stumble, going once to her knees before he wrenched her upright again. Her shoulder, almost to the point of dislocation, protested with agonizing results. The glass-cut toe ached inside the moccasin she was wearing, the thin leather providing little protection.

Perhaps her rage was a good thing. It helped her to bear the pain.

He'd told her to be quiet, but it was he who made the noise. Twigs and pine cones cracked under his heavy tread and with every one, he cursed aloud. Air whistled in and out of his lungs, making her wonder if he had the same sort of disease as Curran. Otherwise, the night's silence felt heavy.

Starlight shone overhead, dappling the shadows along the path. Bushes moved in the slight breeze as if pushed by ghostly hands. Finally, they came to the secondary path leading down to the bay where even at this distance they both heard the rattle of oars in the locks of a boat. But no splash, which probably meant someone was holding the boat close to shore.

"Someone waiting for your wife?" Rio whispered.

Make him hurry, she thought. Make him careless. Make him hurt.

But all he said was, "That cow. She's not my wife."

Not a real surprise. She wondered if Garrity knew.

Where is Garrity? The thought struck hard. Why hadn't he appeared? Had something happened to him? Had Toad happened to him?

He pushed her then, urging her ahead of him. All too soon, the cook shack came into sight. Even at a distance she could see the door was open and light shone inside.

A yank stopped her at the edge of the woods surrounding the compound's clearing and she cried out.

"Shut up." Eino jerked her arm again, drawing a moan before she could stop herself.

The sawmill burner loomed high over by the landing. The barracks were dark, either nobody in residence or asleep at present. The place, except for the cook shack, appeared to Rio to be deserted.

Off in the trees, an owl hooted, the sound making Rio shiver. "Let me go," she told her half brother. "There's no one here. You don't need me."

"Do as I tell you. The shack," he said, "you lead the way," and gave her another of those rough pushes.

But finally—finally—he released the pressure on her wrist and shoulder. Rio tried moving her fingers, numb and nerveless. Her shoulder felt on fire. And although aware of the pistol as a weight in her pocket, she wasn't certain she'd be able to pull the trigger even if she got the chance. Seeing no choice, she headed across the clearing to the shack.

At the doorway, Eino shoved her into the shack ahead of him. Quite as if he expected her to be shot down at once. It struck her that he might be hoping.

Nothing happened. The shack was empty of people. The light came from a lantern left sitting on the table where Li Bai used to make his noodles.

Rio cast a sideways glance at Eino, watching as his face suffused with rage. The stack of wood at the side of the cupboard had been scattered willy-nilly over the floor, flung aside without care. The door to the hatch had been pried open by someone without the know how to smoothly open the sliding section. The saddle-bags, pulled out and left behind, gaped open. The other small case's latches had been sprung, the top flipped back. It, too, was empty.

"She got it. Damn her, the ugly whore got it," Eino ranted, repeating these same words over and over.

Rio didn't say anything. Silently, she edged backward, hoping to move behind her half brother and get outside before he noticed.

Didn't happen.

"The boat." He grabbed her again and pulled her with him. "Come with me. The boat we heard. You were right. It wasn't moving. We can still catch them."

He took off running, panting hard after the first fifty yards or so and, thankfully for Rio, slowing down. At the cut-off, he made her go first, fighting her way through the bushes that overgrew the narrower path. A stone-filled path, if one could even call it that, with an uneven surface of pebbles rolling underfoot with every step, casting her off balance. In spots it was almost straight down, causing them both the slide a few feet on their rear ends. Her toe felt on fire, making it hard to walk.

But Flavia, and whoever her cohorts were, being unfamiliar with the terrain, would've had this same trouble and been slowed as well. Rio hoped they'd given up their quest and managed to get the boat underway by now. Better yet, out of range of Eino's pistol. She didn't want to be around if he started spraying bullets.

Eino in particular, made a great deal of noise scrambling down the rocky path. He went too fast to keep a good lookout, as well. He fell at the exact instant a bullet whizzed past Rio. Had he not, the shot would likely have blown his brains out.

Someone in front of Rio called out, "Got him," evidently believing the fall had been caused by the shot.

Luck may have been involved when purely by accident, he dragged Rio down with him. He left her to fend for herself as he rolled off the path into the bushes and boulders. No fool, Rio copied the movement the other direction.

Whoever had shot at Eino had taken cover only a few yards away. Completely out of sight from where she lay, trying not to move the bushes and draw more gunfire.

"Watch him," a woman said, and a moment later she hurried toward where Eino had fallen. "I'll get it."

Rio held her breath as Flavia passed her. The woman whirled in a circle. "Where are they?" she called to whoever had been in the boat. Then, "There's no blood. You didn't get him Audell. You missed."

"The woman?" a man asked.

Flavia's voice went harsh. "She's gone."

"Dead?"

"No, you fool. Gone. As in, she isn't here."

There was a scramble of bodies before the invisible Audell called out, "Find her, Toad, and bring her to me. Look for them both. Dammit to hell, this business has been a shambles from the get-go."

Toad. Well, Rio knew who she faced now, but what puzzled her most was the connection between Flavia, Curran, and Toad. And Eino? He'd been duped by the woman he'd introduced as his wife? How did it all fit?

Not that she was in any position to ask questions. Probably didn't matter anyway. Flavia began poking a long stick about in the area Eino had rolled toward. Rio took the opportunity to wriggle on her elbows and knees to a bare spot behind a good-sized boulder.

Twenty-Six

Beckett and Quinn, taking advantage of balmy night air, had made their separate ways to the spring where they could be sure of privacy should any of the hotel guests chance to stroll on the beach or do a little night fishing.

They waited there for Rio, each on a stump stool, not talking. Frogs took courage and croaked a song. Crickets chirped; birds rustled in the bushes. Out on the lake, a fish jumped and the pines emitted a sharp smell.

The wait went on a long time. Longer than anticipated.

At last, Quinn spoke, his voice quiet in the dark. "Do you suppose Rio fell asleep? I don't think she's had a full night's sleep since I've been here what with seeing me through the stabbing, that half brother of hers trying to set the barn on fire, and men..." He stopped.

Beckett moved restlessly. "Men what?"

Quinn coughed—an excuse. "Men trying to invade the place. Poking around where they got no business.

306

Somebody always watching the place. Threatening her."

Beckett had the thought there must've been something even more serious. Something this Quinn Callahan was keeping from him. But all he said was, "It's only been a few weeks since I last saw her. I figured she'd be better now but you're right. She's on the edge of exhaustion."

"Did you meet him? Her half brother?" Quinn asked.

"Nope, and I don't want to. His reputation precedes him."

Quinn snorted. "Consider yourself lucky. If you've heard about him, he's...well...he's all that and more. I expect you'll see for yourself if you're staying a while."

Beckett shot him a look. "Then I expect I will." He didn't know what to make of Callahan's expression. "I understand you're staying out of sight yourself."

Quinn nodded. "I'm here because of Eino Salo. And so are some very dangerous men. The ones hanging around the hotel."

"You wouldn't happen to be one of those dangerous men, would you?"

A quirk of a smile helped Quinn's answer. "Not to Rio."

They didn't speak for some time, then Beckett had another question. "You've met Wash Ames?"

"I have." Quinn hesitated. "I'd thought those two, Rio and Ames, were close considering how he helped her establish ownership of this place, but these last few days I've begun to wonder."

"They were close," Beckett agreed, careful to keep his voice level, the words even. That closeness was one reason he'd left here when he did. Before he got in too deep, his feelings for her too intense. The job hadn't been so demanding that he couldn't have— He shut off the track his thoughts were headed for. Again.

They fell silent until Beckett said, "I think you should explain to me exactly what's been going on. Rio told me part of it, but I can tell she's holding back. When I left here, she was out of danger. Now I'd guess she's in worse trouble than ever. I know she's been drawn into her half brother's problems, but so far, no one has said exactly what those are." He paused.

Quinn didn't say anything.

Chuffing, Beckett said, "What can you tell me?"

"I'd rather she told you."

"I'd rather too, if we can ever get together. That woman..." Beckett jerked erect, his head cocked toward the logger's barracks. "Did you hear that?"

Quinn shook his head. "What is it?"

"Gunshot." Beckett's mouth set as he lunged to his feet. "I've got a feeling..." He took off, loping toward the sound and the words were lost.

Quinn got up too, hesitating only a few seconds before following. More shots came clearly then, the sharp crack of revolvers amplified by the water.

Then they stopped.

Who was shooting at whom?

———

SHIVERING, Rio lay huddled on the ground behind the boulder, curled into the smallest package she could be. A nest of pine needles cushioned the stony ground. The rustle of Flavia's stick as she prodded through the bushes covered her own small movements. After a while the sounds of Curran and Flavia's search faded and she risked raising her head far enough to see around the boulder. Those two made enough noise for bull elk as they moved farther away, but what puzzled Rio was where Eino had gotten to. How, as inept as he was in the woods, could he have so thoroughly disappeared so fast?

Reassured to find herself alone, she stood.

A mistake, as it turned out.

"Hah," said a voice from right in back of her. "I knew you was close. Think you're damn smart, don't cha? Well, you ain't."

Rio whirled just as Toad stepped into full view from behind a tree. He held a knife poised as if to throw the second she moved a muscle. She had no doubt the knife would not miss.

"I hear Curran calling for you," she said. "He must need you."

Toad croaked a laugh. "Nope. You don't hear nothing because he ain't saying nothing. He told me to find you." Another of those eerie laughs sounded. "And I did."

Incontrovertible truth.

His knife, a long, narrow-bladed pigsticker, waved her up the hill, his expression long-suffering. Proof he didn't care for traversing the rocky hillside any more than she did.

Did she have a choice?

Up she went, climbing the steep slope using deeply rooted bushes like ropes to anchor her on the way up. Once she turned. Toad was doing the same but using only one hand. He didn't let go of his knife.

At the top of one section, she stopped to catch her breath. "Who is Flavia?" she said to him. "Eino said she's not his wife, but she was living with him like one."

Toad stared at her out of those pop-eyes. For some reason they seemed to shine like beacons even through the dark where only starlight lit the sky. She shuddered, wondering if the question would earn her a stab wound, but he only shook his head.

"She's Curran's stepdaughter, that's who she is. Smart." He paused. "Mean. But not as mean as me."

She hadn't thought him capable of such an encompassing reply in so few words, especially when he added to it.

"She was part of Marciano's gang, her and her ma, back before her ma got together with Curran and the gang kicked the old lady out. She'd worked with the old man himself. Flavia, she just paired up with Curran after."

"After what?"

"I kilt her ma. Too late. She'd already gave Curran the tuberculosis."

Shuddering, Rio turned her attention to the final part of the climb, reaching the path back to the hotel with Toad right behind. She didn't want to hear anymore. Particularly since Toad was gasping from the effort of climbing the hill. The idea had come to her that, like Flavia's *ma*, it was likely Curran had passed his malady on to his loyal Toad.

They stopped while Toad caught his breath, loud as the bellows she sometimes used in the lobby fireplace to encourage the flames.

She'd have to do an extra deep cleaning of the room

he and Curran had stayed in at the hotel. A bit late, perhaps, but she'd feel better.

If she lived.

At last Toad nodded, brandishing his knife as if she'd been the one to demand a rest.

She started off at a brisk pace. If she could get ahead, she could turn and draw her gun from her pocket out of his sight. She'd shoot him, though she dreaded the thought. Another dead man to her account?

But better him than her.

And if she didn't kill him, she might be able to slow him enough to run away. There were people at the hotel. Quinn, Beckett, Win. Even Mr. Perry, the guest who'd witnessed Eino and Flavia's attempt to burn the barn, who was on his return trip home. He might intervene.

Curran and Flavia would surely be too involved with Eino to worry about her. And once there, Beckett could arrest him. He could arrest all of them.

But there'd still be Marciano to deal with.

A sudden "oof" behind her spun Rio around in time to see Toad lying flat on the path. His knife had flown from his hand and lay a couple yards ahead of him, blade shining in the starlight.

That didn't arrest Rio's attention as much as the man standing over Toad grinning at her.

"Garrity! Where did you come from?"

"I been tagging along since you left the hotel. You and your brother." Garrity seemed pleased with himself. "Figured to stay close enough nobody got hurt."

"Do you mean you could've stopped Eino from

taking me with him?" she demanded. And what did he mean, *nobody got hurt*? She'd gotten plenty hurt! "And he's only my half brother."

"Huh." He nodded. "Yeah, I could've stopped him. Figured letting it play out might work better." He shook his head. "Don't know as it did. Maybe."

"So where is my half brother right now?"

"Back at the hotel. I got him away from Curran and Flavia. He's packing his stuff, ready to move on. I'll make sure he goes. After that I'm done with him."

"Leaving me to clean up his mess best I can," she said bitterly. "After almost getting me killed and ruining my business." She looked down at Toad and saw his fingers clench in the litter of pine needles of the path. "What do you plan on doing with him?"

"You do what you want."

"Me?" Rio stared at him. "What am I to do with him?"

Garrity grunted. "Piss ant," he said, succinct as usual. He reached down and pulled the little man up by the collar. "Ah, hell. Forget it. I'll take care of him."

He made a quick search of Toad, discovering three other blades secreted around his person. Rio pointed out the one in a sheath dangling from his neck. Quite the pendant, she thought. Lethal if not pretty.

Holding the little man by the scruff, Garrity marched the frantically threshing Toad off toward the hotel, keeping pace with Rio who confiscated the knives and hurried to get back. Mostly, she figured, just to make sure there was anything left on the premises.

Eino was clever when it came to stealing, seeming to ferret out anything of value even from people and places he didn't know well. He knew the hotel very well indeed. And probably the combination to the safe.

But, Rio thought, if Eino was indeed at the hotel, he should've walked right into Beckett and Quinn. They were sure to have him secured by now. And maybe, if Curran and Flavia had followed him, them too. Still, it was funny, why hadn't Garrity mentioned them.

She spun to Garrity. "When you took Eino to the hotel, Garrity. Did you see anyone? Quinn? Or maybe a dark-eyed man and a younger one who looks like him?"

Garrity frowned. "I didn't see anybody. The boss and I, we came in at the back porch and snuck up the stairs. I told him to stay put. That I'd be back and we'd leave before Marciano or Curran caught up with him. Then I came back for you." He gave Toad a shake, eliciting a yowl of protest. "And him."

She broke into a jog. One fast enough that only a few minutes later, Garrity and his prisoner lagging behind, had her plunging up the steps and passing through the porch.

Inside, the hotel was dark except for one small lantern sitting on the kitchen table. Its wick had burned low. Making a quick sashay through the lower floor, she found the place dark and silent. No strange man sitting in the lobby or dining room waiting to snare her. No Curran and Flavia waiting to take her prisoner. She'd sort of expected them.

She heard Garrity and Toad enter and head for the light in the kitchen. Then Garrity growled, "Sit."

Rio assumed Toad obeyed. Her attention went on to the upper floor. She didn't hear anything from there. Mr. Perry had the room at the farthest end of the hall, she remembered. And the fishing couple from the city the one next to him. She'd kept them as far away from Eino as possible. The last room, besides Eino's and her own where Win and Beckett had lodged, was empty.

From long habit, Rio went up the stairs keeping close to the wall where the steps were less likely to creak and give her away. At the top, she drew her pistol from her pocket and cocked it, thinking the sound of it loud as a thunderclap. Almost before she realized she'd moved, the door to Eino's room loomed in front of her. Beneath the door, a sliver of light showed occupancy as a figure moved between the light source and the door, casting a second of shadow.

She didn't bother knocking. She opened the door.

Eino spun toward her, holding the stove poker out in front of him. "You," he said. "I thought she had you. Hoped she had you. But no. You're like a damn cat. Got nine lives."

"I see you're packed." Rio refused to answer on his terms. Better to state the obvious. His duffel and a leather satchel stood open on the bed, the duffel haphazardly filled with his wardrobe. The satchel contained a wad of money. She had a guess where it had come from.

Deciding not to mention the theft—worthwhile to lose the receipts of two days business that was all she'd had on hand—than to fight him for it. Let Garrity take him and go. And pray he never found his way back.

"Garrity is waiting for you downstairs. I don't know why he is still loyal to you, but he seems to be. If you hurry, you can get away before the others catch up."

His smile was smug. "He owes me."

She shrugged. "Now you'll owe him. Go."

But even yet he took his time putting on his suit

coat and checking the room one more time as if to prevent leaving anything valuable behind. He'd hadn't once, it struck her, mentioned their father while he'd been here. No grief. No regret at ignoring his dying father for the better part of a year. He'd not even showed gratitude for the inheritance of a going timber concern and made no provision for its continued viability. It was as if Elias and Salo Timber Products had never counted.

At last, when she was ready to scream at him to hurry, he said, "I'm ready. Lead the way."

But when they got to the head of the stairs, she motioned to him to go first. Rio wasn't about to turn her back on him.

They found Garrity watching Toad struggle with his bonds. During the time Rio'd been upstairs, the bodyguard had managed to collect his few things and bundle them into a pack to carry on his back.

"They're coming," he said to Eino. "We'll have to go fast."

Eino nodded like an emperor giving an award. "Then let's go." At the door, he glanced at Rio and smirked. "We're not finished, sister. I'll be seeing you."

"Not if I can help it." Rio turned away but Garrity stopped a moment and pointed to a slip of paper sitting on the counter. "You're a good lady," he said quietly. "I'll take care of him."

Only later did it come to her those five words could've meant just about anything—or nothing.

For now, she watched the two of them disappear into the night, heading the long way around the lake to meet with the road leading eventually into Canada. A stage rolled past there every morning along about daylight, she remembered. Or there was a connecting road that angled off over the mountains to the coast. Or the smuggler's road. Or...it occurred to her there were several escape routes. The others were in for a fine old time trying to track him from here.

Or maybe not. Squinting into the dark, as the two went past the barn Rio caught sight of someone else down by the corral. Whoever it was followed, moving like a black wraith.

A wraith trailing skirts, she realized.

Toad struggled and was still struggling when Beckett, Quinn, and Wash, Rio was surprised to see, herded a group of individuals into the hotel at gunpoint. They entered through the lobby and passed through to the dining room where Beckett stopped them and told them all to have a seat.

Rio, standing in the dark, held back, waiting to see what happened.

Marciano and his men huddled together around one of the tables. The two factions glared at each other. Wash guarded from one side, Quinn from the other. Beckett stood in the middle where he could watch them all.

"Now what?" Marciano demanded.

"Now we wait," Beckett said.

"For what?"

"Until everyone is here."

Rio supposed she was the everyone in question. Unless they were thinking Curran and Flavia would show themselves. She knew they wouldn't. They had their target, Flavia no doubt believing Eino had the money. Still, it wouldn't hurt any of them to wait a few more minutes. Silently, she slipped outside and made her way to the blackberry patch, retrieved the fishing creel she'd stashed there, and carried it back to the office. Scattering the contents out on the desk, she divided it into three piles.

After that, she tidied her hair, washed her face and hands, changed her blouse and smoothed her skirt. Deeming herself ready, she checked the pistol in her pocket and selected two packets of money to take with her.

Taking a deep breath, she strode into the lobby, spine straight, shoulders back. Chairs shifted; eyes turned toward her. Quinn winked. Wash looked at her, then away. Beckett's eyebrows lifted.

"There's one more fellow tied to a chair in the kitchen. He belonged with Curran and Flavia."

"You have Toad?" Marciano's voice rose. "I figure he killed Enzo."

Rio ignored him.

"I'll get him," Wash said.

"He's shifty," Rio warned. "I think we got all his knives, but I expect you'd have to strip him to be sure."

"We?" Beckett asked.

"Garrity and I." She made a little face. "I don't think you had a chance to meet him."

Beckett shook his head. "I'll wait for you to explain."

Rio felt the weight of the men's eyes on her as they waited. Oh, yes. And of Marciano's hard stare. She shook her head. Later, it meant.

Beckett lit more lamps.

"Now," Rio said, setting the two packets down on a table. She looked out over the room, worried whether she was doing the right thing.

Then Toad appeared, Wash pushing him along to take his place beside the others. But stopping in his tracks, Toad's pop-eyes scanned around the room, searching. Stopped a moment to examine Quinn's face, then moved on.

"Where is he?" Toad demanded. "Where's Curran?"

Twenty-Seven

First thing, Rio told herself, is to be finished with Toad. Get him out of here so she can take care of the rest.

If, she qualified, they'd be satisfied with money and not demand some kind of retribution from her. And that went for Quinn as well as Marciano. As for Toad—

Rio went to stand in front of the little man. His bulging eyes swiveled up to meet hers. "What is your stake in this?" she asked.

He glowered up at her, those bulging eyes malevolent. "Stake?"

"What do you have to win or to lose?"

He frowned even harder, seemed to be thinking, then shrugged. "Nuthin', I got nuthin'. I just do like Curran says. Or her. I take my orders from them."

He meant Flavia. Ye Gods! What a complete fool her half brother was. But a dangerous one.

"What do you get in return?" He was a raggedy little man. Vile in body habit—as she could well attest to having been much nearer to him than she liked—and vile in intellect.

"They take care of me," he said.

Somebody in the room snorted. *One of Marciano's men*, Rio thought. Or maybe Marciano himself.

Putting a fingertip over her lips, she eyed him. "What would you do right now if you were given the chance?"

"I'd ask Curran what to do next."

"If Curran has left you behind?"

Toad blinked both eyes at once. "He don't leave me. Not for long. I'll find him. I always find him."

It crossed her mind to wonder if Curran truly appreciated Toad's loyalty. From a shifting of Quinn's feet, he might be wondering too.

"So if I were to turn you loose right now, you'd go find Curran?"

"Yeah. Sure. I'd catch up."

Rio eyed him, then turned to Wash. She had an idea. "This man almost killed Mr. Callahan, and he's threatened to kill me. I don't trust him. Can you lock him up in the jail in town, then turn him loose in the morning?"

She wanted to give Garrity a head start. Give him a chance to ditch Eino and go his own way.

Wash didn't look happy about it. "I suppose."

She thought maybe Wash knew she didn't want him here for what came next. A faint smile crossed her face. "Thank you."

The part about getting Toad, clumsy with his hands bound behind him, loaded into a boat with Wash at the oars took only long enough for men's feet to start shuffling, a sign of impatience. Finally, Quinn saw them off, then returned, nodded his head, and Rio took up the business again.

She turned first to Luca Marciano. "Mr. Marciano, I understand my half brother managed to steal twenty thousand dollars from your boss. I don't care that he did. A thief stealing from a thief? I don't have a bit of sympathy. What I care about is getting you away from me, my hotel, and my town." She selected one of the packets and opened it. They all could see it was made up of currency. A lot of currency.

An indrawn breath took most of the air out of the room.

"I found where Eino hid the money and I took it. He and that woman evidently spent quite a lot of it, but there's enough here to return the money he stole from your boss." Saying Eino had spent a lot of money wasn't true. Most of the missing money had been in the stash. A surprise.

She shrugged. "I don't know who your boss is and I don't care. I just want you to accept the money, go away, and never come back."

She handed Marciano the packet. He gazed at the bundle with an astonished air. "Count it," she said.

Marciano might not have been good at some things, but he knew how to total up money in a hurry. "All here."

"You and your men will leave?"

Behind her, Beckett rested his hand on the butt of his gun, which he carried in a holster strapped under his arm. Something, it struck Rio at this odd time, that he had in common with Quinn.

Marciano noticed. His chin lifted. "We'll leave on

the first train. I think there's a freight comes by around midnight. But—"

"But?" Beckett asked.

"What about my cousin? What about Enzo?"

"I don't know anything about your cousin," Rio said, her voice steady. At this moment, she almost believed it herself.

Marciano, to her relief, accepted her word.

Glancing at Quinn, she saw his face was inscrutable. She turned to him, smiling as she picked up the large brown envelope from the table. "Your claim appears to be the most honest one. I don't know if all the bearer bonds are safe in here, but this envelope holds all that were in Eino's saddlebags. Along with a good amount of cash that I believe belongs to the White family."

Under Quinn's astonished gaze, she passed the goods over to him. "That's it. Business is finished. I trust everyone is satisfied."

Marciano held up a forefinger. "Just out of curiosity, how'd you get hold of the goods?"

Quite suddenly, Rio's legs went out from under her and she sat down hard. "Let's just say my half brother isn't nearly as smart as he thinks he is."

She was tired. So awfully tired. Dare she hope these last weeks were done with? That at last she could have peace and concentrate on making her hotel and her restaurant the best in the whole northwest?

Blinking, she became aware of Beckett, his expression concerned, hovering beside her, and of Marciano standing up.

"Are we free to go, lady?" he asked, his harsh features as softened as she had ever seen him.

She nodded.

He tucked the packet of money under his arm and motioned for his men to head for the door. He went last, leaning down and whispering, "Don't worry. We won't be back."

Rio's lips twitched. "For both our sakes, I'm glad to hear it."

He laughed as he walked out. Out the door and out of her life.

The room felt almost empty when just the three of them were left. She, Beckett, and Quinn.

A shiver came out of nowhere, the fine hairs on Rio's arms raising. She didn't know why. A goose walking over her grave?

————

WASH ROWED hard across Painter's Bay, water sloshing up from the clumsy beat of the oars, his heart like lead in his chest. The knowledge of what he'd done to Rio tore at him. He'd destroyed her trust in him, her friendship—maybe more. There'd been a chance of more. Because of his job? He found himself questioning the worth of it. Oh, he knew he'd been successful here. As she'd pointed out, he'd had plenty of other offers from concerns needing a good timber boss. Most had even offered more pay. But he'd wanted to settle here where the Chinese workers looked up to him, made him feel good about himself. White men would never give him that unquestioning respect.

And then Eino Salo showed up as if risen from the dead, saying Wash could keep on as the boss of a profitable timber company. Even pay himself a bit more as long as Eino continued to receive his share. So he'd bent to Salo's will. Well, he'd known Eino couldn't take the hotel from Rio, hadn't he, and been aware Eino wouldn't stay around long?

But he'd also known Salo was a danger to her.

They reached town, the boat rocketing into the dock and throwing Toad off the seat. Wash's teeth snapped together, reminding him of what he was doing. Snagging a cleat on the dock as the boat lurched sideways, he tied the boat and clambered out.

"C'mon. Up. There's a cell waiting for you."

The little man cursed, clumsy in making it over the side when his hands were tied. "Don't like boats. Don't like jails."

"This won't be for long. Miss Salo said to let you go in the morning. It's almost morning. You'll just have time for a nap."

No more than the truth.

Toad grunted.

He'd go to the hotel first thing tomorrow, Wash told himself. He'd apologize. He'd grovel. Beg forgiveness. Knowing Rio, she'd be okay with him after a while. She was that kind of woman. And there was one more thing he'd use to convince her of his steadfastness. It was something Eino had let slip when he bragged of how things were going to change when he took over. He'd said there was something at the hotel he wanted. Something worthwhile.

Wash didn't know what for certain but Rio was bound to be interested. It had to be money. Wasn't that Eino's consuming interest?

Prodding Toad ahead of him, he got the little man stowed in a cell and, sitting in the swivel chair the old sheriff had brought in for himself, Wash settled to making plans for the morning. He wrote a list.

Number one was a cryptic little message, a reminder to himself to stay on track if he wanted redemption.

Tell Rio about the hidden treasure, it said.

———

QUINN FOLLOWED Marciano and his gang— reduced now to himself and three men—through the lobby and out into the night. When sure they were safely tromping off around the inlet toward town, he came back inside and locked the door behind them. Slapping the brown envelope lightly against his thigh, he went to join the others.

"Slick." He grinned at Rio, an admiring expression that made Beckett, standing beside her, shift his weight. "So your brother—" He corrected himself quickly. "Your half brother thinks Flavia made off with the money, and Flavia and Curran believe he has it." He laughed. "What happens if they meet up and find out neither does?"

Rio shrugged. "I can only hope they don't ever meet up. I imagine Curran will be dead before long, and Flavia connected with some other unsuspecting fool. I'm hoping they'll forget about me."

Startled, Quinn gawked at her. "Curran dead? What makes you think so? He's a wily old cuss."

"Have you noticed his cough? The way he looks? I think he's in the last stages of TB."

Sudden comprehension dropped his jaw. "I'll be. You may be right. A lunger."

"Yes. And if we're lucky, he'll have passed it on to Toad. Maybe Flavia, as well." She glanced at Beckett. "Don't think me heartless, but I'm tired of being threatened with fire, with guns, with knives, and just about every other awful thing you can think of."

"I know you're not heartless." Beckett smiled a little.

"Of course she's not. You've every right to look after your own interests." Quinn actually looked pleased. "A lunger," he said again, still amazed.

"What about this Toad person?" Beckett asked, his quiet question sounding a warning. "A sinister-looking fellow if I ever saw one."

Rio's smile wavered. "That's why I asked Wash to give the others a head start. Toad said he always finds Curran no matter where he is. I suspect he does, which means all three will be after Eino. But with Garrity's help, Eino should be able to avoid them long enough to disappear."

Beckett made some kind of sound, one that could've meant anything.

Quinn glanced at him, meeting Beckett's eyes. Eyes so dark the pupils almost disappeared in their depths. He'd known all along he had no claim on Rio and wouldn't make one, although he had the feeling she was the only woman he'd ever met capable of changing his mind. But when he looked at Beckett, he saw something that warned him to take care what he was about.

Not that he intended on letting the other man know he'd read the warning.

"The White family will be most grateful, Rio. Just like I'm grateful to you for saving my life and..." He laughed, genuinely amused. "And for doing my job for me. Those folks will be mighty glad to see me when I get back to New York City."

He glanced at Beckett. "I'll be leaving in the morning."

Beckett nodded.

"After breakfast," Quinn went on. "Sourdough pancakes and a western omelet?"

Finally, he was rewarded with a smile. "Sourdough pancakes and a western omelet," Rio agreed.

And that was that, he thought, striding off to the room that'd been his home during these last few weeks. Except maybe he could sneak one last kiss before he left. Miss Rio Salo had the makings of a mighty fine kisser with a little practice. Too bad he wasn't going to be the one who got to teach her.

———

HAMMERING on the lobby bell brought Rio running from the kitchen where she'd been soaking salt from one of Mr. Golz's smoked hams in preparation for the croquettes she planned as one of the evening's dinner choices.

She'd been working rather mindlessly, weary still from yesterday's drama added to all the previous events. Still thinking of Quinn's goodbye kiss this morning too, rather pleasant although— Anyway, she'd sensed the finality behind it. This had been a permanent goodbye. Was she sorry? She hadn't quite decided.

"What is it?" she called to the person standing at the lobby desk even as she rushed toward him. Just for a moment, she missed the now familiar bump of her pocket revolver against her hip. But all that was over with. Eino, Curran and Toad. Flavia. Marciano. Over with. Wasn't it?

And Quinn. The thought struck at her again.

The person turned from the lobby desk bell. It was Mr. Meadows's white-haired apprentice mortician—she'd forgotten his name—but he was wearing a hangdog expression. She stopped several feet from him. "What is it?" she repeated, hearing the quaver in her voice.

"Mr. Meadows sent me." The apprentice had an unnaturally—or so it seemed to her—deep voice.

Rio simply looked at him, waiting for the message. Maybe not breathing.

"He, Mr. Meadows that is, happened to be passing by the jailhouse early this morning." His eyes shifted away, probably taking note of the way the blood drained from Rio's face. "He noticed the door was open. Saw feet sticking out the opening. Feet attached to a prone body."

Rio was only vaguely aware of someone coming up behind her. Someone who grabbed hold and held her upright as she swayed.

"Whose prone body?" She forced the words out.

"Well," Meadows's apprentice said, dragging it out, "I'm sorry to say..."

"Beck!"

It was Win who held her, Rio discovered. He who bellowed for his brother and interrupted the message.

"Beckett. Get in here." For a fourteen-year-old, Win could be very forceful—and intuitive. He stopped the messenger from speaking further. "Wait a minute. This is gonna be bad, isn't it?"

The apprentice nodded. "It is. You'd all best take a seat."

By the time Win had nursed her over to one of the lobby armchairs, Beckett was there. He'd been shaving. A few drops of blood beaded where he'd nicked himself with the razor at his brother's call. His untucked shirt-tail flopped over his belt.

"What?" he demanded, but Win signaled the apprentice to continue the message.

"It's Mr. Ames."

Rio sucked in a breath.

"He's been murdered."

Her eyes closed.

"His throat'd been cut. Bled out. Mr. Meadows, he hollered for the doc and raised up a bunch of men to go looking for anybody wearing clothes with fresh blood-stains, but there wasn't anything else he could do, what with no sheriff or deputy or nobody hereabouts to take charge. The men," he hesitated over this part, "some of them proved a little reluctant to look with what just happened to a tough logger like Ames. We didn't know why Ames opened up the jailhouse in the first place. Or who mighta done it. But Doc, he thought you might know. Said there'd been some trouble here at the hotel lately. Between you and them strange men staying here."

But Rio wasn't really hearing him. Just enough to hear an accusation behind the message. One she couldn't deny.

Beckett put warm hands on her shoulders. "I'll look into it," he told the apprentice. "Folks may remember me from a few weeks ago with the situation with Sheriff Donaldson. I've got experience and some authority."

An expression of untold relief passed over the man's face. "Good," he said. "Good. I'll row back and let the fellows know. You'll be coming soon? We don't know what to do."

"I'll see to it."

The man skedaddled before anybody tried to keep him any longer. Before Rio's sobs began.

But they didn't begin. Her reaction had more to do with rage.

"I told him to beware," she whispered. "I told him to do a thorough search, that we'd found several knives, but he—Toad—might have more." She looked into Beckett's dark eyes. "I told him."

He nodded. "I know. I heard you." Beckett motioned to his young brother. "Watch over her, Win. I don't know how long I'll be."

Win nodded, even as Rio stood up. "I'm coming with you."

Beckett shook his head. "Not wise, Rio. Let me learn what's being said. Maybe catch up with Toad. Believe me, I'm aware of the danger. You stay here and lock the doors. Don't open up unless you know who is outside."

She swallowed, not missing the warning. Toad might still be around. She might be on his list of victims. After all, it had been her decision to lock the pop-eyed little man up and keep him and Curran separated. He'd be angry.

Chilled by the thought, she knew her first action would be to restore her revolver to her pocket.

"I'm taking a horse," Beckett said. "I may need to give chase."

Rio nodded. "Take the sorrel. He's fastest."

"I remember."

"And I saw Tommy Golz at the barn just a few minutes ago." She stopped and steadied a voice wobbling off kilter. "Tell him to get home and tell his sisters not to come today, that they're in danger too. I'm closing the hotel. I don't know for how long."

"I'll tell him." He beckoned to Win. "Lock up as soon as I'm outside."

With a look at Rio, Win followed him out.

Minutes later showed him urging the sorrel into a lope as they circled the bay to town. Minutes until it was just Win left with her at the hotel, she still dry-eyed and determined not to break down in front of the boy.

Young man, she corrected herself.

Would this nightmare ever be over?

Twenty-Eight

It didn't seem real. Wash dead?

It couldn't be real. Wash couldn't be dead. Not Wash. Over and over, those words kept pounding through Rio's head. She'd just seen him last night. Everything had been settled last night. The bad people, including her half brother, sent on their way to somewhere—anywhere—else. Gone from Painter's Bay.

She found herself staring out the window, over the bay to where she could still see the mortician apprentice rowing slowly back to town, his boat a pinpoint on the water.

Wash dead. A few more words added to the stark message. *His throat cut. Bled out.*

"Rio. Come with me. Let's make sure the hotel is secure. And where's Boo?"

She startled, brown eyes opening wide as she turned to Win. "Boo? Isn't he—"

Win shook his head.

Her little dog had been helping with the ham earlier, begging for a taste although she wouldn't give him any. Not until the salt had been soaked out. Then the messenger had come and she remembered Boo, avoiding the clamor of the lobby bell, had dashed outside.

She hadn't seen him since.

"Get the shotgun," she said, a chill sweeping over her. A peculiar knowledge. "Keep it with you." On the way to the back porch, she retrieved her small pistol from the office. At the kitchen, she stopped and picked up a filet knife, one just sharpened in advance of cutting up a large salmon fresh from the Spokane River. One of the local Indian men who kept her supplied had been here very early.

Win followed her, trying to protest as she unlatched the porch door and stepped outside. "Beck said not to go out."

Rio ignored him. "Boo," she called. "Boo, come."

But he didn't. Didn't bark either. No matter how many times she called. No matter how many times she whistled.

And she knew in her heart of hearts the dog wasn't playing games. Lord, how she wished he was.

"Rio," Win said, shaking. "Come inside. You'll have to leave him."

He knew too.

"Please," he added. "Don't..."

"Don't what?" Dead cold. Dead steady.

"Don't die."

"I don't intend to." She lifted her head, studying the nearby woods. That was where Boo went to do his business. Where something was most likely to happen to him, to take him unaware.

"Hush now, Win. Go inside. Stay there," she said to

him then marched on, spine stiff, shoulders as straight as a soldier on parade. At the edge of the wood, she stopped. Listened. Heard nothing when there should've been something. Raised her nose to smell.

And went on, until she knew she was gone from Win's view.

It wasn't far. A few yards and she was in a little clearing. Boo liked doing his business in the open. Under a tree, yes. Under a bush where on rainy days it dripped on him, no.

Not a concern today, she realized. The sun shone overhead, a glorious day already growing hot.

Boo was there, in plain sight in the open clearing. Not dead, she saw. Not yet, at least. But trussed up like a turkey for the oven with a filthy rag tied around his muzzle. He tried to move when he saw her but only succeeded in ruffling his white fur in the dirt.

"Be still," she whispered to him. Then louder, "I'm here. Come out."

Toad appeared from behind a tree. His stench preceded him, the odor of blood and sweat strong enough she'd already known he was there.

He was grinning, a horror of popping eyes and snaggled teeth. Wash's blood, dry now, splattered his clothing. He pointed at Boo. "I ain't killed it yet. Ain't even hurt it much. Figured you'd want to watch when I finished him."

"Did you? But you'd be wrong. I don't." Did she sound calm? She wanted to. Casually, she put her hand in her pocket.

"You're the one, ain't you?" He lost the grin. "You're the one what took the money. I figured it out. Took it all for yourself. You can't keep it though. The money. It's for Curran. And some of it for me."

She didn't dare look away from him, even though her stomach churned. "Why did you kill Wash Ames? He let you go free this morning."

He shrugged. "I felt like it. That's all."

Felt like it. Sorrow pierced her like the point of a sword. *He felt like it.*

"A mistake on your part," she said. "A big stupid mistake."

He didn't like being chastised. Quite suddenly he was moving. Coming at her fast—so awfully fast—he turned into a sort of blur in her eyes.

But this was not the time to falter. She'd prepared. Her right hand stayed in her pocket and she didn't bother to draw the gun. He ran toward her, his knife blade flashing in the sun and she simply shot through the pocket.

The bullet didn't stop him but she'd prepared for that too. The filet knife pointed up and she held it steady. All she had to do was let him fall into it and finish the job when the bullet finally dropped him.

She staggered back, allowing him to tumble bone-lessly to the ground and barely avoid going down with him.

"Rio!" Win screamed from somewhere behind her and fired the shotgun into the sky.

She stepped away from Toad's body, just in case it came alive again.

But it didn't.

Win ran up, the shotgun loose in his hands. "Rio," he said. "Are you..."

She didn't look away from the body. "You know why he killed Wash?"

He stared at her. Shook his head.

"Because he *felt* like it." Tears came then, a great welling overflow. "He just felt like it."

Win hovered uncertainly. After a few minutes, Rio's tears slowed, allowing her to regain her voice.

"Cut Boo loose, will you please?" she said to Win.

And he, who'd believed the dog dead, hurried to do so. By the time the little dog stood unsteadily on his feet and was shaking the dirt from his coat, the sorrel— Beckett lashing him for speed—pounded into sight. The horse slid on its hind legs as they charged into the clearing and Beckett pulled it to a halt.

He took in the scene at a glance. "I heard the shotgun go off." Beckett grasped his young brother's shoulder. "You all right?"

Win nodded, and Beckett went on to Rio, who by this time was cradling Boo in the crook of her arm and crooning to him.

———

WHEN BECKETT STARTED into town for a second time, it was with Toad's body tied onto a saddled horse they'd discovered not far away. A horse he'd stolen in town for his run to the hotel side of the bay as it turned out.

By late afternoon Rio and Win had begun fretting. They'd had people drop by during the day, some, having heard of Wash's death and with Rio being considered in charge now of Salo Timber Products as well as the hotel, to ask about her intention to carry on with the logging operation.

She had no answer for them.

Some showed up to offer condolences, people having known she and Wash were friends, and that she may have been the closest thing to a relative Wash had. She knew he had a sister somewhere, though they hadn't been close. Someone would have to find the woman's address and notify her. Rio supposed she was elected.

A few came because they were simply curious. More were relieved to hear the recent influx of outlaws and men of murderous intent were gone, hopefully for good. Rio couldn't have agreed more.

And last, there were those who came hoping for dinner. Hoteliers are never allowed a day off, and this proved no exception.

Afternoon was waning when Beckett finally returned. He looked satisfied with himself, but weary.

Rio, having already filled three rooms at the hotel with newspaper reporters from surrounding towns, had realized she'd have to feed them too and was in the kitchen expanding her menu. The boy from the grocer had rowed over with a list of people reserving dinners, probably as much out of curiosity as hunger. In other words, business was back to usual, no matter that a few tears may have fallen into the French onion soup.

The first she knew Beckett had returned was when she straightened from putting a tray of featherlight rolls in the oven to bake.

"I'm back," he said from behind her back.

She turned to face him. "You were gone so long. I was afraid—" She couldn't admit those fears.

Beckett waited, but she didn't continue. "A lot to do. Telegrams to send, investigate the scene as much as possible after a dozen men traipsed through the jail destroying any evidence. See Wash cared for. Write a report on the Toad fellow. I used the sheriff's office. Don't know what will come of it, but it was the best I could do for Wash, for you, and for the town."

She nodded, tears welling yet again.

Beckett gathered her into his arms.

Her head dropped to rest against his chest, her pale hair wisping under his chin. His arms felt so good around her. "Thank you. Without you and Win, I don't know what I'd do."

He smiled crookedly. "You'd manage just as you always do. You're one tough lady, Rio Salo."

Rio didn't believe him. She didn't feel tough. Fact is, she felt like mush inside.

Beckett tilted up her chin with a fingertip, forcing her to meet his dark eyes. "There's something you should know. I would've been back hours ago, but a group of men from town invited me to a meeting."

"A meeting?"

"The doc, the mortician, the grocer, the butcher, the banker. They realize the need for law and order. I told them this trouble would never have gone so far if they'd insisted the county provide someone after the mess with Donaldson. I told 'em it's their fault trouble came down on you like this. The reason Wash got killed. The men agreed. They also agreed to push the commissioners in hiring a temporary officer."

Rio's heart increased its beat. Dared she hope— "You?"

"Me. I'll take the job if they offer."

"You will?"

He nodded. "Temporarily. See how it works out."

There was a promise there.

Rio reached her arms around his waist. "It'll work out," she said, crossing her fingers behind his back. It was past time something did.

She'd make sure of it.

A Look At Book Three

LAST LAUGH

To survive what's coming, she must uncover what was never truly buried.

Rio Salo thought her half-brother—and the chaos he brought—was gone for good. But when strangers descend on the Painter's Bay Hotel in search of treasure he's rumored to have hidden on the grounds, the past comes clawing back. Among them are two men eager to buy the hotel at a suspiciously low price. Rio refuses to sell. She also refuses to believe in buried treasure—until two people are found dead within her walls.

With danger closing in, Rio turns to Beckett Ferris, a U.S. Customs Agent running for sheriff and the one man she's beginning to trust with her heart. Beckett takes on more than a murder investigation—he's determined to keep Rio safe, even as the threat circles closer and the secrets grow darker.

Will Rio protect the legacy she's fought to rebuild—or become the next casualty of her brother's deadly past?

AVAILABLE SEPTEMBER 2025

About the Author

2019 Spur Award winner for *The Woman Who Built a Bridge* and 2020 Spur Award winner for *The Yeggman's Apprentice*, C.K. Crigger lives in Spokane Valley, Washington, where she crafts stories set in the Inland Northwest.

She is supervised by a feisty little dog with a Napoleon complex and ignored—except when he wants to lay on the keyboard—by a reclusive cat. Not satisfied to write only of the historical west, she also writes contemporary mysteries and dabbles in the speculative genre.

A member of Western Writers of America, she reviews books and writes occasional articles for *Roundup* magazine. *Buried Under Books* also features her book reviews.